'With your perm

Theodora allowed Nik...... ....
into the mulberry-coloured pillows and sent up
a swift, if muddled prayer. Tonight she must
give the performance of her life. She must
pretend that she was a virgin and that this was
the first time she had lain with a man. She must
also—God help her—please him.

Were these aims compatible?

She breathed in her new husband's scent. It was
dark and spicy—like him, it was utterly male.
She pressed her lips against a satisfyingly wide
shoulder and covered it with kisses. She took
the tang of salt onto her tongue. *Delicious…
this man even tastes delicious.* And she was
melting with desire. Theodora didn't delude
herself that it was love that was making her
feel this way but, Lord, she had never felt like
this before…

AUTHOR NOTE

For me, the word *Byzantium* conjures images of an exotic medieval empire. It carries with it an aura of magic. Byzantium... I loved learning about it at university, and enthusiastic teachers ensured that for me Byzantium lost none of its shimmer.

These books bring Byzantium alive:

Byzantium, the Surprising Life of a Medieval Empire by Judith Herrin (Penguin, 2008)

Byzantium by Robin Cormack and Maria Vassilaki (Royal Academy of Arts, 2008)

Fourteen Byzantine Rulers by Michael Psellus (Penguin, 1966)

The Alexiad of Anna Komnene translated by E.R.A. Sewter (Penguin, 1969)

Names can be tricky. Without being too rigid, I have used Greek versions of names where possible, and in a couple of cases I have shortened the names of real people.

BETROTHED TO
THE BARBARIAN

Carol Townend

First published in Great Britain 2012
by Mills & Boon, an imprint of Harlequin (UK) Limited.
Harlequin (UK) Limited, Eton House, 18-24 Paradise Road,
Richmond, Surrey TW9 1SR

© Carol Townend 2012

ISBN: 978 0 263 89262 8

Harlequin (UK) policy is to use papers that are natural, renewable and recyclable products and made from wood grown in sustainable forests. The logging and manufacturing process conform to the legal environmental regulations of the country of origin.

Printed and bound in Spain
by Blackprint CPI, Barcelona

Carol Townend has been making up stories since she was a child. Whenever she comes across a tumbledown building, be it castle or cottage, she can't help conjuring up the lives of the people who once lived there. Her Yorkshire forebears were friendly with the Brontë sisters. Perhaps their influence lingers…

Carol's love of ancient and medieval history took her to London University, where she read History, and her first novel (published by Mills & Boon®) won the Romantic Novelists' Association's New Writers' Award. Currently she lives near Kew Gardens, with her husband and daughter. Visit her website at www.caroltownend.co.uk

Previous novels by the same author:

THE NOVICE BRIDE
AN HONOURABLE ROGUE
HIS CAPTIVE LADY
RUNAWAY LADY, CONQUERING LORD
HER BANISHED LORD
BOUND TO THE BARBARIAN*
CHAINED TO THE BARBARIAN*

*Part of *Palace Brides* trilogy

KEEP THIS TICKET PORTION

Crisis Spring Raffle 2016   2406189

£1 per ticket

First Prize
£7,500 cash
or a luxury holiday in Bali

Second Prize
£1,000 cash
or a weekend break to Lake Windermere

Third Prize
£500 cash
or a Flying Experience

Fourth Prize
10 x £50 cash

Draw Date: 8th July 2016
Close Date: 24th June 2016

Thank you for joining in the fun and taking action against homelessness

Crisis Spring Raffle 2016

For your reassurance: Rules of The Spring Raffle 2016

Responsible person: Edward Tait. Crisis, 66 Commercial Street, London, E1 6LT. **Entry:** Prizes are open to all GB residents including Crisis volunteers and employees. It is an offence for tickets to be sold to or by anyone under 16 years of age. **Draw date:** Entry closes on 24th June 2016; the draw takes place on 8th July 2016. **Notification of winners:** Winners will be notified in writing. A list of winners will be available on our website after the draw date – www.crisis.org.uk. Alternatively, send a stamped addressed envelope to: Crisis, 66 Commercial Street, London, E1 6LT to request a winners list. **Winners:** Each winner may be photographed if required, and asked to provide comment on being selected as a winner, to help us promote future fundraising draws. Winners' names, city of residence, and photos may be used to help promote future draws. **Late entries:** Any money received after the closing date will be treated as a donation and used to fund our work. **Unsold tickets:** Please recycle any unsold tickets, thank you.

Crisis UK (trading as Crisis), Registered Charity Numbers: E&W1082947, SC040094, Company Number: 4024938. Registered with the Gambling Commission, licence numbers 000-005009-A-316326-003 & 000-005009-N-303937-006.

gambleaware.co.uk

If you feel you have a problem with gambling visit www.gambleaware.co.uk or call the Gamcare National Helpline on 0808 8020 133

To play online, visit www.crisis.org.uk/raffle

WANT MORE TICKETS? CALL CRISIS, MONDAY TO FRIDAY, 9AM TO 5PM: 08000 38 48 38

To play online, visit www.crisis.org.uk/raffle

28721_TKT

Chapter One

'Constantinople,' Princess Theodora Doukaina murmured, staring into the dark over the ship's guardrail. 'At last we are home.' She clutched her baby to her chest, angling her so that she might have her first glance of the city at the heart of the Empire. Martina was busy sucking a corner of her blanket, her gaze caught by the glow of a lamp nailed to the mast amidships. As Theodora shifted her, easing the blanket from her mouth, Martina's eyes tracked the lamp, not the City. Theodora sighed.

'My lady, with your permission?' Sophia was hovering at her elbow and, as the galley rose on a gentle swell, she slipped a steadying arm under Theodora's cloak and wound it round her waist. The warmth of her lady-in-waiting's body was welcome. It was not yet Easter and out on the Sea of Marmara the wind had bite. 'Perhaps I should take the baby below?'

'No. The sea is calm and I would like Martina to see the city.'

Above them, the night sky glistened with stars. Moonlight from a full moon washed over the deck, playing with the shadows of sailors preparing to lower the sail, stretching and shrinking them with the rise and fall of each wave. Over Constantinople itself, there was not a star to be seen, likely a bank of cloud lay over the City and was blotting them out.

The helmsman's voice rose sharply over the creak of timbers. 'Captain Brand!'

'My pardon, ladies.'

The captain pushed past them, heading for the stern. Theodora barely noticed, she was staring hungrily across the water, throat tight. *We are home. Home.* Her mind was in turmoil. Fear, guilt, hope—she felt them all.

To the north, several lights were spaced out at intervals along a dark, indistinct skyline. That must be the palace wall, it was hard to see tonight. There were domed silhouettes—churches—glowing with an eerie radiance. Puzzled, Theodora stared at the domes; something was out of place, something was missing. She knotted her brow—why could she not get her bearings? She knew the City like the back of her hand. Was that the Palace? She ought to know. Holy Mother, she should be able to see the Boukoleon Palace; the entrance to the Imperial harbour should be lit by the braziers on top of the towers, and a little to the right of that the dome of Hagia Sophia...

A gust of wind wrenched a strand of brown hair from her cloak hood. A chill went through her, a chill that had nothing to do with salt-laden sea breezes. There was something else in the air...something that chilled more effectively than the wind, something other than salt. Theodora's skin prickled. *Danger, danger.*

'Sophia, can you smell something?'

Like Theodora, Sophia was looking landwards, towards the Imperial Palace. Her grip tightened, her nostrils flared as she inhaled. Wide eyes met Theodora's. 'Smoke! My lady, I can smell smoke!'

'The City is burning. Look at that dome, the gilding never glows like that, not even at sunrise. Parts of the city have been fired.' Even as Theodora watched, the dome winked out of sight. A pall of smoke was drifting over Constantinople. That was why no stars were visible in the north.

'My lady...' Sophia flung a worried glance at the stern '...perhaps we should get below.'

Behind them, a sailor swore. Captain Brand snapped an order; there was a sudden flurry of activity, and beneath their feet the galley altered course. Ropes groaned, wind filled the sail. It was then that Theodora heard the screams. Faint screams, borne by the wind across black briny water.

'Sophia, can you hear that?'

Sophia tugged at her arm. 'Please, my lady, I really think we should get below.'

Captain Brand marched up even as Theodora had opened her mouth to object. His face was grim. 'Ladies, it is time to retire, I believe.'

'What is happening, Captain?' Sophia asked.

Their Varangian escort shook his head. 'I have no idea, my lady, but the Palace lighthouse is out. I won't risk sailing into the Imperial harbour tonight.'

Theodora looked at the city skyline, mind racing. The Palace lighthouse—of course, that was why she could not get her bearings! For years, the Palace lighthouse had stood like a sentry next to the Boukoleon Palace. It was lit at dusk each day and for it to have been extinguished before dawn, something appalling must have happened. The wind shifted, pushing at the smoke, and the sea wall swam into focus, a grey ribbon bathed in moonlight. Flames flared like bright flowers on the domed skyline. Then the smoke drifted and the flame flowers, the gilded domes and the sea walls vanished.

Shivering, Theodora hugged Martina close to her breast. 'The City is on fire.' She felt hollow inside.

'We cannot be sure, my lady. It is probably perfectly safe, but we shall not be entering the Imperial harbour tonight.'

The wind buffeted the galley and the sound

of drumming reached them. Theodora gave the Captain a straight look. 'Battle drums, Captain?'

Captain Brand pressed his lips together. 'That seems most unlikely. However, I have been ordered to protect you ladies. My apologies for the delay, but you will not be sleeping in the Boukoleon Palace yet awhile.'

Theodora exchanged glances with Sophia. She wanted to laugh, she wanted to cry. Naturally, in her role as simple lady-in-waiting, Princess Theodora Doukaina did neither; she went meekly below deck, as she had been instructed. There was no sense rousing the good Captain's suspicions about her identity at this late stage.

'Have you decided what you will do with the baby, my lady?'

'Mmm?' Theodora lifted her gaze from the infant dozing in her lap. She and Lady Sophia were sharing a bench in an ill-lit guest chamber in St Michael's Abbey, a few miles outside Constantinople. They were waiting for word on what had happened in the City; they had been waiting for nigh on two weeks. *Two weeks.* Easter had come and gone.

Outside rain was falling, the air smelled dank. Wool-lined slippers made a poor shield against the wintry chill seeping up from the stone floor. Goose-bumps had formed on Theodora's legs and arms. Keeping firm hold of the baby in question—her daughter, Martina—she cocooned both herself and the child tightly in veil and shawl.

Theodora was grateful for this unexpected time alone with Martina, every moment spent with her was so precious. She was achingly conscious that Sophia, who was her friend and lady-in-waiting, believed that she and Martina would soon be separated. Permanently. Protocol would demand it. Protocol was an old foe. Theodora had fought it before, she would fight it again. She did not know how, but somehow she would win the right to keep her daughter.

Sophia gave her a sympathetic smile and tried again. 'Martina. What you will do with her when we reach the Imperial Palace?'

The Princess and Lady Sophia were alone; the other ladies were in a larger guest chamber. Theodora was almost certain that they had managed to secure privacy for herself and Sophia without arousing Captain Brand's suspicions; she was almost certain the good captain did not know she was the Princess Theodora Doukaina. They had taken great pains to make him think she was just one of the many ladies-in-waiting he was escorting to the Great Palace. A niggle of doubt remained. *Has Captain Brand seen through our deception?*

The accommodation at St Michael's was far from palatial, the guest chamber was little more than a monk's cell. The walls were whitewashed and the meagre furnishings—sleeping pallets, bench—were dusty and decidedly rustic. The icon on the wall was shrouded in cobwebs. Since Captain Brand had decreed that none of the ladies could leave the monastery until they received confirmation it was safe to proceed to the Palace, the guest chamber had, in effect, become their prison. Thanks to the rain, even the Abbey courtyard was out of bounds.

Theodora held down a sigh. The voyage back to Constantinople had been fraught with difficulties, not least because none of the soldiers escorting them to the Imperial Palace could know that she was anything more than another lady-in-waiting. Only Theodora's waiting women realised the truth.

The day of reckoning is almost upon me. I am Princess Theodora Doukaina and it is time for me to reclaim my proper identity.

Theodora sat on the bench, stroking her daughter's hair. The problem was that she did not want to reclaim her true identity. Outwardly, her expression was calm—years of training had ensured that. Inside, she felt as though her heart was made of glass, glass that had shattered into a thousand pieces. She could no longer remember what it felt like to be whole. Much as she loved Constantinople, she dreaded her return. If it was discovered that she had a daughter, the scandal would rock the City.

If they discover that Martina is mine, will

they take her away? Holy Mother, that must not happen!

Captain Brand—the Varangian officer charged with ensuring their safety on their journey to the Great Palace—had assured them that St Michael's Abbey would be the ideal place to wait for news. They would not be allowed to set foot outside until he knew it was safe.

Safe. It had been hard not to laugh in the Captain's face. Safe. If only he knew—Theodora had so many secrets she could never feel safe again.

The voyage from Dyrrachion on the Empire's western border had been nothing less than torture. Theodora had been obsessed with the thought that with every day that passed, they were a day closer to the moment when she might lose her daughter. On the one hand, she had wanted the journey to last for ever, so that she could enjoy being with Martina. On the other, pretence did not come easily to her. It was a challenge pretending to be just one lady-in-waiting among many, particularly when the other women knew her to be the Princess Theodora Doukaina and were in the habit of bowing to her every wish. The strain of the pretence was taking its toll on her.

We should be in the Boukoleon Palace—what can have happened?

'Why was the Palace lighthouse out?' Theodora asked, not for the first time. 'It's unheard of. Unimaginable.'

'I do not know. Perhaps the wind…' Sophia trailed into silence.

'The wind…no.' Theodora rocked her daughter and adjusted her wrappings. The bench creaked. Theodora thought about the fires they had seen and the acrid smell of smoke. The screams. The wind had *not* extinguished the Palace lighthouse that night, Sophia knew that as well as she. For the Palace lighthouse to have gone out, and for it to have remained out, something terrible, revolutionary, must have happened in the Palace itself.

'What can have happened?' *Has there been a Palace coup? A revolt of some kind?* Even in Dyrrachion they had heard the mutterings; the Emperor—who insisted on calling himself Theodora's uncle—was not the most popular of men.

Sophia lifted her shoulders. 'My lady, I do not know.'

'It will take time for a messenger to reach the Palace and return, of course.'

'Time? The messenger is certainly taking an age,' Sophia said. 'I don't understand it—isn't St Michael's used as a hostel by the Court because of its proximity to Constantinople?'

Sophia was in the right. St Michael's Abbey sat on a promontory overlooking the Gulf of Lasthenes where their galley was currently at anchor, it really was not far from the City. Theodora forced a smile. 'If something has happened in the Great Palace, we shall soon learn of it.'

She rested her hand gently on the top of her

daughter's head, her thumb absently smoothing the baby-fine hair. Martina was snug in several layers of fine linen and silk. *Safe, my daughter is safe. God knows what is happening in the City, but He has granted Martina and I another day together. For now, Martina is safe.*

Martina was infinitely precious to her, it was terrifying how much Theodora felt for this small bundle of life. Terrifying and marvellous. When Theodora had learned of her pregnancy, she had had no idea she was capable of such powerful feelings. *Martina is mine, I will not let them take her away from me.* Death might have broken the bond between Theodora and Prince Peter—nothing would break the bond between Theodora and her child.

Lady Sophia looked at her. 'It cannot be long until we are back at the Palace, my lady.' And then, even though she and Theodora were alone in the stark little cell, she lowered her voice. 'If you want to keep your secret, it is time to decide what you are going to do with her. You can put it off no longer.'

Tears burned at the back of Theodora's eyes, her heart ached. Sophia spoke the truth, she had hard decisions to make. There was no doubt in Sophia's mind as to what she ought to do—protocol demanded that Theodora give up her child. Theodora ought to pretend that she and Peter had not created this wonderful, mysterious scrap of humanity.

I cannot do it.

However, there were other reasons why Theodora should give up Martina, reasons known only to her, reasons which outweighed protocol, important though that was.

It might be safer for Martina if I do give her up.

It was a powerful reason, but powerful as it was, Theodora would not do it. There had to be a way to keep Martina safe without losing her. She squared her shoulders and looked directly at her lady-in-waiting. 'I cannot give her up.'

'My lady, you must! Think of the consequences if you are found out.'

'Sophia, I have been thinking of nothing else since we left Dyrrachion. I will not give her up.'

Lady Sophia's sigh was loud in the quiet. Outside, Theodora could hear the chanting of the monks; she could hear the scream of a gull as it flew over the gorge; she could hear the spring rain hissing on the paving outside the lodge. Several moments passed.

'Sophia, she's my daughter!'

'I understand, but what will you do? Confess you have had a child out of wedlock? An Imperial princess?'

'I cannot do that.'

'No.' Sophia blew out a breath. 'I suppose you could keep on running. The scouts Captain Brand sent to the City may already have learned if Katerina and Anna arrived safely. You could let Katerina continue the pretence a while longer.'

The pretence. Theodora sighed. She was Princess Theodora Doukaina, but because she had borne a daughter that few people knew about, she had temporarily taken on the guise of a mere lady-in-waiting. Some of her own ladies, already shocked by her pregnancy, had been even more shocked by this pretence. Little did they know. Theodora would take on the guise of a shepherdess if it meant she could keep her daughter.

Sophia tipped her head to one side and looked thoughtfully at her. 'How long will Katerina and Anna be able to keep up the deception?'

'If you are trying to rouse my conscience about asking Katerina to take my place for a time, then I must tell you, you are succeeding.' Theodora reached for Sophia's hand, she needed the contact. She had been bred to do her duty, but duty had never seemed such a ruthless task master as it did today, guilt was twisting her into knots. 'I hated asking them to do it, but I wanted more time with Martina and that has not changed. It never will.'

'What will you do, go into hiding?'

Dread sat heavy in Theodora's belly. She pushed to her feet and Martina stirred, eyelashes fluttering against sleep-flushed cheeks. *That tiny nose is surely the sweetest in the world...*

'It is a tempting idea, but it would be selfish to consider only myself and Martina. I must also consider Katerina, it is not fair to expect her to keep up the pretence indefinitely. Sooner or later she will give herself away. For Katerina's sake, I must resume my position as Princess Theodora Doukaina—I must return to the Palace.'

'I am sure that would be best.' Sophia leaned forward. 'What will you do? If you admit that Martina is yours, perhaps Duke Niko—'

Theodora cut Sophia off with an imperious jerk of her head. 'Sophia, I should not have to remind you, that would not be safe for Martina.'

'What will you do?'

Theodora frowned at the closed door of the guest chamber. There were too many unanswered questions for her to be as decisive as she would like. *How long do we have? What has been happening at the Palace? Does Captain Brand suspect...?*

'Have the men in our escort shown any curiosity about Martina?'

'Why, yes, my lady.'

'What did you say? Did you claim her as yours?'

'Mine?' Sophia's eyebrows shot up. 'I am unwed, my lady, so, no, I said nothing of the sort. I told them Martina's mother had died in childbirth and that one of our maidservants was acting as her wet-nurse.'

Theodora let out a snort. 'Her mother died in childbirth, eh? Well, it's certainly true that I am no longer the woman I was.'

Red-cheeked, Sophia hastened to reassure her. 'I meant no insult, my lady, truly, but I could not claim Martina is mine. If my mother heard rumours…the very thought of me giving birth to an illegitimate child…it would kill her.'

'And the entire Court would probably ostracise you. Don't worry, Sophia, I am painfully aware what it is like at Court—the rules, the protocols. I understand.'

'If you so command, I could pretend Martina is mine,' Sophia said, doubtfully. 'It is just that my mother…'

'We are about to return to the Great Palace and you are willing to assume responsibility for my transgressions? You are very loyal.' Theodora shook her head. 'I appreciate your generosity in making such a suggestion, Sophia, but it will not be necessary. If there is any shame to be borne over my daughter's existence, it is I who must bear it.' She stared thoughtfully at the whitewashed wall. 'I am in hopes that we shall be able to avoid shame. Let me think. Take Martina, will you?'

Carefully placing Martina in Sophia's arms, Theodora went to stand in the shaft of light coming through the window slit. A light breeze played over her cheeks. The stone walls of the building opposite were blurred by rain, the opening was too narrow for her to see much else. After a moment, she turned. 'Sophia, I like your story about Martina's mother dying. We shall embroider it a little and with luck I shall be able to convince everyone at the Palace that I am exactly what I ought to be…a dutiful, obedient princess returning home from a vassal state to meet my fiancé.

'When I resume Princess Theodora's mantle, we must take pains to ensure that I appear perfect. Pure. Duke Nikolaos must have no idea that I am not the virgin he has been promised.'

Sophia glanced at the infant on her lap. 'And little Martina? What of her?'

'Martina shall be the child of a slave who has died in childbirth. Princess Theodora has taken it upon herself to care for her.' Her smile twisted. 'That way I may keep her. No one will question her presence in the entourage of an unmarried princess.'

'Very well, my lady,' Sophia said, slowly. 'If you think that will work.'

'You might look a little more convinced. This *will* work, it has to. Martina is my life, I cannot give her up.' Theodora brightened her tone. 'I shall say I have adopted her. Stranger things than that have happened in the Great Palace, I can assure you.'

'And the Duke of Larissa? What if he objects? A good princess, a perfect princess, must obey her betrothed.'

Theodora bit her lip. She had almost managed to put Duke Nikolaos of Larissa out of her mind. She had yet to set eyes on the man whom the Emperor had decreed she must marry. 'If fortune favours me, I shall not meet him for some time.'

Sophia nodded. 'I heard the Duke was recalled to Larissa.'

'Yes, his mother is gravely ill,' Theodora said.

'Thank goodness.'

'Sophia!'

Sophia grimaced. 'I am sorry, my lady, that did not come out quite as I meant it. Please don't think I wish illness on the Duke's mother, it is just that it must have occurred to you that the Duke's absence from Court will be a relief to Katerina and Anna.'

Theodora nodded—that had occurred to her. It had also occurred to her that with any luck the Duke might remain in Larissa for some time and her meeting with him would be delayed. A reprieve of any sort would be most welcome.

Sophia looked at Martina. 'I pray he lets you keep her.'

'I shall make sure of it.' Theodora spoke confidently, even though she was convincing herself as much as Sophia. In truth, she had no idea how her fiancé would react to news that Princess Theodora Doukaina had a baby in her entourage. Duke Nikolaos was a noted general in the Imperial army, a man surely more given to command than to being persuaded. What might he say? What might he do?

She dreaded the moment of their meeting. She wished she could avoid the marriage.

Sophia looked up at her, eyes large with concern. 'Will you marry him, *despoina*? Will you be able to after Župan Peter…?'

Theodora's gaze misted. Swiftly she looked away and was vaguely aware of Sophia's hand fluttering apologetically in her direction.

'Theo—my lady, my apologies. I have hurt you by mentioning him.'

Theodora swallowed down the thickness in her throat. 'Prince Peter is never out of my mind.'

'Of course not.' Sophia bent over Župan Peter's child. 'Are you ready to marry Duke Nikolaos?'

Blinking rapidly, Theodora lifted her head. A strand of brown hair uncoiled and fell across her breast, briskly she tucked it back in place. 'I am as ready as I shall ever be.' Her voice became a thread of sound. 'No one can replace Peter. But, despite my many failings, I remain a princess of the Imperial House. If the Emperor insists that I marry Duke Nikolaos of Larissa, I shall obey him.'

Lady Sophia nodded and adjusted Martina's shawl. 'Of course. I am glad we have thought of a way you may keep this little one.'

Theodora sent Sophia a watery smile. 'I have you to thank for that. We are simply embroidering your story.'

'Yes, my lady. I am pleased to have been helpful, but…'

'Yes?'

'I want you to be happy. Can you be happy with Duke Nikolaos?'

'I shall strive to be,' Theodora said, firmly. 'I am the Princess Theodora and it is my duty to cater to my husband's happiness. My happiness will depend on his.'

Sophia opened her mouth to reply, but brisk footsteps sounded outside the lodge.

'Hush, that will be Captain Brand.' Deftly, Theodora dragged her shawl over her brown, simply dressed hair, arranging it so most of her features were concealed. 'We have come this far without him realising that I am the Princess— we must not fall at the last hurdle.' When she was satisfied that all Captain Brand would see was a pair of dark eyes, she nodded at Sophia to admit him. Not wishing to draw attention to herself, Theodora tried to speak to him as little as possible.

'Come in,' Lady Sophia called.

The latch clicked and Captain Brand stepped on to the threshold. Theodora nodded distantly at him. He was Anglo-Saxon, as were many men in the Varangian Guard. Because of his origins, to those born within the Empire, the Captain was as much a foreigner as Peter had been. A barbarian, an outsider. Pain twisted Theodora's insides, a sudden cramp. She recognised the pain for what it was, an impossible longing for Peter to be brought back to life, for her life to have continued in Rascia.

Peter, why did you have to die?

She kept her features clear of emotion. She had been trained.

As had Captain Brand. Even though the man had been born in England, far beyond the reach of the Empire, he had a firm grasp of Palace protocols. In the Imperial Palace, men and women lived almost separate lives unless they were married. The unmarried women's quarters were in one section of the Palace, the men's in another. And Captain Brand, God bless him, had displayed his understanding of the protocols during the voyage from Dyrrachion. He had spoken to Theodora and her ladies only when absolutely necessary, and then never when one of the ladies had been on her own.

It was all so different from the friendly informality of the Rascian Court. And doubtless, when they finally reached the Imperial Palace, everything would become even more formal. Theodora's days of freedom were over.

'So, Captain…' Sophia smiled politely at him '…have you discovered what was happening the night our galley reached the City?'

'Yes, my lady.' The Captain remained on the threshold. He was carrying his helmet and his hair was rain-dampened. He looked over his shoulder. 'It is a…delicate matter.'

'Come in, do,' Theodora said, her hunger for news temporarily overcoming her resolution to play the part of a quiet, shy lady. 'We are not back at Court yet.'

The Captain's eyes widened, nevertheless, he did as he was asked, closing the door behind him.

Sweet Mary, the news must be grave indeed. And I was too forthright. I must take care not to betray myself. It was a struggle constantly having to pretend, particularly when she was impatient to learn what had been going on in Constantinople. *I must keep Martina. Somehow I will find a way to keep Martina.*

'Ladies, as you know, I sent scouts back to the City after we arrived here.'

Captain Brand's accent betrayed his foreign, barbaric birth, yet he was perfectly comprehensible. In any case, Theodora had had much practice in understanding barbarians.

'The lighthouse, yes, of course,' Sophia said, correctly interpreting Theodora's subtle nod as meaning that she should take over and speak for her. 'And the fires, the smoke drifting across the water—you thought we were in danger.'

Captain Brand nodded. 'I was afraid there may have been some…' he was picking his words with care '…unrest in the City.'

Theodora cut in, despite herself. 'Captain, the Palace has its own walls, its own fortifications. Surely unrest in the City would not penetrate the Palace?'

'I did not wish to take the risk, my lady. Not with Princess Theodora's entourage. As it turns out, my instincts were right.' His voice became confidential. 'Ladies, my scouts tell me that, while we were at sea, there has been a palace coup.'

Theodora's breath left her. Indeed, she was so startled she loosed her grip on her shawl and it fell away from her face. Irritably, she retrieved it. Until she was once again the Princess Theodora Doukaina, she must keep hidden. 'A revolution?'

'Yes, my lady. One of the generals has seized the throne.'

Theodora exchanged stunned glances with Sophia. *Has the Emperor been murdered?* It had happened before. Theodora's mind began to race and her next thought was, shamingly, that perhaps the tide had turned in her favour. If the man who called himself her uncle was no longer Emperor, she might not have to marry Duke Nikolaos.

My secret will be safe, Martina will be safe. Finally, she found her voice. 'One of the generals? Which one?' *It could not be Duke Nikolaos. It must not be the Duke. If it is the Duke...*

Her mind seized up. It was bad enough to consider deceiving a general, but the thought of deceiving an Emperor...

'Alexios Komnenos is now Emperor,' the Captain said.

Not Duke Nikolaos. Thank God. 'And what of my unc—?'

A sharp kick from Sophia had Theodora's mouth snapping shut just in time. As she herself had said, they had made it thus far without mishap, it wouldn't do to fall at the last hurdle. 'What of Emperor Nikephoros? What has happened to him?'

'He abdicated, my lady, about two weeks ago.'

The Emperor had abdicated.

'Two weeks ago,' she murmured. 'That would have been about the time we sailed past the Palace.'

'Yes, my lady. His Imperial Majesty Alexios Komnenos was enthroned on Easter Day. Both he and his wife—Empress Irene—have been crowned.'

Theodora struggled to control her expression, but this news had turned her world upside down.

Sophia gave her a subtle nudge and smiled sweetly at the Captain. 'Empress Irene is a cousin of our princess, is she not?'

'Yes, my lady, so I understand.'

Theodora shifted. This would take time to absorb, her young cousin was wearing the Imperial crown. 'Captain, do you know if Emperor Nikephoros has come to harm?'

'He is safe, we were informed he has retired from public life. I believe it was at the instigation of the Patriarch.'

Theodora nodded. That made sense, the Patriarch was Bishop of Constantinople, one of the most influential men in the City. That the Patriarch had suggested Emperor Nikephoros should abdicate bore testimony to the weakness of her 'uncle's' regime, he had never been popular. She sighed, not much about Emperor Nikephoros had filtered back to Rascia. He was old, that much she did know.

Theodora had no genuine blood ties with Emperor Nikephoros. The man had seized the throne from her real uncle, Emperor Michael, forcing him to abdicate and retire to a monastery. He had then legitimised his claim to the throne by marrying Emperor Michael's wife.

'How ironic that Emperor Nikephoros should himself be forced to abdicate,' Sophia observed.

Theodora's thoughts raced on, the coup changed everything. It might invalidate her betrothal to Duke Nikolaos… The old Emperor had pushed for the marriage, but if he were gone…

Can I escape the marriage? Theodora looked longingly at the infant on Sophia's lap. *If I escape marriage with Duke Nikolaos, it will surely be easier to keep Martina.*

'General Alexios Komnenos has become Emperor,' she murmured.

She might have to revise her plans. Alexios Komnenos was nothing like his aged predecessor. Theodora had a chance of hiding what she had done from the old Emperor. But the new one? Alexios Komnenos was young and vigorous, he was reputed to be highly intelligent. Holy Mother, the last thing she needed was a young, vigorous and intelligent emperor! It would be hard, if not impossible, to pull the wool over his eyes. And extremely dangerous if she were found out…

'Yes, my lady,' Captain Brand said. 'Komnenos had the backing of the generals. The army was camped outside the City walls for weeks.'

'The army?' Theodora went very still. She had gone sharply, horribly cold. 'I don't suppose you know if Duke—General—Nikolaos of Larissa was with them?'

The Varangian Captain reached for the door latch. 'Yes, my lady, I believe he returned from Larissa shortly before the coup. Duke Nikolaos is loyal to Emperor Alexios. He is his Commander-in-Chief.'

'Where is he now?'

'The Emperor?'

'No, Duke Nikolaos, the Commander-in-Chief.' Theodora watched Captain Brand's eyebrows lift, her question had surprised him, as well it might. She rushed to explain. 'I…I was wondering if you had heard whether…whether the Princess and the Duke have had a chance to meet?'

'My lady, I have no idea. But if you would care to warn the other ladies about what has happened at Court, I would be grateful.'

'Certainly, Captain,' Sophia said. 'Thank you for keeping us informed.'

The Captain bowed. 'Lady Sophia, please ask the ladies to gather their belongings together. We shall board within the hour. It is only a short sail down the Bosphoros. The galley should reach the Palace Harbour early this evening.'

'Thank you, Captain, I shall inform the others.'

When the door clicked behind the captain, Theodora sank on to the bench. 'Holy Mother—he's in the City! Duke Nikolaos is *already* in the City.'

Sophia nodded. 'Yes, my lady.'

Martina gave a small murmur. Theodora's throat tightened, somehow she straightened her spine. 'I can put this off no longer, there must be no more delays. We must get to the Palace, and quickly. I can't expect Katerina to meet the Duke in my stead.'

Chapter Two

⚬⚬⚬

Duke Nikolaos of Larissa, dark hair whipped by the wind, was riding like a demon into the mêlée on the Palace polo field when he realised his man-servant Elias had returned and was waiting for him by the sea wall. Reining in sharply, Niko-laos wheeled Hermes about and spurred away from the action.

'Devil take you, Niko! What are you playing at?' a team-mate cried, with scant regard for formality, as the ball hurtled across the turf. Duke Nikolaos was General of the Athanatoi Cavalry and Commander-in-Chief of the Imperial Army, but he had made it clear that in this practice session, he was playing with friends. He was not on his warhorse today. Hermes was small and light-boned. Hermes was built for speed.

'Niko.' Another player leaned out of the saddle and took a wild swipe at the ball flying beneath his horse's hooves. Missing the ball, the man righted himself with difficulty.

'Damn you, Niko,' he bawled, as his general trotted from the field.

Nikolaos swung his mallet over one shoulder and grinned. 'A thousand apologies, I have business to attend to. In any case, I fear the girth is going on this saddle.'

A chorus of shouts and groans went up. 'We're a man short.'

'Curse it, Niko, you can't retreat mid-game.'

'Keep practising,' Niko said. 'There's less than a month before the tournament—the tournament, I remind you, that the Athanatoi shall win.' He gestured at a lad standing with the reserve horses on the edge of the field. 'Zeno?'

'General?'

'Take my place, will you?'

The boy's eyes lit up and he vaulted on to the back of one of the horses. 'Gladly. Thank you, my lord.'

'It's your first time in the field, isn't it, Zeno?'

'Yes, General.'

'It looks like a game and so it is. But one word of warning, it's a ruthless one. Take no prisoners. Those miscreants…' with a grin, Nikolaos jerked his head at the men he had assigned to the opposite team '…will show you no mercy. Remember that, and there's a chance you will keep your seat.'

'Yes, General.'

Nikolaos swung from the saddle, tossing the

reins to Elias. His stallion's brown coat was flecked with foam. 'You delivered my message?'

'Yes, my lord.'

Elias looked troubled. One of the reasons Nikolaos had kept Elias as his manservant for so long was that he never dissembled or lied to him. And that, as Nikolaos had learned, was a rare and precious quality. 'Don't tell me, the Princess is still ailing?'

'Apparently so, my lord.'

A cypress at the edge of the polo ground was swaying slightly in the onshore breeze. Nikolaos scowled at it. 'That's twice I've sent messages to her apartment. I take it you saw no sign of her this time either?'

It had occurred to Nikolaos that Princess Theodora might be hiding from him, but that would seem absurd. She was an Imperial princess and the former Emperor, the man who had married her aunt, had approved their marriage.

She could not have taken a dislike to me, since we have never met.

Elias was shaking his head. 'Not as much as a glimpse, my lord. All I saw was a handful of maidservants and a guard assigned to her apartment. Other than that her chambers were quiet.'

Nikolaos tapped his thigh with his mallet. 'You left my message with the guard, I take it?'

'Yes, my lord.'

'What regiment was he?'

'Varangian.'

Nikolaos grunted. 'Should be reliable. Did you get the man's name and rank?'

'Kari. A trooper.'

'Very well. My patience is wearing thin, but I shall give the Princess till this afternoon to respond. And then, if she continues to ignore my existence, I will have to speak to His Imperial Majesty. Our betrothal was made at the behest of his predecessor. Perhaps Emperor Alexios has decided he has other plans for her.'

Removing his gloves, Nikolaos tucked them thoughtfully into his belt. He could not decide whether Princess Theodora's illness was genuine or whether it was an excuse designed to keep him at a distance. Nikolaos wanted this marriage. He had seen other men's careers blighted by innuendo and rumour and he was determined that was not going to happen to him. Marriage with an Imperial princess was a great honour, it would bolster his position at Court. Was it possible that Emperor Alexios had changed his mind?

Turning his back on the polo field and the turreted wall that protected the Great Palace from both sea and invasion, Nikolaos began walking towards the stables. Elias and Hermes kept pace. 'It is odd, though,' Nikolaos said, raking a hand through windswept brown hair, 'you would think that His Majesty would have mentioned any concerns he has over my marriage arrangements when I was asked to organise the polo tournament.'

'Didn't he confirm that your marriage was to go ahead shortly after he was crowned?'

'He did, he did indeed. Why, then, is the Princess so elusive?'

'I do not know, my lord. Perhaps she really is unwell.'

'Or a reluctant bride,' Nikolaos said. 'Think about it. First, she refused to return to Constantinople when the old emperor summoned her from Rascia, and when she does return, she hides away like a nun.'

'You should give her the benefit of the doubt—she could really be unwell, my lord.'

Nikolaos gave Elias a straight look; he and his manservant had been together since Nikolaos was a boy and there was a strong bond of affection between them. Nikolaos could discuss anything with him. Nikolaos's gut tightened—well, almost anything. 'I have been giving her the benefit of the doubt for some days,' he said, drily. 'It occurs to me that Princess Theodora has no wish to marry.'

'You cannot assume that, my lord.'

'True. I am ready for this wedding to take place, Elias, but if my bride is reluctant?' Nikolaos grimaced. 'Lord, no.'

Nikolaos wanted this marriage. It would signal to the world that he was firmly ensconced with the new regime. And he wanted it soon, before anyone else got wind of his mother's unexpected confession.

I am illegitimate.

The man Nikolaos had always thought of as his father was the late Governor of Larissa, Governor Gregorios. But according to his mother, Lady Verina, Gregorios was not his father. Nikolaos had received his mother's confession as something of a body blow; her marriage to Gregorios of Larissa had seemed blissfully happy. They had been the perfect, loving couple with Governor Gregorios idolising his wife. And Nikolaos would have sworn the affection had not been one-sided, his mother had given every appearance of adoring her husband in return. The intense grief she had displayed at his death could not have been mere pretence. And yet…

I am illegitimate. I have no blood ties with Governor Gregorios.

Dear God, better men than he had their careers wrecked because of their birth. That would not happen to him.

'Will you ask His Majesty for another bride, my lord?'

'I may have to, if Princess Theodora continues to show reluctance.' Nikolaos sighed and ran his hand round the back of the neck. In view of his mother's confession, he needed this marriage more than ever, but…a reluctant bride? No.

'Your mother will be disappointed. She was delighted when you were chosen for the Princess.'

Nikolaos felt his face stiffen, it was hard to keep the anger from his voice. 'Naturally my mother would be pleased. Such a marriage would appease her conscience, if she has one.'

Elias frowned. 'You have had a disagreement with Lady Verina?'

Nikolaos let out a bitter laugh. 'You might put it like that.'

'My lord, I thought—'

Nikolaos silenced Elias with a look. 'Yes, old friend, you are right. My mother was delighted. I never thought we'd hear the end of it. But I will not marry a reluctant bride, however highborn.'

'Duke Nikolaos?'

'Mmm?'

'If the Princess continues hiding away, will you ask Emperor Alexios to release her from the betrothal?'

Hermes clattered across the paving stones as they passed through a fountained courtyard. Water jetted from the mouths of a shoal of bronze fish; rainbows shimmered in the spray. 'I am undecided. It was the previous Emperor who gifted her to me. If Princess Theodora really does prove reluctant, it should be easy enough to persuade His Majesty to give me another bride.' He smiled at Elias. 'I shall give the Princess until this afternoon to respond. Come, let's get to the stables, Hermes needs a rubdown and that girth needs checking.'

'Yes, my lord.'

* * *

That afternoon, Elias carried a third message to Princess Theodora's apartment in the Boukoleon Palace. When he came away, he knew exactly where to find his master. Duke Nikolaos had told him he would be in one of the saddlers' workshops outside the Palace walls.

The saddlers' workshops were clustered together in a narrow street that cut away from the Mese—Middle Street—the main street of the City. Sure enough, Hercules, the Duke's black warhorse, was tethered outside, next to an animal usually assigned to one of the grooms. Entering the workshop, Elias nodded at the groom and leaned against a wall to wait for the Duke to conclude his business.

'But, General—' the saddler's voice was high and tight, his fingers shook as he examined the girth '—it is not as though you take this saddle into battle.'

Nikolaos shook his head. 'You should not underestimate the rigours of the polo field, it's an important part of training for my officers. Use stronger leather next time. Look—' he pulled at the offending strap '—see here?'

'That's a natural flaw, General, part of the animal's skin. You can't avoid natural flaws.'

'Nonsense! Even an untrained eye could see that this section of leather is weak. It should have been discarded. It has no place in a saddle of this quality—of any quality, come to think of

it. Serious injuries can be caused by workman-
ship like this. If it happens again, I shall take my
custom elsewhere. And I shall certainly ensure
that the officers in my regiment know to avoid
your merchandise. That said, I am sure you'll
put it right...'

'Yes, General.' The saddler flushed dark red.
'My apologies, it shall not happen again.'

Nodding at the man, Nikolaos stepped back
into the street and smiled at Elias. 'Well? I can
tell from your face that you had no luck at the
Princess's apartment.'

'No, my lord. This afternoon she is apparently
a little recovered, but there is no message for
you.'

Nikolaos tucked his thumbs into his belt.
'Does the total lack of response strike you as
odd, Elias?' The Princess might be reluctant, but
surely she would have to be gravely ill to ignore
so many messages from the man to whom she
had been betrothed?

'My lord?'

The skin was prickling at the back of Nikolaos's neck. It was the sort of prickling he usually
had on the eve of battle. His instincts were trying
to warn him...of what? Danger. Danger to him?
No, he did not sense that the danger was to him.
To the Princess? That did not seem possible, yet
his instincts had not let him down before.

He looked at the groom. 'My thanks, Paul,

that is all. I shall walk back. Take Hercules back to his stall, would you? Elias, you are with me.'

'Yes, my lord.'

'Something's wrong,' Nikolaos murmured, once the groom had taken the horses and was well out of earshot. He followed the route the groom had taken, turning into the street that led past the Hippodrome, back to the Palace.

'I agree,' Elias said. 'It seems extraordinary that after sending several messages, you have received no response from Princess Theodora.'

The walls of the Palace loomed over them. 'The former Emperor appeared keen, even eager, to promote my marriage to Princess Theodora,' Nikolaos murmured, thinking aloud.

Elias, probably realising that this remark did not require a response, said nothing.

Nikolaos let his thoughts run on, thoughts which he was well aware a few weeks ago would have bordered on treasonous. He had not held the previous Emperor in high regard. Emperor Nikephoros had been weak and ineffective—unscrupulous courtiers had wasted no time in manipulating him. With little strength of will, and almost no understanding of military matters, the man had made a disastrous head of state. Which was why Nikolaos had supported Alexios Komnenos in his bid for the throne. The Empire needed a strong hand at the reins.

With regard to his marriage to Princess Theodora, Nikolaos had been led to believe that Emperor Alexios would honour the arrangement made by his predecessor.

The guards at the Palace gate jumped to attention, saluting as they passed through and entered the first of the courtyards.

'What will you do, my lord?'

'I have had enough of delays and evasions.' Nikolaos grinned at Elias. 'I shall visit the Princess's apartment myself.'

Elias flung him a startled look. 'You would go to the women's quarters in person, my lord?'

Nikolaos lifted his shoulders. 'Why not?'

Elias began to splutter. 'But, my lord, you cannot...not the women's quarters! They...they are sacrosanct...only a close relative may enter...and the Princess...a cousin of the Empress...'

Smiling, Nikolaos waited for his manservant to stutter to a halt which he did, with a final 'My lord, you cannot visit the women's quarters, particularly not those of the Princess.'

Nikolaos sighed. 'Elias, these days it is almost impossible to gain an audience with His Majesty. Ever since the coronation, he has either been deeply involved in affairs of state, or else he is doing penance for seizing the throne.'

'I had heard about the penance. Forty days of fasting and sackcloth and ashes.' Elias pulled a face. 'How much of the penance is left?'

'A little over three weeks. The polo tournament comes towards the end of it. Until then, it is possible to arrange an audience with His

Majesty only for the most pressing of matters. I must resolve the question of my marriage myself.' Niko gestured ahead of him. 'Lead on, Elias, I am hazy about which staircase leads where in the Boukoleon.'

'My lord, you do recall that Princess Theodora's apartment is watched over by Varangian Guards?'

Nikolaos lifted a brow. 'I remember. And I am sure they have sworn allegiance to Emperor Alexios and are as loyal as they have always been. As I am. May I remind you that my own regiment supported His Majesty? I doubt I will be questioned.'

'Yes, my lord, I know. But…but…she is a princess.'

By now Nikolaos and Elias had left several courtyards behind them and had passed the stables and the lighthouse. An imposing building rose before them, with walls like cliffs. The Boukoleon Palace. On the upper levels, Nikolaos could see the stone balustrades where terraces overlooked the gardens and courtyards. On the other side of the Boukoleon, the balconies looked out over the Sea of Marmara.

Nikolaos and Elias reached a columned portico where a broad flight of marble stairs led upwards. 'The women's quarters, Elias?'

His manservant's throat worked. 'This way, my lord.'

* * *

Some hours earlier, Theodora's galley had docked at the Imperial harbour. By the time the sun began to sink, she and her entourage were busy exploring the Princess's apartment at the top of the Boukoleon Palace.

It was a magnificent apartment and had been reduced to chaos by their arrival. Slaves and servants ran in and out of the great double doors, laden with packing cases and trinket boxes. Others bore ewers of water and linen cloths. Trays of refreshments were set out on side-tables for travel-worn ladies. There was something to suit all palates—goblets of wine; milk sweetened with honey; cold meats and soft cheeses; shelled hazelnuts, almond cakes, dates. The gleaming marble floor was hidden under untidy heaps of baggage; ladies' cloaks were strewn over gilded chairs, across inlaid tables and painted screens. Braziers had been lit to lift the chill from the air; and there, on another side-table, perfumed smoke wreathed from a golden globe—roses and the rich scent of incense mingled with the slight tang of salt blown in from the sea.

The time had come for Theodora to end the deception. She must stop pretending to be a lady-in-waiting and become, once again, Princess Theodora Doukaina. The transition from lady-in-waiting to Princess would be tricky, though. There was much to take account of…sins both real and assumed.

'It is time, Sophia,' Theodora murmured as they stood in the light of a large window.

Martina was held fast in Sophia's arms. Filmy purple drapes hung from ceiling to floor, silk hangings that shifted in the breeze coming off the Sea of Marmara. Imperial purple. Theodora bit her lip as guilt rushed through her. Theodora had not herself been 'born in the purple'. This meant that she had not been born in the Purple Chamber, the great birthing room in the Palace that was lined with purple marble and set aside for the confinement of an Empress. Notwithstanding this, she had been allocated this wonderful apartment decorated with the Imperial purple. It was a great honour.

It is an honour I do not deserve, I was not born in the Purple Chamber. Worse, I have deceived everyone. Worse still, I have every intention of continuing to deceive them.

Theodora was as heavily veiled as a Princess of Persia, her gown was voluminous and hid her shape. Until she had successfully reclaimed her place as Princess Theodora Doukaina, she would have to go on hiding behind shawls and veils. Until she found Katerina, the maidservant she had sent on ahead to impersonate her, she must continue to conceal her identity.

Theodora and Katerina were completely unrelated and it was by chance that they might be taken for twins. They had the same dark hair, the same dark eyes, the same slight frame. Some of the ladies had said the Princess and her maidservant were as alike in features and build as two peas in a pod. And until Theodora was once again in her own shoes, until she knew what had been happening in the Palace in the past few weeks, she was not prepared to be seen by anyone save her ladies.

But, Holy Mother, what a mire she had walked into! Katerina seemed to have vanished and so, too, had Lady Anna of Heraklea. Lady Anna was the lady-in-waiting Theodora had sent to accompany Katerina. Theodora had charged Lady Anna with ensuring Katerina had everything she needed to convince the Court that it was she who was Princess Theodora Doukaina.

'Where do you think Katerina and Anna have got to, Sophia?' she asked, conscious of the Varangian Guard standing by the great polished doors, watching them. She edged away from him. 'Why is that guard staring at us? Do you think he knows where they are?'

Sophia gave the Varangian a surreptitious glance. 'You are imagining it, he is simply curious to see the Princess's ladies. I do not think it is more than that.'

'I wish I could agree with you. Where are Katerina and Anna? Why aren't they here?'

'The guard mentioned they were visiting friends.'

'Which friends?'

'He refused to say.'

'Why? Why would he not say?'

'Perhaps he does not know.'

Theodora sighed. 'Perhaps. Lord, it would have been better if Katerina and Anna had kept themselves to the apartment.' She rearranged her veil, making sure the guard could only catch a glimpse of her. In Rascia, she had received many comments about the uncanny resemblance between herself and Katerina. It would not do for someone here to look too closely. Not yet.

My deception must not be discovered, the transition must happen smoothly, Martina's welfare could be at stake.

Theodora reached for her daughter. 'Let me hold her.'

'Are you sure, my lady?' Sophia tipped her head at the watchful Varangian and the army of servants and slaves. 'There are many eyes here.'

'Sophia!' As Theodora took her child, a measure of peace settled over her. Martina gurgled. A chubby hand reached out, pushed Theodora's veil aside and reached for an earring. Theodora's heart squeezed. 'She has her father's eyes,' she murmured. 'Thank heaven we found a suitable wet-nurse—I like Jelena.'

Sophia nodded.

Theodora felt stinging at the back of her eyes. She had enjoyed feeding Martina herself, a sentiment that would surely shock most ladies in the Great Palace, Princesses did not usually feed their babies. But since she had been sent to

join the barbarians in Rascia, it would seem she
had become something of a barbarian herself. It
had been more painful than she cared to admit,
handing Martina over to the wet-nurse. It had
taken time. Weaning Martina had been as painful physically as it had been emotionally. Theodora's breasts had hurt, her heart had ached. The
sacrifice had been necessary though, no one at
Court must suspect that she had borne a child.

Setting her jaw, she stared out of the window, out past the Palace Harbour to the Sea of
Marmara. The sea was as grey as the sky. Ships
were sailing past the promontory—merchantmen,
dromons, rowing boats. Seagulls were circling a
fishing boat; she could hear their thin mewing.

'The lions and oxen are still there,' Sophia
said. 'I had forgotten about them.'

'Hmm?'

'The statues on the Imperial quays. I had forgotten how impressive they are, like sentinels.'

'It is certainly a change from Rascia,' Theodora said, wistfully. She caught a flutter of gold,
a couple of galleys were flying the Imperial standard. The same flag was flying on the towers on
either side of the entrance to the Palace Harbour
and the double-headed eagle was plainly visible
on both of them. There was no doubt of it, she
was home. She sighed and wished she did not
feel so torn. The coup had changed everything.

*What will I say if I am summoned to meet Em-
peror Alexios?* It was one thing to have planned

to deceive a weak and ageing Emperor, but Emperor Alexios was strong and in his prime. Intelligent. *God save me.*

Sophia was fingering the delicate purple curtains. 'I have never seen such hangings, my lady, all silk. Everything in your apartment is silk, silk and marble.'

'This apartment is not mine,' Theodora reminded her quietly. 'Not until I have reclaimed my identity.'

She risked another look at the Varangian by the doors. He had stood at his post like a rock since their arrival. His gaze was alert. Too alert. Several ladies had returned with her to the Palace, but it was she whom he was focused on. *He has noted the resemblance between me and Katerina.* 'That man knows exactly where Katerina and Anna are, and I would swear he knows who I am, too. Why will he not answer our questions?' Anxiety clawed her insides. 'Do you think they are safe and well? Do you think they have been found out? Arrested?'

'Sweet Mary, I hope not.'

'Then where are they? I took pains to tell them to be discreet until we arrived. I shall never forgive myself if they have come to harm, but I had to wean Martina on to the wet-nurse, I had to—' she broke off as the guard's gaze never wavered.

Enclosing Martina's tiny hand in hers, Theodora pulled her veil across her face and presented the Varangian with her back. She was on the point of handing Martina back to Sophia when there was a disturbance at the entrance.

The shining double doors were flung wide. The guard stood firmly in the centre, feet braced as he challenged someone out on the landing.

'I am sorry, General,' the Varangian said. 'You may not enter these chambers—they are assigned to Princess Theodora.'

'I am aware of that.' The newcomer's voice was cultured. 'Why do you think I have been sending messages here these past few days?'

Theodora froze. She could not see the man on the landing clearly—the doorframe blocked full view of him—but she caught the impression of height. He sounded confident, even arrogant. A jewelled sword-hilt flashed, a gold ring gleamed on a strong, well-shaped hand. Oh, no! If this man was permitted to bear arms in the Palace, he must be trusted indeed. And for him to have been sending messages to the Princess's apartment, he must be...

'Duke Nikolaos,' Sophia hissed. 'It must be your general.'

Theodora's heart started to race. If it was Duke Nikolaos, he was breaking with the conventions by coming in person to an apartment in the women's quarters. She was not prepared to meet him. And yet...curiosity flared into being, undeniable curiosity... What did he look like? If she were careful...

Martina firmly in her arms, Theodora went

to the door. It might not be Duke Nikolaos, she told herself, it might be that this man was one in a long line of courtiers who had come to pay his respects to the Princess. Katerina could simply be hiding away because she had been overwhelmed by the part she had been asked to play.

The man was tall and broad-shouldered. He had strong features and a Roman nose that would not have looked out of place on an ancient coin. His hair was thick and dark and in need of a trim. Theodora received the impression of much energy, energy that was barely contained. He had a faintly disreputable air, despite the patrician profile. His jaw was square and he had high cheekbones. Bold, dark eyes.

Noticing her looking at him, he smiled. His teeth were white and even, the smile practised.

Theodora's belly lurched. She had time to notice a small scar beneath one of those dark eyes. She had time to notice how good-looking he was—if you found dark men who ought to have visited a barber a week since attractive. Which she, of course, did not. She had time to notice his clothes. They were those of a nobleman. His tunic was olive-coloured samite, a heavy silk, lavishly embroidered in silver and gold thread. Theodora's gaze lingered on his sword. The grip was leather, the pommel was gold and set with an emerald of exceptional clarity. The sword looked like a dress sword, but the wear on the grip warned that this sword was more than mere ornament. This man might be dressed as a nobleman, but he was clearly more warrior than courtier.

Duke Nikolaos of Larissa, General of the Athanatoi Cavalry regiment—the famous Immortals—Commander-in-Chief of the Imperial Army. He had come to the very doors of her apartment. Captain Brand had been correct—the coup had brought the Duke racing back from Larissa in support of his fellow general, Alexios Komnenos, now Emperor.

Mouth dry, Theodora lifted her gaze. Dark eyes were fixed on her, the intensity of his gaze was vaguely unsettling. He inclined his head.

'My lady?' He glanced briefly at the baby in Theodora's arms. 'I take it you are one of the Princess's ladies-in-waiting?' His voice had a thread of steel running through it; it was the voice of a man who had the habit of command, of a man whose commands were always obeyed. And his mouth, now she looked at it, was held in a tight line. The veneer of politeness was thin in this man, his manner was verging on insolent.

Theodora ignored the frantic tug Sophia gave to her sleeve and her murmur of protest; she was *not* going to retreat. 'Please take the child,' she said, placing her daughter in Sophia's arms. Secure in the knowledge that her veil was wrapped tightly about her and that only her eyes were showing, she turned back to the man in the doorway. 'My lord? You are addressing me?'

The dark eyes sharpened, her tone had been

too peremptory. A lady-in-waiting, as she was purporting to be, would never address a nobleman in such a tone. Certainly not before she found out who he was.

'Yes, you.' Shouldering the startled Varangian to one side, he occupied the doorway. 'Where is your mistress?' His tone moderated. 'I have been trying to arrange an audience with the Princess for some days, but I have been told she is ailing. I trust she is not seriously ill?'

Theodora gave him a diplomatic smile. Cool, formal, and slightly distant. She would not let him annoy her. 'Princess Theodora is, as I am sure you have already been told, not receiving guests today. I will, however, ensure your message reaches her. May I know to whom I am speaking?'

He bowed, and as he did so Theodora couldn't help but notice how his mouth had eased as she answered him. His lips twitched. As though he were laughing at her! 'I am Duke Nikolaos of Larissa and I am entirely at your disposal, my lady. And you are…?'

It *was* Duke Nikolaos. Inclining her head to hide the rush of emotion—this was the man her uncle had decreed she must marry—Theodora affected not to have heard his question. 'Please come back tomorrow, my lord.'

He looked her up and down. Theodora was confident her veil was still in place, so why had she to resist the urge to adjust it? Thankfully, he wouldn't see much of her. Just her eyes. With luck, he would assume he was speaking to one of the more modest of Theodora's ladies. She stared at the toes of her slippers as though her life depended on it. She could not let him study her, lest when he met her as Princess Theodora, he realised that she was the same woman who had told him the Princess was not yet well enough to meet him.

This man is a commander, a general of the Imperial Army. I must say as little as possible. Duke Nikolaos had an air of ruthlessness about him, a man such as this would not hesitate to dispense with Palace protocols if it suited him. That he had come to the apartment in person proved it. *This man is dangerous.*

Theodora effaced herself, backing away, her gaze fixed on the marble floor tiles. For the first time in her life she was grateful for the rigid rules and conventions set up to protect unmarried women. Even as she prayed they would keep him at arm's length, an odd thrill of uncertainty shivered through her. *Protocols mean nothing to this man, he is a rule-breaker.*

She retreated with Sophia into a room that opened out from the reception chamber and overheard him exchanging remarks with the guard. When she looked back, the great double doors were closed, Duke Nikolaos had gone.

Martina began to whimper. 'It is time she was fed,' Theodora said.

'I will take her to Jelena,' Sophia said. 'One moment.'

Theodora found herself standing alone in the large bedchamber. It was so lavishly appointed that her jaw had dropped when she had first arrived at the apartment and seen it. A huge bed filled much of the space, liberally festooned with mulberry hangings. There was yard after yard of gold braid and fringing; there were silk mulberry sheets, gold and mulberry-coloured cushions. Marble-topped tables were set against the walls; there were golden basins and ewers; there, on the floor, was one of the travelling chests she had given to Katerina to help her play her part as Princess.

This is my bedchamber, or it will be when I am Princess Theodora Doukaina once more. Her heart missed its beat. *If I marry Duke Nikolaos, that bed is where we will consummate our marriage.*

The great bed was a world away from her bed at the Rascian Court. In Rascia, Theodora had had her own chamber, as befitted a Princess of the Empire, but her bed there had been very different to this one. The bed in which she and Peter had loved each other had been furnished with plain linens, not silks and damasks and…

The air shifted behind her, Sophia had returned.

'Martina is feeding well, my lady, she… Good Heavens,' Sophia said faintly, looking at the bed.

'Quite.'

'What are you going to do?'

Theodora glanced at the door and lowered her voice. 'First, I shall reclaim my identity. I shall make that Varangian tell us where Katerina and Anna have gone. And then I shall once again be Princess Theodora Doukaina.'

'Will you marry him?'

Theodora stared at the mulberry-draped bed in the centre of the chamber and bit her lip. Marry that handsome, ruthless-looking stranger? 'Only if I have to.'

Chapter Three

Sophia moved so she had clear sight of the apartment entrance, anxiety clouding her expression. 'Oh, dear, Duke Nikolaos did seem rather... rather...'

'Overpowering?'

Sophia nodded. 'Perhaps you should seek an audience with the Emperor, my lady, he may look kindly on a request to set the arrangement aside.'

'I wish I had your confidence. Emperor Alexios is a soldier, he is more likely to expect blind obedience. Oh, Lord, of all the times for there to have been a coup, this is surely the worst! The last thing I need is a strong emperor.' Theodora jerked her head in the direction of the Varangian posted at the entrance. 'And I had forgotten the extent to which women here are cloistered. Life here is going to be somewhat different from

life in Rascia. Just look at that man. Is he there
for our benefit, or is he spying on us?'

'Married women have more freedom than unmarried ones, Princess.'

Theodora shot her lady-in-waiting a sharp
look. 'You think I should marry the Duke.'

Sophia lifted her shoulders. 'It is hard to tell on
a first meeting, but Duke Nikolaos did not strike
me as a…conventional man. Such a man would
not care for the opinions of others…'

'You are saying he would let me go my own
way?'

'I do not know. Perhaps.' Another shrug.
'However, if you do marry him, he will soon
discover you are not…not as innocent as he believes.'

Theodora sighed. 'Were I to marry him, I
would simply have to pretend.'

'You would act the virgin?'

'I shall be as pure as the driven snow.'

'He would know,' Sophia said, firmly. 'A man
like that would surely know.'

'I disagree. He's a general, a warrior…he
didn't strike me as being particularly…subtle.
Surely I can convince him I am innocent?'

'If you say so, my lady.'

Giving Sophia a curt nod—her doubts were
irritating—Theodora strode back into the reception chamber. *'Guard!'*

The Varangian looked warily at her. 'My
lady?'

'I have questions and this time you will give me the truth. When we arrived, you told us that the Princess was visiting friends—is that not so?' The guard flushed dark red and opened his mouth, but Theodora swept on. 'You also told Duke Nikolaos the Princess was sick. Why? Where is she?' When the guard would not meet her gaze, but stared woodenly at the wall behind her, she went to stand directly in front of him. 'Look me in the eye, when I am speaking to you. The Princess is not sick, nor is she out visiting friends. *Where is she?*'

The guard's throat worked.

It struck Theodora that the Varangian was young to be in such a position of such responsibility, she softened her voice. 'Do not be afraid. It is my belief you are acting on orders. It is also my belief that you know the whereabouts of the Princess.' Her foot tapped. 'You will tell me. This instant.'

The young man stared at her and gave a slight nod. With a lurch Theodora realised that he had been studying her while he made up his mind about her. *He realises I am the Princess.*

'Very well, my lady. If you wish, I can send her a message. I am sure she will join you shortly.'

Theodora let her breath out in a rush. 'Thank you. Please send the message at once.'

The young Varangian was as good as his word. Scarcely an hour later, when Theodora was in the bedchamber supervising the unpacking of her belongings with Sophia, someone scratched on the door.

'Enter.'

Katerina burst into the room. She was swathed in shawls and silk veils and escorted by a man wearing the uniform of a Varangian officer. The officer followed her right into the bedchamber and scowled at Theodora.

Theodora's heart sank, she knew this man. He was Ashfirth Saxon, Commander of the Varangian Guard. She had last seen him in Dyrrachion on the outskirts of the Empire.

Theodora had never actually spoken to the Commander, because it had been in Dyrrachion that she and Katerina had switched places. They had deceived him into thinking that he was escorting the Princess back to the Palace, whereas in truth he had been escorting Katerina.

Does the Commander know that rather than escorting me, he was duped into escorting my maidservant? Is that why he is looking so coldly at me?

'My lady!' Katerina dropped to her knees and bowed her head, several veils slithered to the floor. 'It is so good to see you! Oh, my lady—'

Afraid that Katerina might mention Martina, Theodora held up her hand. 'A moment, Katerina, we are not alone.'

Commander Ashfirth gazed at her with cool, assessing eyes and stepped fully into the bedchamber. Reaching behind him, he shut the door with a snap.

Theodora stiffened. 'What do you think you are doing?'

'My lady, you are the Princess?' the Commander demanded, voice curt. Holy Virgin, he knew about the deception practised upon him.

Does he know about Martina?

Katerina scrambled to her feet. 'Of course this is the Princess.' She laid a hand on the Commander's chest. 'Ash, all is well. The Princess is home at last and I need to speak to her, in confidence.'

'You want me to go?'

'If you wouldn't mind waiting in the reception chamber.' Katerina smiled. 'I will introduce you properly when I have brought the Princess up to date with everything that has happened since we last saw each other.'

Commander Ashfirth nodded at Katerina, gave Theodora a grudging bow and left the bedchamber.

Theodora looked thoughtfully at Katerina. Katerina had had an unhappy past. Indeed, it had been Theodora who had saved her from a life of abuse as a slave and had freed her. The Katerina whom Theodora knew had been extremely wary of men. 'You are very familiar with Commander Ashfirth.'

What has she told him?

Katerina's smile lit up the bedchamber. 'Yes,

my lady, and with very good reason—the Commander is my husband.'

Theodora's eyes went wide. 'You *married* Commander Ashfirth?' Theodora had never thought Katerina would be able to trust a man again, never mind marry. 'So soon?' It had only been a few weeks since Theodora had persuaded Katerina to take her place. And now she was married?

'It was not a difficult choice, my lady, *despoina*. Ashfirth is an honourable man, and thanks to you I am—' her chin inched up '—a free woman. I have every right to marry.'

Theodora smiled and touched Katerina's arm. 'Of course you do.' Her hand fell away. 'You must tell me everything. First, if you please, you must tell me how much you have told him.' She lowered her voice. 'Does he know about Martina?'

Katerina shook her head and a twist of hair, as dark as Theodora's, trembled at her temple. *'No.'*

Theodora felt her tension ease. 'Thank God.' She frowned at the closed door. 'Is Anna outside? I should like to see her, too.'

Katerina grimaced. 'Princess, I…I'm afraid that is impossible, Lady Anna has left the City.'

'I beg your pardon?'

'Lady Anna left Constantinople several days ago.'

Theodora groped for the bed, she had to sit down. 'Anna *abandoned* you when I charged her with looking after you?' Katerina had little knowledge of the ways of the Court, which was why Theodora had asked her lady-in-waiting, Anna of Heraklea, to go with her. Anna was meant to have taken Katerina under her wing; she had promised to explain the intricacies of court protocol to her...but if Anna had left the City...?

'Princess, Lady Anna knew I was safe. By the time she left, she knew that Commander Ashfirth and I...that we...' Katerina glanced at the great bed and coloured 'She knew I was safe.'

Theodora rubbed her forehead. 'What on earth happened? Blessed Mother, you had best start from when you arrived at the Palace.'

'All went well, at first. I was nervous, of course, but Lady Anna was a great help and Ash...the Commander...was kind. We did not make much of a show of ourselves, nor did we plan to do so. But almost as soon as we had arrived, General Alexios staged his coup and his mercenaries overran the City. For a few days all was chaos.'

Theodora shook her head as Katerina told her about the old Emperor's downfall, as she learned how Katerina and Anna were caught up in the unrest at the time of the coup and had to flee marauding mercenaries. Theodora did not have to be a seer to realise that Commander Ashfirth had helped Katerina, but her jaw dropped when she learned that Anna had been saved by a Frankish knight she had bought in the slave market.

Theodora held up her hand. 'You are saying

that Anna bought a cavalry officer at the slave
market? A Frank?'

'Yes, my lady, *despoina*.'

When Katerina proceeded to explain that
Anna had fallen in love with the slave and had
sailed off to Apulia with him in order to escape
an arranged marriage, Theodora fell back against
the mulberry pillows.

'Anna let a Frankish cavalry officer carry her
off to Apulia?'

'Yes, Princess.'

Theodora could not help but groan. 'I don't
know what I expected when we returned and
found the apartment empty, but this…' She
caught her breath. 'The knight will not hurt
Anna, will he?'

'I believe that he loves her, he intends to marry
her.'

'That at least is something to be thankful for.'

'I am sorry, Princess. Everything was going
smoothly until His Majesty, the new Emper—'

'Yes, yes, I am sure you did your best.' With
a sigh, Theodora pushed herself upright. She
needed no reminder that the dawn of the new
regime changed everything. 'In truth, Katerina,
in the circumstances you did well. There is one
slight problem…'

'*Despoina*…?'

'Duke Nikolaos came to this apartment in person this afternoon. He was looking for me. As I
understand it, he arrived in Constantinople with

His Majesty and he has been sending me messages for some days. The Duke is not pleased to have been, as he sees it, ignored.'

'Oh.'

'Exactly. Oh.'

Katerina clasped her hands at her breast. 'Princess, I am deeply sorry not to have been here. Ashfirth felt it was too risky. I have been at his house in the City; he refused to let me leave.'

'And you were happy to fall in with his wishes.'

'I...yes.'

What must it be like to be loved in such a way? A painful twinge that felt alarmingly like envy shot through Theodora. *What must it be like?*

Katerina was staring at a swirling pattern in the marble floor, twisting her fingers together. 'My apologies, Princess, I would have insisted on being here if I knew the Duke was in the City. Ashfirth didn't tell me.'

'Never mind, he was probably trying to protect you. And you are here now, which means we can each step back into our own shoes. It will be a relief to you, I am sure. Katerina, tomorrow the Imperial Court is going to find that Princess Theodora Doukaina is much recovered. She is going to make something of a show of herself and we need to discuss how she is to go about it. Once we have done that, you must take me into the reception chamber. I should like to thank your husband for all he has done for you.'

* * *

Next day, the bells for morning service had barely faded when courtiers in the Great Palace were at last granted clear sight of Princess Theodora Doukaina. She trotted out of the Imperial Stables at the head of a glittering entourage. Her stallion was the colour of milk, its flowing mane and tail had been neatly plaited with violet ribbon made from the same delicate fabric as her gown. The Princess had, so the word went, been up and about since dawn.

Princess Theodora led her cavalcade through the spring sunlight to the Mangana Palace, where she dismounted and went inside with a handful of ladies-in-waiting. She was doubtless reacquainting herself with her aunt, the former Empress. No one could say how the meeting went, the Princess had simply dismounted and gone inside. She emerged some half an hour later, climbed back into the saddle, and set about reacquainting herself with the City.

Princess Theodora Doukaina rode out through the Palace gates and no one had seen the like of it in years. A contingent of Varangians marched alongside her, fearsome battle-axes flashing in the light. Her outriders were wearing the uniform of Palace Guards and Lady Sophia, a favoured lady-in-waiting, was riding at her side. With the rest of her attendants riding a horse-length behind, the Princess processed down the entire length of the Mese—Middle Street.

Her next stop was at the Church of the Holy Apostles for prayers. Then she and her retinue paraded about under the arches of the aqueduct that carried fresh water into the heart of Constantinople. Citizens and slaves stopped in their tracks. From streets and alleyways, from windows and doors, heads craned to look.

There was no mistaking Princess Theodora Doukaina on that milk-white stallion. Some of the onlookers half-expected to discover that the Princess who had lived so long among the barbarians—ten years, imagine!—had grown horns and a tail. But there were no horns, just a jewel-encrusted diadem that had been set on elaborately arranged brown hair. Pearls swung on pendants dangling from the diadem; matching pearls hung from her ears. There was no tail, either, just yards of flowing violet silk. Princess Theodora's smile was gracious and her brown eyes sparkled. She looked happy to be home.

Behind the Princess and her lady there was always that long and colourful train of ladies and maidservants. In short, the Princess was seen with enough attendants to satisfy the needs of a dozen princesses, let alone one. Silver glittered at wrists and fingers; gold shone on headbands and jewelled cloak-pins. Shawls fluttered, bright as butterfly wings—pink, blue, green, crimson. The ladies' eyes were, as was seemly, downcast;

they were talking to each other non-stop, chattering like sparrows. Harness jingled; hooves struck sparks from the paved streets.

Word spread like wildfire, the crowds grew. Everyone wanted to see for themselves that Princess Theodora was back. She was clearly enjoying perfect health and looked every inch the Princess. For those hoping for a scandal, she looked disappointingly normal.

'So that's what she looks like,' one man muttered to his slave. 'She was hidden away for so long, I thought she must be hideously scarred, but she's lovely, quite lovely.'

'That stallion is no lady's mount,' observed the young wife of one of the generals.

'She's controlling it well,' the general said. 'And given it only returned yesterday with her women, that is no mean feat, it must be champing at the bit for a good gallop.'

At last Theodora rode back to the stables, she was aware that all eyes had been on her—she had expected nothing less. *They hoped for a pageant. I trust this has satisfied them.* She felt exhausted.

'Princess, we can leave the horses at the Boukoleon portico,' Sophia said gently. 'A groom will walk them back to the stables.'

'I prefer to walk,' Theodora said, realising, too late, that her tone had been curt. A slave-girl watching from one of the doorways lifted her eyebrows. Theodora made a note to soften her voice. She was not going to enjoy the restrictions that would be imposed on her, but there was no point snapping at poor Sophia because she was unused to being the centre of so much attention. 'Besides, I have yet to inspect the stables. I want to speak to the head groom, there may be days when I am unable to ride and the horses must not be neglected.'

Sophia nodded.

Theodora gestured for one of the accompanying guards. 'Captain Brand?'

'Despoina?'

'There are orders for the head groom that I should like to deliver personally. Lady Sophia will accompany me.' She gestured at the train of attendants. 'Be so good as to tell the other ladies they may return to the women's quarters. You may escort them.'

'Yes, my lady.' The Captain exchanged words with a couple of sergeants and turned back to her. 'Princess, I must tell you I have orders myself. Commander Ashfirth insists that I remain with you until you are safely in your apartment.'

Theodora kept her irritation from her face. Yes, this was how it was going to be. Already it had started; she was hedged in by rules, by other people's expectations. Her days of freedom were truly over.

'Very well, Captain.'

In a tack room in the Imperial Stables, Duke Nikolaos was checking his equipment with Elias and one of his grooms. That faulty girth had been weighing on his mind. His gear was regularly checked, both by himself and his groom, it seemed unlikely that they should have missed such an obvious flaw.

'This saddle is fine, my lord,' Elias pronounced.

'This halter also,' said the groom.

Nikolaos looped the bridle he had been examining on to its hook with a sound of exasperation. 'And this. I simply don't understand how we could have missed that girth.'

'Everything here is in order, Duke Nikolaos. Shall I return the saddles to the racks?'

'Please do.' Nikolaos waved at the heap of harness. 'Put it all away, Paul, there's nothing wrong with any of it.' He paused. 'On second thought, leave out gear for two horses, I have business in the City; afterwards I shall take a gallop through the countryside. Elias, saddle up, you are coming with me.'

Nikolaos hefted a saddle at his manservant and together they headed for the stalls.

'Where to, my lord?' Elias asked, slipping the bridle over the brown mare that had been his gift from his master some years previously.

Hercules harrumphed and whickered a greeting as his master entered his stall. 'We shall go to Cleo's first and then—'

'Cleo's?' Elias looked faintly uncomfortable. 'Are you sure you want me with you?'

'I shan't stay long,' Nikolaos said, slinging the saddle on to his horse and tightening the girth.

'You are going to tell her about your marriage.'

'She knows about that already. I am going to bid her farewell.'

Elias went very still. 'Really?'

Nikolaos gave his manservant a rueful look. 'I cannot afford to alienate a princess, Elias. Remember, she is a Doukas—cousin to the Empress.'

'Yes, my lord.'

'It strikes me that, if I am to be married, I should start by trying to do the right thing. Cleo must go.' Lady Verina had given Nikolaos a mistrust of women; nevertheless, he wanted to at least start his marriage by trying to do the right thing.

Light footsteps approached. Voices. A shadow formed in the doorway. One of the stable boys was hanging about outside, watching someone in the stable yard.

Elias muttered under his breath.

'What's that, Elias?'

'Nothing, my lord.'

Niko narrowed his eyes. 'You don't believe me.'

Elias leaned against the black's neck. 'You and the lovely Cleo go back a long way, that is all, she is more than fond of you. Do you want me to take her a message?'

'No, I must tell her myself.' The voices ap-

proached and more shadows darkened the doorway. 'Cleo will understand, she's a practical
woman. If only all women—'

Elias glanced towards the door and blanched.
'My lord,' he hissed, with a swift, silencing gesture that had the black mare toss her head. 'We
are no longer alone.'

A diminutive lady was silhouetted in the doorway. Her features were in shadow, but Nikolaos
could see that she was wearing one of the finest
gowns ever to grace the Imperial Court. Violet
silk. His heart lurched. Her gown wasn't the deep
purple that was reserved for the Emperor's closest family, but violet such as might be worn by...
Princess Theodora Doukaina?

Holy hell. First sight of his betrothed would
have to be when he had been talking about Cleo.
And the Princess was well within earshot...

A golden diadem sat on glossy, elaborately arranged brown hair, pendant pearls glowed in the
sun. Yes, this could only be Princess Theodora
Doukaina.

Involuntarily, Nikolaos reached a hand towards her and stepped out of the stall.

Her head turned, the pearls swung on their
pendants, and a pair of dark eyes flashed in his
direction. Head high, she gave Nikolaos a cool
look and turned away. A woman—one of the ladies he had seen yesterday in the apartment—
trotted after her.

With a groan, Nikolaos shoved his hand

through his hair. 'Don't tell me, that was Princess Theodora.' He hadn't been able to see her properly, but she had looked vaguely familiar. Her dark eyes... He might be imagining it, but her eyes were extremely similar to those of the heavily veiled woman he had spoken to yesterday in the Princess's apartment. A man noticed a woman's eyes when that was all he could see of her, particularly when those eyes were unusually fine. And those long, sooty eyelashes and lustrous brown eyes were exceptional. 'Blast it, she heard me mention Cleo.'

Striding to the door, he leaned on the frame. Violets, he could smell violets. There was a rustle of silk as his betrothed picked up her silk skirts and crossed the yard. He noticed she was crumpling the costly material with little regard for its rarity, which was interesting. Was she angry? Irritated? Yes, he would swear that anger was there in the set of her shoulders, in the way she never looked back...

Very interesting. Could this be the same woman he had spoken to in the Princess's apartment yesterday? If so, why had she made such a mystery of her identity? True, convention demanded they met officially before they spoke together, but she could surely have been more open with him. What was going on?

I spoke to the Princess yesterday, those eyes are unforgettable. As was the scent of violets. Yesterday he had barely noticed it, but a spring-like fragrance had hung about her, cutting through the heavier scents of musk and roses.

The anger was a puzzle. He was not the first unmarried general to have taken a mistress and he would not be the last. Since he and the Princess had yet to form a bond, she could not be jealous. Pride might explain it. She was a proud princess and learning of Cleo had angered her. Yes, pride was probably at the root of it. Which meant that she knew who he was. *So I did speak to her yesterday—why the mystery?*

Thoughtfully, Nikolaos watched the violet silk whisk along the sunlit path. It seemed he must watch his step where his Princess was concerned. He must watch her. It occurred to him that for her to risk ruining that priceless violet gown—Imperial silk—in a stable yard, she must like her horses. 'We have that in common, at any rate,' he muttered.

'My lord?'

'The Princess likes horses.'

As Princess Theodora gained the path that led towards the Boukoleon Palace and vanished behind an antique statue, Nikolaos glanced back at Elias. 'Did you recognise her?'

Elias looked blankly at him. 'My lord?'

'She's the lady we spoke to in the Princess's apartment.'

'I don't think so, my lord.'

Niko shrugged. 'I can't be certain it's the same woman, but why else would she be angry?'

Elias began to splutter. 'That's obvious, my lord, you mentioned your mis— Cleo. Everyone knows that whenever you are in the City, you go straight to Cleo.'

'Exactly. Think, man. It's one thing for me to recognise the Princess in all her finery, but how did she recognise me?'

'I...I don't quite follow.'

Nikolaos gestured at his plain brown tunic, at his workaday chausses and scuffed boots. 'We have yet to be introduced. Unless she was the lady we spoke to yesterday, how would she know me?'

With a sigh, Nikolaos returned to the stall, unbuckled his saddle and heaved it off Hercules.

'We are not riding, my lord?'

'Later. Since Princess Theodora has at last emerged from hiding, the least we can do is go and greet her.'

'And Cleo?'

'Cleo will have to wait.'

'Did you hear him, Sophia?' Theodora demanded, taking the stairs up to her apartment in the women's quarters. Captain Brand dogged their heels. 'My betrothed probably has women hidden all over the City.'

At the landing outside the apartment, sight of her jewelled diadem had the guards jumping to attention—they saluted, they bowed almost to the floor. The polished doors swung open. Brushing past the guards, Theodora made straight for the small room at the far end of the reception chamber. The room had one slim window and was little more than a closet, but Theodora had decreed that it should be Martina's nursery. She wished it might be more spacious, but to have given anything grander to a child who was supposed to have been born to a slave would certainly rouse suspicions.

The wet-nurse Jelena was sitting next to a wooden cradle, folding baby clothes. Jelena had been with them since Dyrrachion and she had that morning been informed of Theodora's Imperial connections. However, she remained ignorant of the fact that Theodora was Martina's mother.

Bending over the cradle, Theodora ran her finger down a lightly flushed cheek and stroked her daughter's hair. Martina had recently begun to teethe, and since Theodora was in the habit of spending most of the day with her, she had been concerned that the baby might be upset with only her nurse for company.

'She went to sleep without fretting, Jelena?'

'Martina has been fine, my lady, *despoina*. She began to fuss, but I found a coral teether and that did the trick.'

'Thank you, Jelena. How long has she been asleep?'

'Not long.'

Theodora nodded. It was dawning on her that even if she managed to keep her daughter, her duties as a princess would separate them more than she would like. However, Jelena was both caring and competent, and if Martina was happy with her, that was what mattered.

Lightly, she touched Jelena's arm. 'I am glad you came with us.'

'Thank you, *despoina*.'

Theodora rubbed her forehead, her head was thumping. 'I shall come back to see Martina later, when she is awake.'

'Yes, my lady.'

Theodora left the nursery, nodding at the smiling, curtsying ladies who awaited her pleasure in the reception chamber. Her head ached so much, it was a struggle to remember that the servants were always watching and she must give lip service to the lie that some of her ladies would not have spoken to her for some weeks. *I must remember, I am meant to have returned to the Palace some weeks ago and my ladies sailed in yesterday.*

'Thetis, are you well?' she asked, smiling.

Thetis curtsied and followed Theodora's lead. 'I thank you, *despoina*, I am very well.'

'And Cassandra…' Theodora made her voice warm '…how are you?'

'Never better, my lady.'

'That is good to hear.' For the benefit of the servants and any guards not under Commander Ashfirth's orders, Theodora raised her voice. 'It is such a relief to be reunited with my ladies at last—I have missed you. You shall tell me about your voyage in due course. First, I would speak alone with Sophia. Come, Sophia.'

Retreating into the opulent bedchamber, Theodora dragged the diadem from her head and tossed it on to the mulberry bedcover. With a groan and a grimace, she began massaging her scalp. 'I had forgotten the weight of that thing.'

Sophia clucked her tongue and retrieved the diadem, the pearl pendants had become entangled. Reverently, she straightened them.

Theodora began to drag the pins from her hair and Sophia watched the destruction of the elaborate hair arrangement she had taken so long to create with rueful resignation. Hairpins went the way the diadem had gone, bouncing off a tasselled cushion. Theodora's hair rippled as it was released, a glossy dark cascade which hung to her waist.

Aware she was frowning, Theodora searched her hair for more pins. 'Did you hear my betrothed? He knows our official meeting must be soon, yet he is arranging assignations in the City.' She thrust her shawl and a couple of stray hairpins at Sophia. 'She must be his mistress.'

'You don't know that, my lady.'

Theodora let out a sound of vexation. 'You don't need to be a soothsayer to read Duke Nikolaos. A man like that will have women scattered all over the Empire, waiting on his pleasure.'

Carefully, Sophia set the diadem and hairpins

on a gilded side-table. She shook out the shawl. 'A man like that?'

'A...a man of...vigour and experience.'

'Vigour. Experience. Hmm.' Sophia shot her a penetrating look and pursed her lips. 'Certainly, Duke Nikolaos seems extremely...vigorous.'

Theodora held down a blush and paced to the window. Sophia knew her too well. She had realised that Theodora found the Duke handsome, she knew Theodora was carnally attracted to him. And as for his vigour...his energy...that, too, was attractive. She sighed. What would it be like to be loved by a man of experience, rather than a boy? The thought seemed so disloyal, she pushed it away. *I loved Peter, I do not love the Duke and he does not love me. If I bedded with the Duke, of course it would be disappointing...*

There. That was better, that was much more loyal. If only she could believe it.

Resting her arms on a window ledge, she found herself gazing out over one of the Palace courtyards. She could see the Palace walls that separated them from the city she had once been so sad to leave. And beyond the walls lay the huge stone oval of the Hippodrome, the great arena where chariot races and circuses were staged.

She turned and caught Sophia's eye. 'The Duke is nothing like Peter.'

'I don't suppose that he is, my lady, but you have only spoken to him once and, don't forget, he is unaware he spoke to you yesterday.'

'I cannot marry him.'

'Why not? It's obvious he intrigues you.'

'It is no good, I cannot marry a man like that. I shall have to seek an audience with the Emperor.' *Yesterday Sophia said that a man with the Duke's experience would know at once that I am no virgin. She was right. He will expose me. I was dreaming to think otherwise.*

Sophia put Theodora's shawl on the bed. 'His Majesty is doing penance for usurping the throne, many of his duties have been set aside until his penance is over.'

Theodora frowned. 'How long a penance?'

'Forty days, my lady. There is more than three weeks left of it and—'

'The Emperor must still govern! I shall insist on seeing him.'

'Are you sure that's wise? It might be better to go ahead with the marriage as planned.'

'I cannot marry that man.' Theodora had reached the window again. Heavens, there were soldiers everywhere. Varangian Guards, Palace Guards…she recognised the uniforms of several local regiments. 'The army is here in force, the grounds are bristling with soldiers.'

Sophia came to lean against a mulberry-coloured curtain and murmured agreement. 'I don't remember half as many when I was last here.'

'The army will want to make the most of the regime change. Emperor Alexios is himself a soldier, I expect the military are delighted the balance of power has shifted in their favour.' Theodora sighed. 'It may be no bad thing that the Emperor has decided to do penance for so many days. In truth, Sophia, I was dreading the moment I must meet him. A reprieve will be most welcome.'

'Look, my lady.' Sophia pointed. 'Duke Nikolaos is by that fountain.'

For a moment Theodora was able to study her betrothed unobserved. He stood casually, a boot on the rim of the fountain, exchanging jokes with a Varangian officer. When they flung their heads back, their laughter reached the apartment. The Duke's teeth were white and even, his dark hair was ruffled. He was dressed as he had been in the stables, like a groom. Even at this distance Theodora could see that his brown tunic was fraying and worn. The Duke should have looked out of place among the immaculate uniformed officers. It was mildly irritating that he did not. The brown tunic stretched across wide shoulders, a worn brown belt cinched a slim waist. The man was big, but he carried not an excess ounce. And he was wearing his sword—he was the only non-uniformed man in the courtyard to be doing so.

She felt a pull on her skirt. 'He will see you watching him, *despoina*.'

'Too late,' Theodora observed, as that darkly handsome face turned up to the window.

Duke Nikolaos grinned and, with something of

a flourish, gave her an elaborate bow. He clapped the Varangian officer on the arm and continued towards the steps that led into the Boukoleon.

'I wonder if he's coming to meet you?'

'Dressed like a stable hand? He wouldn't dare.'

Sophia gave Theodora a look that told her that Sophia believed the Duke would dare anything. In her heart Theodora knew Sophia was right.

'He is not in the least like Peter,' Theodora murmured.

'No, my lady, I do not believe he is.'

As Theodora pondered on the nature of the Duke's character, a nervous shiver shot through her. She really did not think she could marry him.

Chapter Four

The formal introduction of Duke Nikolaos of Larissa to Princess Theodora Doukaina did not take place until late that afternoon. Lord Basil, the Palace Chamberlain, was in charge of the ceremony and Lord Basil was not to be hurried; the ceremony must be perfect. In the Palace courtyards and gardens, shadows lengthened to allow for final preparations. Theodora was left with hours to consider how Emperor Alexios might react if she were to repudiate his most trusted general in public.

Sophia and Thetis took her to the bathhouse on the ground floor for another bath. They hustled her back into the apartment to redress her hair, and all the while Theodora found herself worrying over the matter of her impending marriage. She fretted almost as much as Martina fretting over a new tooth.

Theodora had sent a subtle plea for help to her cousin, Empress Irene, in which she confessed to having misgivings over the match. Her message had been carefully worded, to avoid giving offence to the Emperor's most loyal general. All afternoon, Theodora waited anxiously for the reply, praying she would not be summoned to meet either her cousin or the Emperor. She was not prepared to lie to them, and if she were asked about Peter or Martina, she did not know what she would say.

Empress Irene's reply came when Theodora was in the windowless dressing room adjoining her bedchamber. Clad in her undertunic, she was peering through the jumpy light of a sputtering wall lamp at a violet silk gown Sophia had picked out for her. 'Not that one, Sophia, I have never liked black braiding.'

'Excuse me, Princess.' A maidservant stood under the arch that led back to the bedchamber, holding out a silver salver with small scroll on it. 'From the Empress, *despoina.*'

Snatching up the scroll, Theodora ran her nail under the seal and moved nearer the wall lamp.

'What does it say?' Sophia asked.

Theodora stared in disbelief at the formal reply, a reply which made her wonder if the Empress had read her message properly. It was not much help. 'The Empress thanks me for my good wishes on her husband's accession. In return she sends heartfelt congratulations on the occasion of my betrothal.'

'Congratulations? She is attending the betrothal ceremony?'

'Empress Irene begs to be excused, she is sure I will understand. She has joined His Majesty in doing penance for the unrest that took place in the City before his enthronement. She does not consider it would be appropriate for her to attend such a joyful celebration.'

Sophia sent her a concerned look. 'It sounds as though the Empress approves the match.'

'It would seem so, for she goes on to say that a marriage between myself and the Duke would be in the best interests of the state. She understands that I feel nervous—nerves are natural, she says. I must be strong. My cousin will pray for me.' Theodora looked blankly at another gown Sophia had unearthed from one of the packing cases. 'Thank you, Sophia, that one will do.'

It would seem there was no escape. Yet.

'The Empress is very young, my lady,' Sophia said. 'It might have been better to have written to the Emperor...'

Theodora shook her head. Duke Nikolaos was known to be close to the Emperor, it was likely His Majesty's reply would have mirrored his wife's. 'In the circumstances, I have decided not to draw attention to myself.'

'That might be wise, my lady.'

'Lord, it seems I have little choice but to attend the ceremony and pray the right moment comes.'

'The right moment, *despoina*?'

Theodora looked down at her hands, astonished to see they were shaking. Nerves.

Nervousness was not something that Theodora usually experienced and she did not like it. It was the Duke's fault.

'I shall know the right moment, when it comes.'

'Do you think your aunt might attend, *despoina*?'

'I hope so, but I am uncertain. She may not consider it appropriate. As wife to two previous Emperors, both of whom have been ousted, her position at Court is tenuous.'

It was a pity, because Theodora would have welcomed some moral support. An afternoon of thought had confirmed her decision. She could not marry the Duke. Such a man, a man of experience, would find out first one secret, and then another, and then...

If only she could be the virgin he expected...if only... But, no, Theodora would never wish her daughter unborn.

Sweet Mother, His Majesty would not thank her if she repudiated his most powerful general in public. Yet given that they were not supposed to meet until formally introduced, what choice did she have?

How will the Duke react?

'Excuse me, Princess?' The maidservant was

back under the arch. 'Duke Nikolaos is waiting to greet you in the small throne room.'

Theodora swallowed. 'I shall be down directly.'

She stood like a statue in the middle of her dressing room, arms held out slightly from her sides, and submitted to being eased into another violet gown. Her ladies were efficient. Thetis twitched the gown into place; there was a sharp pull on her scalp as Sophia adjusted a hairpin. Finally, the hard weight of a gold diadem settled on her head. She grimaced.

'You are fortunate to have such thick hair, my lady,' Sophia said. 'It cushions the weight.'

Thetis fluttered about, swiftly slipping amethyst rings on to her fingers, pushing a heavy enamelled bracelet on to her wrist, finding earrings to match the rings. 'The Chamberlain Lord Basil will be there, my lady,' Thetis said. 'And there will be other generals besides Duke Nikolaos, I am sure.'

'No doubt.' Theodora looked down as Sophia lifted her feet, one after the other, to push on her silk slippers. 'In her letter, the Empress says she is sending a couple of her ladies to wish me well.'

'That is kind of her,' Sophia said.

Theodora took a violet and gold fringed shawl and draped it about her shoulders. Her stomach was churning. 'Please attend me, both of you.'

Heart pounding, head high, she led them through the double doors. Pearls swung from her diadem; amethyst earrings gently tapped the side of her neck.

Ladies had emerged from all corners of the women's quarters to see her, the marble hallway was lined with them. Indeed, half the population of the Palace seemed to be crushed into the stairwell. Theodora had known what to expect, but she had led a quieter life in Rascia and it was something of a burden to feel the pressure of so many eyes. It had been the same this morning when she had paraded about the City. It had been exhausting. With a flash of insight it came to her that the real reason for her exhaustion was not that she had stepped back into her life as an Imperial princess, it was that she was hiding so many secrets. *Secrets are exhausting and I have too many of them.*

'Congratulations, my lady.'

'All blessings upon you, Princess!'

'Princess, I wish you a happy marriage—'

'A *fruitful* marriage.'

'With many children...'

Someone tittered.

Children...if only they knew...

So many people had come to see her. Feeling as though she were walking to her execution, Theodora nodded to right and left and walked calmly on. Her violet skirt billowed and frothed about her ankles like sea foam. She went down past the ancient statues that lined the stairs;

down past the painted frescoes—Diana, Achilles, Ariadne…

All this fuss and I will bet my life that the Duke comes to greet me with the stink of horses still upon him.

The thought brought a slight smile to her lips, a smile that was still there as, with the train of her skirt hissing behind her, she swept into the throne room.

The throne room was as crowded as the stairway and filled with a murmuring that sounded like the hushing of waves on a distant shoreline. A phalanx of guards formed a human screen between her and the mosaics on the walls. Noblemen and courtiers jostled each other, vying for places, vying for attention in finery that was bright as a rainbow. The air was still and stuffy, the scent of clashing perfumes overwhelming.

At Theodora's entrance, the murmuring cut off abruptly. She was surrounded by faces and did not recognise a soul. It had been too long since she had been at Court, and if her aunt was present, Theodora could not see her.

And then Duke Nikolaos was before her, taking her hand, bowing over it, smiling at her with those disturbing dark eyes. An irritating tingle shot up Theodora's arm.

She lifted an eyebrow. In the hours since she had seen him, Duke Nikolaos had changed. The transformation was undeniably pleasing—his long court tunic, a blue damask liberally banded with silver embroidery, seemed designed to make the most of his masculine form. Underneath those clothes, Theodora was sure the Duke's body would be honed to perfection. It would be that of a warrior, of an athlete in his prime. His belt had a jewelled buckle; there was a gleam of gold at his throat as well as on his fingers. No sword. Since this was the small throne room, that did not surprise her.

'Princess Theodora,' the Duke said, kissing the back of her hand.

This time, Theodora was prepared for the effect his touch had on her and she managed to squash the irritating tingle before it had time to reach her belly. 'Duke Nikolaos.' Theodora barely noticed the heavily bearded Lord Basil as he unrolled a beribboned scroll and began the ritual of the formal introduction—listing their titles and rank, their more illustrious forebears…

'…Duke Nikolaos of Larissa, General of the Athanatoi Cavalry Regiment, Commander-in-Chief of the Imperial Army…'

Theodora kept her head up while the Chamberlain ran through the rites. She was supremely aware of the strength in the hand holding hers. She had not realised that the Duke had command over so many regiments, nor that he was governor of so many provinces. Covertly, she watched him.

His eyes were so dark as to be almost black, and now she could study him, perhaps they were not so…unsettling as she had first thought. Something had amused him. *Dancing eyes, he has dancing eyes.* And to Theodora's astonishment, a tight knot somewhere in the region of her gut eased.

'I am overjoyed to meet you *at last,*' he murmured.

Was it her imagination, or had the Duke laid particular stress on the words *at last*? *Holy Mother, let him be referring to the glimpse we had had of each other in the stables and not to the earlier encounter in the women's quarters. It would be dreadful if he realised that I am the woman he spoke to in the apartment—he might become suspicious...*

'And I you, my lord.'

The mosaic walls glittered, hard and cold as glass. Compared with the Duke's dancing dark eyes, the eyes of the staring courtiers looked equally cold. *I cannot refuse him, not so publicly.* There was thudding in her ears.

'My lord...?'

'Princess?'

She cleared her throat. Lord Basil was breaking the seal on another beribboned scroll, about to make some announcement about her dowry. The parchment crackled as he began to read. Theodora had quite forgotten she held title to so much land. His Imperial Majesty had been generous, too, there were lands on the list that were new to her. Proof, if she did not already know it, that His Imperial Majesty more than approved of this marriage, he was eager for it. Duke Nikolaos had supported Emperor Alexios in the recent uprising and she was his reward.

'My lord…' she looked desperately up at the Duke, voice as quiet as she could make it '…I need to speak to you most urgently. I cannot… we cannot…'

She looked past those broad shoulders to where a group of noblemen were pushing closer, greedy for her every word. She couldn't refuse him, not here.

The Chamberlain rolled up the scroll and smiled benignly at them.

Duke Nikolaos nodded briefly at her and set her arm on his blue silk sleeve. 'Lord Basil?'

'Duke Nikolaos?'

'I am sure you will understand, Princess Theodora and I wish to walk in the gardens a while.'

The Chamberlain's beard quivered, his eyes bulged. *'Alone?* You ought not to be alone with the Princess until after the marriage ceremony.'

'Nevertheless, we wish to walk outside.'

Lord Basil's mouth opened and closed. Nodding smoothly at him, Duke Nikolaos made for the door. Theodora gripped the dark silk of his sleeve and tried not to think about the strength in the arm she could feel beneath it. With much bowing and scraping, the courtiers edged back, the sea of faces parted.

She smiled tentatively at the Duke. 'Thank you, my lord.'

As she left the throne room on the arm of Duke Nikolaos, Theodora heard the Palace Chamberlain grumbling into his beard, 'Most unseemly, most unseemly.' She could hear him urging Sophia and Thetis after her. 'Ladies, follow the Princess. *Guards!* You, too. On the double.'

Behind them Theodora heard a desperate scrabbling as her ladies, the Empress's ladies and several armed men formed a hasty escort.

Thus it was that Princess Theodora Doukaina and Duke Nikolaos, General of the Immortals, found themselves leading a ludicrous train of ladies-in-waiting and courtiers through the Palace courtyards. The military escort would have done His Imperial Majesty proud, the walls echoed with all the footsteps. Snowy-white ibis flapped out of the way; doves flocked on to roofs, wings whirring.

As they took the path towards the gardens, the Duke covered her hand with his. 'What is it, Princess?' His dark eyes searched hers, they were no longer dancing. 'You do not wish for this marriage?'

Theodora felt her colour rise. He was studying her so closely that for a moment she felt sure he knew her for the lady he had met the previous day. She looked at his mouth and quickly looked away, face burning even hotter than before.

This man unsettled her. The Duke's reputation had not led Theodora to expect any sensitivity in him, but here he was, the Emperor's general, offering to listen. There was sympathy in his eyes. Was it possible that he was not quite as ruthless as his reputation had painted him?

'My lord, I confess to some trepidation.'

He drew back. 'Why did you not say something sooner? You returned to the Palace before Easter—you could easily have sent a messenger.'

'I...I...' Theodora was floundering. She could hardly tell him that it had not been she who had returned just before Easter, but Katerina. And she certainly could not tell him that she had been finding a wet-nurse for her daughter.

'Princess, how hard would it have been to reply to my messages? I entered Constantinople with His Majesty, and as soon as I learned you were in the Palace I sent several—you must have received them. Why did you not reply?'

The dark features were thoughtful; his smile remained polite, but Theodora realised the Duke was struggling to treat her with the respect he felt was owed an Imperial princess. Not far below the polite veneer, she sensed impatience. And if he had indeed been sending messages that had been unanswered, his impatience was not entirely unjustified.

Nikolaos was determined to hide his irritation.

Holy hell, what was the matter with the woman? It was bad enough that she had ignored repeated requests for an audience, but now they had met—in full view of half the court—she chose to tell him she was reluctant. He had suspected that this might be the case, but it was a blow to have his suspicions confirmed. With the Emperor's backing, it was likely their marriage would go ahead eventually, but any reluctance on her part could cause delay. Marriage to a princess was a high honour, but Nikolaos knew he had earned it. He did not want there to be any delay. If the Princess came to hear her betrothed was illegitimate, she might feel she had even more cause to reject him.

She might not cavil at my barbarian parentage, for apparently she had loved Prince Peter, but illegitimacy...?

'*Despoina*, far be it from me to press you, but I would know now rather than later. Also, there are others to consider. Lord Basil has informed me we are to be honoured with a betrothal feast next week. Preparations are well in hand, invitations have gone out.'

Briefly, Princess Theodora's beautiful eyes were lit by surprise. Since this could not be the first time she had heard of their betrothal feast, it seemed a little odd. Nikolaos felt a quickening of interest such as he had not felt since before the coup, when his energies had been channelled into supporting Alexios Komnenos in his bid for the throne.

Ever since his ambitions had been met, Nikolaos had been conscious of a sense of...not boredom exactly—far be it from him to become a warmonger for the sake of entertainment. However, until the Emperor put the seal on Nikolaos's proposals for reform of the army, there were only so many reviews and inspections a man could make, only so much training to be supervised. The Princess intrigued him. *She has secrets...*

'My lady, what is troubling you?'

'It...I...I do not know you.'

They had come to a latticed gate, from there the path led to a grassy area and the wooded grounds beyond.

He smiled. 'I do not know you either, my lady, but I am prepared to take the risk.'

Her lips twitched and she shot him a look through eyelashes that were long and luxuriant and had been darkened in some mysterious way. 'You! Frightened of me?' A small crease appeared by the side of her mouth, she was trying not to laugh.

Nikolaos nodded gravely, his irritation pushed aside by the temptation to see how she responded to teasing. 'When Emperor Nikephoros first broached the subject of our marriage, I must admit, I was disconcerted, if not overwhelmed, to find I had been chosen as your husband. Since then, Emperor Alexios has ratified the original agreement and I am well pleased.' He squeezed her hand. 'Princess?'

When she looked up, he saw that her mouth had for the first time relaxed into an actual smile. It was very pretty. Almost as pretty as those exotically darkened eyes. 'My mother tells me it is time I married,' he continued. 'Naturally I have no wish to force an unwilling woman into marriage, but if you refuse me, my mother will be sorely disappointed.'

A seagull flashed past them. They walked on and Princess Theodora Doukaina gave him another of those slanting, assessing glances. Her eyes were huge in the afternoon light and the pearl pendants in her diadem trembled. She was not a tall woman—without the diadem she would barely reach his shoulder—but when their eyes met, she had a way of filling his vision. The rippling notes of a blackbird floated down from an oak tree, along with the mutterings of their entourage.

'But not you, my lord. You will not be disappointed, surely?'

It was a question that could be taken a number of ways. It might be an invitation to flattery but, looking at her, Nikolaos did not think that that was the case. It might be an invitation to flirtation, but his instinct told him that that was not so either. He decided to take the question at face value and give her the truth. Part of it.

'I will be disappointed. I am flattered to have been given a princess as a bride, it is a high honour.'

Her brow wrinkled, she waved at the fluttering ladies-in-waiting. 'As the Emperor's right-hand man, surely there are others...?'

Shaking his head, Nikolaos continued down the path. 'I want you,' he said and was startled to realise he meant it, he really meant it. *I want this woman.* 'What is it, *despoina*? Do you want a prince? Is it that you feel I am beneath you?'

Her eyes widened. 'Beneath me? Why, no, my lord, you could not be more wrong. It is just as I said, I do not know you.'

'That can easily be remedied. You did not know Župan Peter when you were sent to Rascia.'

She bit her lip, a tiny movement which caught his attention. 'That is true, but I was younger then and Prince Peter, he was not at all…not…' Her voice faded, her cheeks went pink and she jerked her gaze away, focusing on one of the guards patrolling the sea wall.

They came to a halt. They were at the edge of a grove of cypresses and their entourage stopped a few moments after they did. A lady-in-waiting caught his eye and sent him a simpering smile; a nobleman gave him an obsequious bow. Blowing out a breath, Nikolaos shoved his hand through his hair. 'This is intolerable.'

She started. 'My lord?'

'How in hell am I meant to speak to you with that rabble on our heels?'

Her smile reappeared. Hesitant. Tentative. It had potential did that smile. When Nikolaos found himself exchanging an understanding glance with her, his gut clenched.

'I feared it would be like this, once I had returned to the Palace,' she murmured, eyes sparkling with fellow-feeling.

Oh, yes, he thought, as his gut responded instantly. Serious potential. He cleared his throat. 'You had more freedom in Rascia, Princess?'

Turning those mysterious brown eyes on their audience, she gave a slight nod. 'There is no comparison.' Without warning, her fingers clenched on his sleeve, the sparkle in her eyes was gone.

'Princess, what is it?' She was ashen. Her gaze was caught—no, transfixed might be a better word—by someone among the attendants. 'Princess?'

Her breath was uneven, the pearl pendants trembled. The tassels on her violet shawl shimmered and it was not the wind causing the movement, it was her. The Princess was shaking from head to toe, *shaking*.

'Princess?' Taking her firmly by the hand, Nikolaos glared at their entourage. 'We need a little privacy.' He pulled her with him into the trees. Manoeuvring her out of sight behind a cypress, he had taken her by the shoulders before he recollected that she was Princess Theodora Doukaina, cousin to the Empress.

'My apologies, Princess,' he said, letting his hands fall away. He did not wish her to think he was attempting to constrain her, but what was going on? She was still shaking. 'What is it? *Tell me.*'

The diadem tipped back as she searched his

face. She took her time over it and it came to him that she had not really seen him before. Her chest lifted, her breath came and went several times while overhead the gulls wheeled and screeched. Violets. Nikolaos inhaled, he could smell violets.

'I saw someone.' Her voice was a thin whisper as she twisted to peer round the tree and her eyes scoured the crowd. 'A man I had left behind in Rascia. I cannot see him any more, I may have imagined it. I pray so, for I dislike him intensely.'

'You fear him,' Nikolaos said and it was not a question. He managed to catch her eyes. 'And you dislike me. That is why you will not marry me. So be it.'

Vehemently, she shook her head and set the pearl pendants swinging. 'My initial refusal had nothing to do with you.' She paused. 'My decision to allow you to offer for me, however, does.'

His heart lifted. 'You are now saying you will accept me?'

Brown eyes looked deep into his and for a moment he could not breathe. When her small, beringed hand reached towards him, he enfolded it in his.

'My lord, I think…' she swallowed and held herself very straight '…our discussion has reassured me. Duke Nikolaos, I am delighted to inform you that I would be happy to accept you as my husband. Indeed, I look forward to it.'

For a moment Nikolaos simply looked at her. The mysterious Princess Theodora. Sometimes she seemed to be shielding her beautiful eyes from him, while at others she gave the impression she was watching him with minute attention. His lips curved. No matter. This was the outcome that he hoped for, she had agreed to the marriage. There would be time to learn what she was hiding. It seemed unlikely that he would discover anything that might overset the state, for all her secretiveness, the Princess had a guileless air to her.

However, for His Majesty's sake, and that of the Empire, it would not hurt to have her watched. Rascia's loyalties were not in question, that could not be said of neighbouring principalities. The Princess had spent most of her life within a stone's throw of several princes whose interests often clashed with those of the Empire and she had been absent for ten years. *Who knows what friends she might have made?*

Having her watched would only be a precaution, Nikolaos was almost sure he would find nothing.

None the less, he felt a prickle of unease; he would prefer a wife with whom he could be completely open. Nor did it sit well with him that she was most likely accepting him because she thought she had seen someone in that mill of people whom she feared. He supposed it was something that she was prepared to trust him on so brief an acquaintance. It was a start—not a particularly auspicious one—but it was a start. He found himself looking at a large amethyst on the back of her diadem. She had turned away and was gesturing at the track that led deeper into the copse.

'Shall we, my lord?'

Nikolaos crooked his arm at her. 'I am delighted we are agreed, Princess,' he said. 'I shall do my utmost to make you happy.'

She strode on, walking through the trees with such purpose and energy that Nikolaos had little doubt that she hoped to lose their attendants and whoever it was who had alarmed her. He glanced back. Ladies, guards and nobles were tripping over each other, frantic to keep up. 'I don't think they will be got rid of that easily, *despoina*. They are determined to protect your virtue.'

She gave a small choking sound and shot him a swift glance he was unable to interpret. The wind teased the fringes of her shawl and blew bright colour back into her cheeks.

'That's better,' he said. 'You were as pale as death earlier.'

She made another choking sound and shook her head. With her face averted, Nikolaos could not see much of her. She genuinely fascinated him. A princess. And she was his. A princess in an amethyst and pearl studded diadem. She had a strong profile, her nose was well formed and her mouth was full and had a slight pout to it. A man might enjoy kissing a mouth like that, but it was too soon for him to be thinking about such things. Never mind that convention dictated they should not enjoy carnal knowledge of each other until eight days after their wedding day—she was an Imperial princess and he must not forget that. For all her assurance, for all that she bore the trappings of her position with dignity, she was far more nervous than he had expected.

Innocent. She is likely to be a total innocent. That could explain much of her nervousness. She is shy. When we come to bed, I shall have to take care with her.

Nikolaos had never made love to a virgin and it occurred to him that it was something of a responsibility. It wouldn't do to alienate his wife. Her skin was olive in tone, smooth and flawless. Her hair was very dark. Currently it was confined in some extravagant arrangement, doubtless intended to set off the diadem. He wondered how long it would be when loose. At a guess it was wavy. His fingers ached to touch it, to find out for himself.

Princess Theodora might have a nervous temperament, but in looks, at least, she pleased him greatly. It would be a pleasure to initiate her into the pleasures of the marriage bed. It was a pity she was so secretive. His mother's face swam before him and his lips twisted. Secretiveness in a woman was not an admirable trait.

On the surface, however, the Princess was utterly charming. He would, on the surface, allow himself to be charmed. Her shyness, that occasional inability to meet his gaze, was strangely arousing. Thank God she had lost some of her reserve and had agreed to their marriage, although he wouldn't mind knowing who she thought she had seen among the attendants.

In the meantime, perhaps this was the time to ask about Brother Leo. Cousin to Nikolaos, Brother Leo had been dispatched to Rascia at the same time as the Princess. He had been Princess Theodora's confessor and Nikolaos understood he had also become confessor to Prince Peter. It had been some time since Nikolaos had had news from his cousin and he was concerned.

'Princess, I have been meaning to ask you about Prince Peter's—' At once, the light went out of her. 'I am sorry, my lady, I am too blunt. It is a soldier's fault, I fear.'

'No, no,' she said, looking back the way they had come, an anxious frown between her brows. 'It is all right, please continue.'

'Did you love him?' Nikolaos had not intended to ask, but since it had slipped out, he was curious to hear her answer.

She gave him a direct look. 'I…yes, yes, I did. Very much.'

Nikolaos folded his arms across his chest. 'You mourn him.' He did not expect a response, but the Princess surprised him. She stepped up to him and laid her hand upon his sleeve.

'All that is in the past—it is over a year since he died. You are my future.'

He smiled and, taking her hand, a perfectly manicured, beringed hand, he pressed a kiss to a neat fingertip. He knew what was expected of him and the words emerged surprisingly easily. 'Princess, you make me the happiest man in the Empire.'

Her lips twitched into that bewitching almost-smile that he was learning to tease out of her. It was a so delicate, so evanescent. Nikolaos did not want to risk losing it by asking about Brother Leo just yet. There would be plenty of time for that later.

In complete accord, they turned and promenaded in the grand manner back up the path through the trees. The entourage parted before them like the Red Sea, and together they endured stares and coy smiles as they led the way through the latticed gate and back into the courtyards.

They parted at the steps of the Boukoleon. Their betrothal feast, set for the following week, would go ahead as planned.

Chapter Five

Theodora took refuge on the great mulberry bed, lying against the fringed cushions with her eyes closed, massaging her temples. The pearl and amethyst diadem was so beautiful it would not have been out of place in a fable, but it could not be worn for long. It was heavy and the padded velvet lining did nothing to lessen the weight. Every time she wore it, her head felt as though it had been in a vice.

Theodora rubbed her brow, bitterly conscious that her headache had not been caused solely by the weight of the diadem. Her mind had been taken over by one thought—Prince Djuradj's man, Boda, was in the Great Palace. His was the face she had seen in the crowd when she had been talking to Duke Nikolaos. What was she to do?

She heard a soft clunk. Sophia was busy in the dressing-chamber, securing the diadem in a strongbox. The air shifted. Soft footsteps came up to the bed. Theodora opened an eye and hoped she did not look as desperate as she felt.

'So, *despoina*...' Sophia smiled as she sat on the edge of the bed '...you decided to marry him. I thought you would.'

'Did you indeed?'

Sophia's smile became speculative, almost teasing. 'Duke Nikolaos is...well...he is...'

'Yes?'

'He...he...' Flushing, Sophia began playing with a gold tassel on the bed-hangings.

Theodora pushed herself a little higher on her cushions and stared at her lady-in-waiting. Sophia was never coy. Sophia never seemed to take much notice of men and, if she did, she never mentioned it. It was one of the reasons Theodora favoured Sophia, she disliked it when her ladies giggled and gossiped in corners. The women in her entourage who did so were, with good reason, deliberately kept at a distance. 'Sophia, you have gone bright red.'

'Well, he is handsome, my lady, you cannot deny it. I ought not to say this...' Sophia trailed off, shaking her head.

'Sophia, finish what you were saying, if you please.'

'He...the Duke is as well formed as Apollo.'

Theodora snorted. 'He is far too dark for Apollo.' Privately, Theodora was beginning to agree with Sophia—the Duke's looks and form

were striking—but she was not going to admit it.
Particularly when she could barely see past the
pounding in her temples. 'Lord, my head.' She
touched Sophia's hand. 'Sophia, I need your full
attention, if you please.'

'My lady?'

'Boda is in the Palace.'

Sophia's jaw dropped. 'Prince Djuradj's man?
No! Where did you see him? When?'

'He was among the attendants when Duke
Nikolaos and I were walking in the grounds.'

'Among the attendants? That is not possible.
Princess, are you sure you weren't mistaken?
If Boda had been in the entourage, I am sure I
would have seen him.'

'Perhaps, perhaps not. He's cunning; Župan
Djuradj would not have despatched him if he
were not.'

'It couldn't have been Boda, I am sure I would
have seen him.' Sophia repeated.

The throbbing in Theodora's head was merci-
less. Lifting a hand, she resumed her careful mas-
sage of her temples. 'Sophia, I am almost certain
it was Boda. He will know you from Rascia, it's
likely he has made it his business to recognise
my closest ladies. He will have made a point of
keeping out of your line of sight.'

'Why, then, should he let you see him? Why
hide from me and not you?'

'I don't know. He might have been afraid you
might raise the alarm. He knew I could do little

whilst talking to the Duke. Boda wants to intimidate me.' She bit her knuckle. 'I have to say, he is succeeding.'

'Princess, you are surely not thinking that one of your ladies will have betrayed you? We have been so careful. Everyone has been discreet. Only your ladies know the truth of Martina's parentage.'

'I hope so.' She sighed. 'I cannot shake the thought that, somehow, Župan Djuradj has found me out.'

Sophia glanced at the door. 'I pray you are mistaken, Princess. I also think you are mistaken about Boda.'

'Sophia, I saw him!'

'If he is in the Palace, he will not get past your guards. To set your mind at rest, we could move Martina and her cradle in here. I cannot think Boda would hurt a baby, but…'

Theodora shook her head, flinching as the pounding intensified. 'Much as I would like it, we cannot bring Martina into my bedchamber. I risk enough raising of eyebrows if word is put out that I am adopting the child of a slave—imagine what would be said if the Court learned a child's cradle was set up next to my bed…'

Sophia grimaced. 'That's a point, not many princesses would permit a baby to wake them in the middle of the night, unless—'

'Sophia, it would ease my mind if *you* slept in the nursery tonight.' Theodora wanted to appear calm, she could not be certain it had been Boda she had seen among the courtiers, but the mere possibility that he had followed her to the City—worse, to the Palace itself—struck fear into her heart. If Boda and his master, Prince Djuradj of Zeta, knew about Martina's parentage, they might decide they had good reason to harm her. *They might kill her!* 'At all costs, Martina must be safe.'

'Very well, my lady, I shall sleep in the nursery, alongside Jelena.'

'Thank you, Sophia.' Closing her eyes, Theodora held down a groan. 'Draw the curtains, if you please. I need to think.'

The mattress lifted. Long skirts whispered as they skimmed the marble floor, curtain rings rattled.

'Princess?'

'Mmm?'

The mattress dipped. A cool hand touched her forehead. 'I see why you changed your mind about Duke Nikolaos, *despoina*. Your fears for Martina led you to accept him.'

'The Duke is strong and honourable,' Theodora murmured. She felt instinctively that Duke Nikolaos was worthy of the honour of caring for Martina. She could not confess all to him yet—the Duke would have no idea what he was taking on when he married her—but that could not be helped. Despite this, she was certain he would do his duty. *If some accident befalls me, Martina will need a strong and honourable protector. When the truth emerges, Duke Nikolaos will do his duty by Martina, even though he had no idea what he was taking on on our marriage day. His honour will not allow him to do otherwise.*

'My lady,' Sophia broke into her thoughts. 'I don't think you need worry so. Župan Djuradj has an evil reputation, but—'

Theodora's eyes snapped open. 'An evil reputation? He is a murdering swine!'

'I know, my lady, I know.' Sophia spoke in so soothing a tone that Theodora found herself gritting her teeth. 'However, we are a long way from Zeta and I cannot see why you are so certain he would harm Martina…'

Theodora didn't answer. What could she say? *Sophia thinks I am in the grip of hysteria, but Sophia does not know everything, she does not know my deepest, most sinful secret.* It did not seem possible that Prince Djuradj should have found that out. Theodora and Peter had been so careful. But if Prince Djuradj *had* found out…

She fought down a sense of rising panic. In a sense, it mattered little whether the Prince of Zeta knew her deep secret or not—either way, Martina was in danger.

'You want Duke Nikolaos to protect you.' Sophia's tone brightened. 'It is a good thought, my lady. And I have just had another one.'

'Oh?'

'You could appeal to Emperor Alexios for

help. He will not permit Prince Djuradj's bullies near you.'

'Sophia, Boda is in the Palace!' She moderated her tone. 'He will have come here in the guise of an envoy.'

'If you spoke to His Majesty, I am sure he would deploy extra guards in the women's quarters. The Prince of Zeta is no match for Emperor Alexios.'

'Sophia, Župan Djuradj is one of the most cold and devious men to have walked the earth; he will do anything to achieve his ends. He murdered Peter and a monk in Holy Orders. He is utterly ruthless. If he has realised that Martina is Peter's daughter, God knows what he may do.'

'I understand your fears, my lady.' Sophia bit her lip. 'And, naturally, you do not want His Majesty to learn you have an illegitimate daughter. What will you do?'

'I have told you, Sophia, I shall marry the Duke.' Struck by a new thought, Theodora bolted upright and gripped Sophia's arm. 'Sophia?'

'*Despoina?*'

'Do you think Duke Nikolaos would agree to bring our marriage forward?'

'He might.' Sophia's brow creased. 'My lady, I truly hope you are wrong about Boda being in the Palace.'

'He's here all right, I only caught a glimpse of him, but I am certain it was he.'

'I am thankful that you have agreed to marry

the Duke. I think that you already trust him, you feel safe with him.'

Theodora pushed away the image of dark, dancing eyes and shrugged. 'Up to a point.' *I can't tell him everything.*

Sophia leaned earnestly towards her. 'Did it set your mind at rest to speak to the Duke, or are you still concerned about his reaction should he learn that Martina is yours?'

'That remains a concern.'

'Rather that rushing on with the marriage, my lady, wouldn't it be best to get to know Duke Nikolaos a little better first, to allow a…a fondness to grow between you? Then when…if he realises you are not a…not a…'

'Virgin is the word you are groping for,' Theodora said, drily.

'*Despoina*, do I have your permission to speak bluntly?'

'Of course.'

'Do you trust the Duke enough to allow him to consummate the marriage? My lady, if you bring your wedding forward, tradition will allow him to consummate your union eight days after the wedding. Are you ready for that?'

Theodora stared at Sophia, though in truth she was looking right through her. She was seeing a pair of intense dark eyes set in an angular, masculine face. 'I think,' she said, on a startling flash of insight, 'that however he reacts, I would feel safer with Duke Nikolaos as my husband.'

'Safer than in here?' Sophia's wave included the entire apartment. 'Here you have guards, day and night. No man may enter without passing them.'

'I can trust the Duke,' Theodora said softly. It would be hard to explain to Sophia the sense of confidence she had in him. They had so short an acquaintance, she barely understood it herself. 'His Majesty trusts him, I am sure I may do the same. And whether or not Boda gets into this apartment, my instincts tell me that Martina and I will be safer under the Duke's protection. The sooner I marry him, the better.'

As the words left her lips Theodora felt as though a weight had lifted from her—she and Martina would be safe under the Duke's protection. She shifted to the edge of the great bed and stood.

'Tomorrow morning I shall speak to the Duke and see what might be arranged.'

The evening after his betrothal ceremony, Duke Nikolaos paused by the wall outside his mistress's house. Above the City, stars whirled across a midnight sky; a row of glowing lanterns lined the street. Conscious of the need for discretion now he and the Princess were in agreement, Nikolaos had chosen to walk rather than ride. A nobleman on horseback drew more attention than a man on foot. Nikolaos had taken off his finery and was dressed unobtrusively; his cloak was as dark as the night.

The house he had bought for Cleo stood well away from the Palace on the other side of the Hippodrome. The street was one of the quieter ones that ran parallel to the Mese. Tonight, a woman's singing floated over the wall of her house; it was a plaintive song, of lost love and lost lives. A song that was fitting for the night's work.

Nikolaos had never deluded himself that he was in love with Cleo; nevertheless, he was fond of her. He had been content with her; it had been an easy relationship on his part, with no messy emotions to muddy the waters. Cleo had needed a protector and he had needed a woman. He had paid for his pleasure.

Nikolaos felt faintly uncomfortable. Cleo was not going to like what he had to say, she had told him she loved him, more than once. Whether or not this was true, he had no idea; he suspected her love had been engendered by thankfulness at the life he had saved her from. Cleo had been the ideal mistress, never demanding more from him than he had been able to give, and for that he was grateful. At times, and particularly since his mother's recent revelation, Nikolaos wondered if love was ever unencumbered by need or ambition. He doubted it.

Sighing, Nikolaos found his key, unlocked the door in the wall and strode across the starlit courtyard. His footsteps echoed into the dark. He knocked on the main door. It opened so swiftly she must have been waiting for him.

Warm hands reached out and pulled him inside. 'Niko! It's been too long. I missed you.'

He was wrapped in a jasmine-scented hug, soft lips pressed briefly against his.

Reaching on her toes to unfasten his cloak clasp, Cleo took it from him and draped it over her arm. Heeled sandals clicked on the tiled floor as she tugged him across the entrance hall. Her hair was, as ever, carefully oiled and curled; it hung down her back in dark waves.

'I hoped you would come,' she said. 'Your favourite spiced lamb is simmering in the kitchen, we have Cretan wine and...'

Chattering non-stop, she handed his cloak to a servant and headed for the dining room. The oil lamps were lit and the low table was set for an intimate supper—bread, olives, glasses. The air was heavy with the mouth-watering smell of spiced lamb and rosemary...

He felt a twinge of guilt. Had she waited for him like this every night since his return to the City?

'Niko, do remove your sword—surely you are not going to eat wearing your sword?'

'Cleo.' Closing the door softly behind them, Nikolaos took her by the shoulders. *Best get this over with quickly.* 'Cleo, I have not come to eat.'

She looked up at him for a moment. Her eyes

filled and she pulled swiftly away. 'Niko, you are tired, let me pour you your wine.'

She reached for a flagon and Niko caught her hand, gently, but firmly. 'No. Cleo, I am sorry.'

A tear gleamed on the end of her lashes and she took another backward step. When she disengaged her hand, he let her go. Head high, she gave him a long look and shook her head. Eyes brimming, she gripped her hands together. 'I knew this day would come, of course.'

A slight sob had him closing the distance between them.

She warded him off. 'No, Niko, it is all right. I understand. It is true that I have been dreading this day, but I have known it was inevitable from the beginning. I hoped we would have longer together, but once I heard about Princess Theodora, I knew our time was almost done.'

'It is a matter of politics, Cleo, I cannot afford to offend the Doukas family.'

'You belittle yourself, Niko. Don't. You are not a man to marry and maintain a mistress behind your wife's back. The hourglass has run dry for us, my love.'

'Cleo, I am sorry. I shall miss you. I shall not forget you.'

Her smile was sad. 'Liar. The love between us was always one-sided,' she murmured.

'I *am* fond of you, Cleo.' Nikolaos tried to smile back, but his lips felt stiff.

Cleo nodded and sniffed and wiped her eyes.

'Well, I shall not cause you any trouble, you have treated me well.' She held out her hand. 'Farewell, Niko. I shall leave directly.'

'Leave?' He took her hand and squeezed her fingers. 'Cleo, the house is yours.'

Her eyes widened. 'Mine?'

'It always has been, I told you long ago.'

She bit her lip. 'I didn't believe you.'

'The house is yours. And you will have enough money to ensure that you never have to return to your former way of life.' He pressed the door key into her hand and she stared down at it for a moment before her fingers slowly curled round it.

'I thank you, Niko.'

With a bow, he turned to go. 'George will see me out.'

'Niko?'

He looked back.

'Thank you, Niko. For everything.'

'Take care of her, will you, George?' Nikolaos murmured as he took up his cloak and crossed the hall.

'Of course, my lord.'

Nikolaos swung his cloak about his shoulders. 'Walk me to the gate, I should like you to lock it behind me. I am not entirely convinced that the mercenaries who entered Constantinople with the Emperor have gone and I want Cleo safe.'

'Of course, my lord.'

George was far too polite to ask him what he

had done with his key. He was also far too good a servant to be left in the dark. At the gate, Nikolaos held out his hand. 'This is farewell, George. I won't be seeing you again, at least not unless we chance to meet elsewhere.'

George flung a worried glance back at the house. 'I am sorry to hear that, Duke Nikolaos. She knows?'

'She knows. George, I should like you to know that the house is hers and I have set some money aside for her use.'

'I am sure you have been more than generous, my lord.'

'Stay with her if you can, George, she will need you.'

'I'm not going anywhere.'

'Good man. Furthermore, I would like you to remember that if ever you, or Cleo, find yourselves in need, I should be honoured to help. You know where to find me.'

'Thank you, my lord. God bless you.'

'Farewell.'

Nikolaos waited outside the gate in the wall long enough to ensure George had locked it behind him. Constantinople was no longer in ferment as it had been in the immediate aftermath of the coup—the mercenaries who had caused the trouble had been recalled—but he didn't want to take risks. There might be stragglers.

The key turned, the door rattled. 'Good night, my lord,' George's voice came over the wall.

'Good night, George.'

It was done. Satisfied that he had done the right thing, and relieved that Cleo had not made a fuss, Nikolaos walked past flaring torches in the direction of the Hippodrome. It was a relief to know that George would be there to look after Cleo, but he would have Elias keep a quiet eye on her in the weeks and months to come.

Above him, the stars had wheeled a little further across the sky. The woman who had been singing had fallen silent; he could hear nothing but his own footfall. He had almost reached the outside wall of the Hippodrome when a shadow moved at the head of the street. It was a swift, covert movement that rang alarm bells in his head. An owl hooted. A signal?

The hairs stood on the back of his neck. It had been too peaceful, he should have known—the City was rarely this quiet. Flicking back his cloak to ensure his sword would have full play if he needed it, he gripped the hilt.

Mercenary stragglers? Runaway slaves? Thieves? Nikolaos glanced behind him, working out the distance from where he was to the other end of the street, the way that led west into the tangle of alleys and tenements between Cleo's street and the Forum. If the shadowy figure by the Hippodrome was one of a pack, which seemed possible, others might be stalking him. He could see no one behind him. There was nothing he could do but continue towards the better-populated streets by the Hippodrome, so he strode confidently on, carefully noting the height of the walls on either side and the precise position of a discarded clay amphora. If needs must, it would make a good missile...

Two shadows took shape in front of him, like wraiths from the underworld. Moonlight flashed on naked steel.

His sword rasped as he whipped it from its scabbard. 'Hold, and state your business,' he said. His heart banged against his ribs. In the poor light he could not judge whether the wraiths were wearing chain mail, but he thought not.

The shadows froze. 'Duke Nikolaos?'

'Who in Hades are you?' Nikolaos could see nothing but two silhouettes backlit by torchlight and two long, moon-silvered swords pointed directly at him. They knew him?

'We don't want a fight, my lord.'

'You choose a pretty odd way of demonstrating it. Give me your names.'

'Our names would mean nothing to you, they are irrelevant. Our...master has sent you a message.'

'Your master? And he would be...?'

'It concerns Princess Theodora.' The man had a strong foreign accent that Nikolaos could not place. 'Our master bids us tell you that you would be wise to reconsider your marriage. If I were you, my lord, I would heed his advice. Refuse her.'

The reference to his marriage to Princess Theodora caught Nikolaos off-balance, and it was a moment before he could speak. If only he could see their faces. 'I most certainly will not.'

'My lord, my master is concerned for your welfare. It would not be…safe for you to marry the Princess.' A silvered blade shifted as the man gestured about the empty street. 'We know you do not always keep the company of your men.' His shoulders lifted. 'It would be too easy for an accident to befall a confident man like you, a man who likes to walk the City streets alone and—'

Nikolaos took a step closer. 'You are threatening me?' If only he could place that accent. What *was* going on? 'I will have your master's name, if you please.'

The men edged back. Nikolaos could smell fear on them, they were all bluster. And they were, thank God, working on their own—no one had come up behind him.

'For your own sake, let the Princess marry someone else,' the man said. 'Refuse her, or suffer the consequences.'

An ear-splitting whistle cut through the night air; it came from the maze of alleys at his back and set dogs barking behind one of the courtyard walls. The two wraiths melted into the dark. Nikolaos stood like a stone for a moment, listening to the dogs.

Refuse her, or suffer the consequences. What was that about? Blowing out breath, Nikolaos sheathed his sword and his heartbeat settled into its normal rhythm.

Tomorrow, he would seek out his betrothed. The questions were piling up thick and fast and he suspected that Princess Theodora could supply him with most of the answers.

In the event, Princess Theodora contacted him first. Nikolaos was roused from sleep just before dawn.

'My pardon, my lord,' Elias said. 'I have received word that Princess Theodora would like to speak to you as soon as you are free.'

Nikolaos flung back his blanket and rubbed his face. A grey light was filtering through the barracks window. 'She rises early.'

'Indeed, my lord.' Elias picked Niko's cloak from the floor with a sound of disapproval and shook it out. 'Her messengers are waiting for your answer. Will you meet her this morning?'

'Assuredly,' Niko said, thinking of all those questions. 'Tell her...hell, there's a review at dawn and after that I'm inspecting the armoury. Tell her I shall come to her apartment at noon.'

Elias shot him a look. 'The apartment, my lord? Princess Theodora's messenger suggested the Fountain Court in the Boukoleon.'

'The Fountain Court? I would rather walk with her in the grounds.'

'It is overcast, my lord, it looks like rain.'

'Very well, the Fountain Court it is. At noon.'

* * *

Remembering the courtiers who had trailed in their wake the last time she had spoken to Duke Nikolaos, Theodora had ordered that the Fountain Court be clear by noon. The Varangians were efficient, and when she arrived with only Sophia and Thetis as her attendants, it was empty.

The Fountain Court adjoined the eastern wing of the Boukoleon Palace. Square in shape, it was open to the sky and resembled an abbey cloister, a cloister with three fountains at its heart. The columns in the colonnade had been cut from porphyry, the walkway was covered and faced with granite. One side of the Fountain Court opened on to the Palace grounds and Theodora had asked that two guards be posted by the garden entrance to prevent interruption. The Chamberlain Lord Basil would doubtless tear his beard out when he found out that she had broken with convention in arranging this private discourse. Theodora did not care, she needed to be alone with the Duke when she spoke to him.

It was raining when Theodora stepped into the cloister and she held her blue skirts clear of the ground in case water had blown in. Even on a day as dull as this, the mosaic tiles around the central fountains were twinkling in the wet.

Not all the walkways were deserted. The Duke was ahead of her, leaning against a purple pillar. He must have had regimental business that morning, for his tunic was dazzlingly white, with the gold and silver braiding that proclaimed him General of the Immortals.

'Princess Theodora.' Pushing away from the pillar, he took her hand, and bowed over it. 'It is a pleasure to see you again so soon.'

'Duke Nikolaos—my lord—I hope that it is, I can see I have dragged you from your duties.'

'It is my pleasure, Princess.' His mouth edged into a smile. 'Believe me, meeting with my betrothed is infinitely preferable to inspecting the armoury with my sergeants.'

When he retained her hand, Theodora's stomach gave a nervous jump. His smile had a similar effect on her. The Duke's eyelashes, now that she was close enough to study them, were extraordinarily long and dark. Peter's had been fair. Looking up at the man—a stranger—whom she had agreed to marry, Theodora realised that dark lashes on a man, thick dark lashes, were not in the least feminine. On Duke Nikolaos they were utterly masculine—like his height, and the strength in those broad shoulders, and—

'Princess? There was something particular you wished to discuss?'

The dark gaze moved past her, reminding Theodora that they were not yet alone. 'My ladies-in-waiting,' she said. 'Lady Sophia and Lady Thetis.'

'My pleasure, ladies.' The Duke released her hand and made his bow.

Theodora should not have noticed that he had

released her to greet her ladies, but she did. She should not have cared. The sight of his capable fingers holding hers had made her feel safer than she had felt in an age. *This is why I am marrying him.* How he did it, she did not know, but there was something in his character that gave her hope that her life might one day be more than lies and pretence. It was a heady feeling.

'Princess.' Sophia gave a little curtsy. 'Do you wish us to stay?'

'Thank you, that is all for now.' She waved her ladies away. 'You may wait for me at the end of the corridor.'

The corridor back into the Palace proper was lined with statues. Theodora waited until Sophia and Thetis had reached the last of them before meeting those dark eyes. His eyes were not dancing this morning, they were watching her with a particular intensity that was most unsettling. The small scar beneath his left eye seemed more pronounced. 'My lord, I wanted to speak to you about the date of our marriage. We discussed our betrothal feast but not the actual date of our marriage.'

'The date? I understood it was set for two months hence.'

'Two months!' Panic flared inside her. She could not wait that long. She had scarcely slept for worrying about Boda, and what Prince Djuradj knew about Martina. The uncertainty was nothing less than torture, and the thought of two more months of such uncertainty was insupportable.

'Insupportable,' she murmured, before she could stop herself.

His eyebrows came together. 'Insupportable? How so?'

Flushing, Theodora clasped her hands. She had not realised how awkward this would be. Last night when talking to Sophia, the idea of asking Duke Nikolaos to bring the date of their wedding forward had seemed so easy. But now...

Tipping her head to one side, she studied him. *What will he think?*

'It...I...' clearing her throat, she strengthened her voice. 'I should like our marriage brought forward, my lord.'

'Brought forward? Surely two months is not so far distant?'

'It is too long. I would like to be married as soon as possible.'

'Why?' For a moment his eyes were fierce. 'Why do you wish to bring our marriage forward?' Then his face lightened and he reclaimed her hand, his thumb moved gently across her knuckles. 'A few days ago you were hiding away in your quarters like a hermit and refused even to meet me. And now you want to bring our marriage forward?'

'I...I was unwell when I arrived in the Great Palace,' she said, clinging to the tale that had been put to him.

'Were you?'

She drew herself up. 'Are you calling me a liar, my lord?'

'I am not sure,' he said, quietly. 'I am not sure what you are. Or, more importantly, what you are doing.'

'My lord?' Theodora's heart gave a great lurch, beneath that searching look she wanted to squirm. She held fast. He shook his head—he was trying to read her. And he was not playing fair when his own face was unreadable.

'So, my lady, you wish to marry soon?'

Theodora swallowed, wondering how she might go about convincing him without rousing his curiosity further. 'Indeed. As I have already mentioned, I was…nervous before we met. I see now how wrong I was.'

He laughed. His teeth were very white, very even. 'No, no, Princess, that won't do. I want the truth.'

Blessed Mother, help me.

Chapter Six

'I want the truth,' Nikolaos repeated, resting his shoulder against a marble pillar. 'My lady, after our betrothal ceremony, you confessed that you loved Prince Peter. I would be the first to acknowledge that the workings of a woman's mind are a mystery to me, but it beggars belief that you could have transferred your affections so quickly.'

'Prince Peter died a year ago,' Theodora said.

It was a comment that might mean anything. Her voice was shaking. Grief? Nerves? She was an enigma. Nikolaos narrowed his eyes, every time he saw this woman, more questions bubbled up inside him. Faint smudges under her eyes hinted at fatigue, fatigue which might be explained by an indisposition, or even the excitement of her homecoming. Or could it? His betrothed seemed highly strung, even for a princess. Conscious that he had little experience in handling princesses, Nikolaos decided to tread carefully. 'Princess, I am not saying I will refuse your request, but I would like to know why you are suddenly so eager to marry.'

Her gaze dropped. She was gowned in blue today, a blue so bright it was almost lapis. With the toe of a slipper fashioned from kidskin dyed to match, she began tracing circles on the granite floor. It occurred to him that she looked smaller than she had when they had walked together in the Palace grounds.

'No diadem,' he murmured. It was the lack of the diadem that made her appear smaller and more fragile. In truth, Princess Theodora was more fragile than most women, but she still had a way of filling a man's vision.

She raised her eyes, they looked confused and troubled. Nikolaos had the wild fancy that her thoughts had taken her to some dark and dangerous places.

'I beg your pardon, my lord?'

'You look smaller without the diadem.'

A tentative smile appeared, it was very similar to the smile he had teased out of her during their promenade through the grounds.

'I hate that diadem,' she said. 'It is most uncomfortable.'

'I imagine it might be. I have never worn one myself.'

Her smile deepened and he felt himself warming to her. He wanted to warm to her, he did not want to be harbouring suspicions about her. *Until I know more about her, I must remain wary with this woman.*

'Diadems and crowns are somewhat…restricting,' she said.

'Restricting?'

'You have to stand with a straight back when you are wearing one, you must walk with decorum. My lord, you will see. You will have to wear a crown on our wedding day, it is tradition.'

Nikolaos grimaced. It was customary for men and women—and not only noblemen and women—to wear crowns during the marriage ceremony. This was particularly true when the wedding was a public ceremony, as theirs would be. Nikolaos also knew that it was traditional for the bride and groom to continue wearing their wedding crowns for eight days after the ceremony. The wearing of the wedding crowns was seen as an outward and visible symbol that the couple was adhering to the prescribed eight days of chastity.

'I had forgotten about the wedding crowns,' he admitted. 'Though they can't be worse than a helmet.'

'You might be surprised.' By now Princess Theodora's lips were curving so temptingly that Nikolaos felt his groin tighten. He found himself wondering what his chances were of persuading her to remove her wedding crown *before* the eight days were over.

Slim. At the moment. Now there was an interesting challenge...

'Princess...' He laid a hand on her shoulder.
The shadows under her eyes made him think
twice, but he had to know why his reluctant bride
had suddenly become so eager. 'Why the rush
to marry?'

He had been warned off marrying her in that
darkened street behind the Hippodrome. Was this
new and inexplicable haste in some way con-
nected to that warning? What was going on?

Nikolaos was beginning to see that His Imperial Majesty had been wise to uphold the marriage arrangement his predecessor had made for
the Princess. Was it possible that at some point
during her years away from the Imperial Court,
this woman had become a threat to the Empire?
With her bloodlines, that would seem impossible.
She was a member of the powerful Doukas family; the Emperor was married to her cousin. None
the less, doubts remained. *Is she to be trusted?*

Nikolaos regretted his doubts, he was strongly
drawn to her. Of course, if any action of hers put
the state at risk, Nikolaos would have to denounce
her, even if they were married. The Duke of Larissa, General of the Athanatoi Cavalry, Commander-in-Chief of the Imperial Army, was, first
and foremost, loyal to Emperor Alexios.

'Why the rush?' He hoped he was imagining
her anxiety. She was an Imperial princess and it
was unthinkable she was embroiled in some plot

against the Empire. And yet there had been that moment in the gardens when the Princess had lost colour; there had been that incident outside Cleo's house; and—lord, how could he have forgotten?—before he met her, there had been that broken saddle girth on the polo field…

Nikolaos wanted to be imagining her anxiety. He wanted maidenly modesty to be the cause of her nervousness. It was possible. *She is shy and innocent.*

Dark eyes held his, they were flecked with tiny green lights. Her chin lifted. It was a determined chin—Nikolaos recognised steel beneath the nervousness.

'Why? Because I have realised how well you will…suit me, my lord.'

Her cheeks brightened, and when she lowered her lashes, Nikolaos realised that she had been looking at his mouth. On her mouth that subtle, enticing smile was back. In truth, he did not know what to think about her—she had his thoughts in knots.

Nikolaos knew a moment's confusion when he was unable to decide whether she genuinely wanted his kiss or whether she was merely using the appearance of wanting his kiss as a distraction. Either way, what did it matter? He knew what he wanted. Shifting his hand to her chin, he lowered his lips to hers.

He kept it light and easy, as a first kiss should be.

Her lips were warm and soft. Nikolaos was at

once lost in a cloud of scent, in a complex blend of violets and musk. She didn't open her mouth and he didn't press her. An unmarried princess such as she, a modest virgin, would need careful handling.

No one will have touched her. He must not alienate her by rushing her. When Nikolaos drew back he was aching and more than a little dazed for wanting more. Startled brown eyes met his, her cheeks were rosy. She had felt it, too, that visceral jolt of connection. *Good.*

He tucked her hand in the crook of his arm and reminded himself that he must remain on his guard, all the more so because it seemed that every moment he spent in her company made him less inclined to interrogate and more inclined to seduce. He began walking with her down one side of the colonnaded cloister. Long blue skirts trailed behind them, hushing over the granite stones. Through the arches, the rain was slanting down in the central courtyard.

'Why the change of heart, *despoina*?' When her hand trembled, he covered it with his. 'I will have it out of you. If I am to become your husband, it would be best if you learned to trust me.'

That subtle smile appeared, it was utterly disarming.

'Already I trust you far more than I expected, my lord.' The smile vanished, her voice tightened. 'Have you given any thought as to where we shall live after our wedding? Shall we return to Larissa?'

That was a change of subject if ever there was one. His princess was determined to give nothing away.

'Princess Theodora.' Nikolaos kept his tone gentle. If she was to become his wife, she must learn that he was equally determined. Some secret was weighing on her soul and sooner or later he would prise it out of her. 'Princess, something unexpected happened last night. I was in two minds as to whether to tell you. I do not wish to alarm you, but since we are to be married I shall tell you.'

She smiled politely up at him, but her eyes were intent and, once again, those slight fingers clenched on his arm. 'Unexpected?'

One colonnade came to an end and they turned to process slowly down the next. In the shallow bowl in the centre, spray from the three fountains was mixing with the rain, spotting the entire surface of the water. With a flurry of white, a dove landed and began washing itself.

'Yesterday evening,' Nikolaos said, 'I was walking in the City when I was accosted by two men I had never seen before.'

Slowly, she unclenched her fingers on his sleeve. He sensed it took effort and noted how she had creased the white fabric. 'Yet they knew you? Who were they?'

'I thought you might tell me—they delivered their message at sword point.'

Her gasp, though quickly smothered, was audible over the hiss of the rain and the splashing of the dove. 'Two men, you say? They did not attack you?' She gripped his arm; the delicacy of those ringed fingers was deceptive. She had strength.

'They did not attack me.'

'Where were you when this happened?'

Nikolaos felt himself flush. 'That is irrelevant.'

'Is it?' Her fingers dug into his sleeve, her gaze was needle-sharp, her voice imperious. 'My lord, I must know…were you in the Palace when this happened?'

Slowly, he shook his head. 'It happened in one of the streets behind the Hippodrome.'

Dark eyes bored into his and he saw the instant she made the connection. Lord, she had heard him in the stables, she knew about Cleo and she realised whom he had been visiting. Her jaw set and she broke away to frown at the dove in the water. 'I also want the truth, my lord. Were you visiting your mistress? I heard you had one.'

Guilt twisted in his gut, even though he told himself that there was no need for guilt. 'I did have a mistress,' he spoke firmly. 'I have one no longer. I have ended our…association.'

She looked coolly at him. 'At any rate, I am glad you were unhurt.'

'Those men were not intent on a fight. And had they been…' he shrugged '…frankly, they were not much of threat. They were nervous, which argues for no great skill at swordplay.' He moved closer and lowered his voice. 'They were almost as jumpy as you. What are you hiding, my lady?'

She drew her head back, her gaze did not waver. 'What did they say?'

'Their master wanted to let me know I would be ill-advised to marry you.'

Her lips worked. 'Their master?'

She appeared calm, but she was twisting her fingers together so tightly Nikolaos could see her bones. Taking her hand, he stilled the movement. 'They refused to give his name. But you know who he is, don't you? You know who sent that message.'

When she tried to pull free, he was ready for her. He tightened his hold.

'Who sent that message, Princess?'

Her eyes flashed. 'Unhand me, my lord.'

'I will, as soon as you have told me the name of their master. You know it, I am sure.'

She shrugged. It struck him the gesture was hunted rather than casual and his heart twisted in sympathy, he had to steel himself to remain detached.

'It might be anyone,' she said. 'A princess of the Imperial House has many suitors, my lord.' She looked pointedly at the hand constraining her. 'And most of them know that this is not the way to court her. Unhand me.'

Theodora's stomach had sunk to the ground.

Boda! It had to have been Boda who had accosted the Duke. And Boda was not alone. Her mind raced as she tried to pull free. 'My lord, I am not prepared to accept rough handling. Release me.'

Nikolaos shook his head and a lock of dark hair fell across his forehead.

What could she say? Theodora had been quick to discover a liking for this man who was to be her husband; however, liking was not complete trust. Not yet. Martina might suffer if she trusted him too soon.

'I...I, my lord, *please*!'

Where were Sophia and Thetis? Could they not see she was in need of rescuing? Theodora craned her neck, but her ladies were out of sight, they had taken her at her word and withdrawn down the statue-lined passageway into the Boukoleon. They were trying to be tactful. They had divined that she liked the Duke and were giving her a chance to build on that. Irrationally, she felt a flash of anger against them. Why weren't they watching her more closely?

Instead, it was Duke Nikolaos who was watching her. Those long-lashed dark eyes were shrewd. They were not unkind, but they were not dancing. They were disturbing. So watchful. He gave her an encouraging smile and it reached deep into her belly. The Duke was, curse the man, far too handsome and Theodora suspected he knew it. That kiss...the heavy-lidded, *knowing* way he looked at her...the way he gentled his voice...

He was using every weapon in his armoury to encourage her to open her heart to him. And he was, she realised, far more determined than Peter had ever been. Complete silence on her part was not possible, he was too intelligent to settle for that. Without mentioning Martina, she would have to give him something.

'My lord, it…in Rascia, Prince Peter had enemies.'

As soon as she began speaking, he relaxed his grip and allowed her to pull free. Pausing, she made a play of rubbing her hand, even though he had not hurt her. 'What do you know about Prince Peter, my lord?'

'I know he died unexpectedly. My lady, a moment ago you mentioned that you had many suitors? What suitors? I was unaware of any suitors…'

'I shall come to that in a moment. Prince Peter was killed, my lord. Murdered. He had violent enemies, enemies whose one thought since then has been to punish me for my relationship with him.'

The Duke tipped his head to one side. 'You are saying Prince Peter's murderers followed you here?'

'My lord, I have no proof as to their guilt, only suspicions, but, yes, I believe Prince Peter's murderers have followed me here. I thought I saw one of them in the Palace gardens yesterday—I believe you observed my reaction. In light of what happened to you last night, I am convinced it was he. He is called Boda, and he is Djuradj's creature.'

'Djuradj? The Prince—the Župan—of Zeta?'

'The same.' Theodora took a steadying breath. 'Prince Djuradj is not cast in the same mould as Prince Peter—'

'Prince Djuradj is ungovernable,' the Duke broke in, frowning. 'The man is impossible to deal with.'

'He is certainly ambitious and hostile to Byzantine interests. My lord, I believe Prince Djuradj has sent men to Constantinople because he wants to marry me.'

Nikolaos went still. 'The Prince of Zeta dared approach you with an offer?'

'Yes, my lord.'

'When was this?'

'He arrived at the Rascian Court shortly after Peter's death. In fact, he arrived so swiftly that I came to suspect...'

'You are saying that Prince Peter was killed because he stood in the way of Prince Djuradj's ambitions?'

Theodora nodded. 'That is my belief. I have no proof.'

'Jesu.' Lightly, the Duke touched her hand. 'You must have been terrified.'

Theodora's eyes stung. 'I was, yes.' She felt a most inappropriate longing to confess exactly how terrified she had been, but sin sat heavily on her conscience. Duke Nikolaos was such a stickler for honour, he might reject her if he knew the truth. *I need him.*

'Princess, you are home now, you are safe. It beggars belief that Prince Djuradj approached you in your hour of grief with an offer of marriage. And he must be aware that Byzantine princesses usually marry within the Empire, your betrothal to Prince Peter was exceptional.'

'Yes, it is rare for a princess to marry outside the Empire,' Theodora said quietly. 'When I was originally told of my betrothal to the Župan of Rascia I…I was surprised, I admit it.' Theodora had been more than surprised—she had been devastated. It had been such a shock to have been sent away from everything she had known, she had cried for a week. *I felt like a piece of merchandise being shipped from one side of the Empire to another.* Her first weeks in Rascia had felt like exile.

The Duke was shaking his head. 'The effrontery of the man! Even Župan Djuradj must realise that the only reason you were betrothed to Prince Peter was because of Rascia's long and friendly association with the Empire. There is no such association with Zeta. And to think that Župan Djuradj approached you directly—' he made a sound of disbelief '—his proposal should have come via the Emperor. The gall of the man!'

'I expect he thought to gain the advantage by securing my agreement first. My refusal infuriated him. My lord, Prince Djuradj was so insistent I went into hiding.'

'That is why you took so long to return home? You were fleeing Prince Djuradj?'

Theodora nodded. Tension was tight inside her, it was uncomfortable giving this honourable man half-truths. *I have no choice. For Martina's sake, the Duke must only have half-truths. I can hardly tell him I went into hiding because I was pregnant.*

'My lord, Župan Djuradj is violent—violent and vindictive. He was jealous of Rascian ties with the Empire and I believe he wants to punish me for refusing him and agreeing to marry you.' She found herself moving closer, looking earnestly up into his dark, dark eyes. She found herself speaking the truth. 'My lord, I am glad to be home again and glad that I am marrying you. It is such a relief to know that the Emperor trusts my husband. I am tired of hiding.'

His mouth twisted. 'You want a protector.'

'With Boda in the Palace, I need one.'

'Princess, I shall make enquiries as to why the man has been allowed in.'

'It is likely Boda will be here on the pretext of establishing some kind of rapport with the Empire. There have been many border disputes.'

Nikolaos gave a burst of contemptuous laughter. 'Border disputes? That I can well believe. From what I hear, Djuradj has an extremely flexible view of where his principality ends and the borders of our Empire begin.'

'One does not reason with Djuradj,' Theodora said fiercely. 'He is a lying, murderous swi—'

Warm fingers lightly touched hers. 'He shall not harm you—I shall not let him. Rest assured, my lady, his men will not touch my bride.'

The sincerity in his voice went some way to reassure her—thinking about Prince Djuradj invariably panicked her. It was hate. It was fear.

'Prince Djuradj has a long reach,' she murmured.

'You are safe, Princess.'

Theodora tipped her head back to look up at him. Duke Nikolaos of Larissa was tall, much taller than Peter. And darkly handsome where Peter had been fair. In truth, Duke Nikolaos couldn't be less like Peter if he tried. The two men were different in more ways than their looks, though. *This man is strong, he is a survivor.* The thought came out of nowhere and caught her by surprise. It had not been Peter's fault that he had been murdered. Nevertheless…this man would protect her—Martina would be safe.

'I trust you, Duke Nikolaos,' she said, and hoped he could read the sincerity in her voice. 'I am thankful that we are to marry.'

He smiled and lifted her hand. As Theodora looked at the unfamiliar head bowing over it, she was struck by the most unsettling thought. His hair was so dark, so thick—what would it feel like? Curling her other hand into her skirt, suddenly afraid that Duke Nikolaos might divine what she was thinking, Theodora tore her eyes away. When he straightened and looked at her, she was studying the acanthus leaves on an elaborately carved capital.

'I am thankful, too,' he murmured. Tucking her arm in his, in a possessive way that was already becoming familiar to her, he resumed his slow perambulation round the Fountain Court.

Theodora allowed herself to relax, giving him half-truths seemed to have allayed his suspicions. It had been surprisingly easy to tell him about the proposal of marriage she had received from Župan Djuradj. Thankfully he didn't seem inclined to probe further. Martina, for the time, was safe.

She cleared her throat. 'So. How soon may we marry, my lord?'

'We could try for next week. With your permission, Princess, I shall seek His Majesty's agreement to the change of plan.'

'Next week would be most satisfactory,' she said. She had kept Martina safe for several months, she must be able to manage another week...

He caught her eyes and lifted a dark eyebrow. 'Provided you can wait that long, my lady.'

His comment caught her off-guard. She was hesitating, wondering how best to respond, when she saw the flash of his teeth, the teasing grin.

'You are very sure of yourself, my lord,' she said. 'My lord?'

'Hmm?'

Strong, warrior's fingers were exploring hers, straightening them. He ran his thumb along their length, playing with her rings. His actions, simple though they were, set off a slow curl of nervousness, low in her belly. She frowned and willed it away. 'Duke Nikolaos? You never did say where we shall make our home. Will we be joining your mother in Larissa?'

His fingers stilled. 'No, my lady, we will not.'

The curt response set alarm bells ringing. There was anger there, definite anger. What had she said? 'If we marry next week…' she said slowly, trying to work it out '…there will not be sufficient time to notify Lady Verina of the change of date. She may not be able to reach the City in time and might miss our wedding. This upsets you?'

He did not answer for a moment. And though he smiled, his eyes were carefully blank. 'If our marriage takes place next week, my mother will accept it.' He gave another pause. 'Lady Verina wishes for this marriage, she will be glad. And now, if you would excuse me, my lady, I shall go and find a scribe and compose our letter to His Majesty. We shall need his blessing on the altered timing.'

He gave her a brief bow and strode off in the

direction of the gardens, boots clicking on the paving.

Thoughtfully, Theodora watched him go. Something…there was something in his voice when he spoke of his mother, if only she could put her finger on it. Duke Nikolaos had the reputation of being a dutiful son, a reputation that had been borne out during Lady Verina's recent illness—he had rushed back to Larissa to be at his mother's bedside.

There is some difficulty with his mother, I know it. Where does the anger come from? What has caused it?

Unless… Could it be that he was irritated with her for asking that the date of their marriage be brought forward? No, she did not think that was it. He had agreed easily enough.

One week—in one week's time, we shall be married.

Many matters had yet to be resolved. If they were not to make their main residence in his family holding of Larissa, where would they live? In the Boukoleon Palace? They could not stay in her apartment in the women's quarters. A man in the women's quarters would not be tolerated. Theodora stared at the dove splashing about in the fountain. She had only just arrived in her seaside apartment, but if the Emperor agreed to change their wedding date, she would soon be moving out.

One thing was certain—she refused to join the Commander-in-Chief of the Tagmata in the barracks.

In his quarters in the barracks, Nikolaos stared blankly at the scribe. The man had been reading the letter he had composed to His Majesty and Nikolaos hadn't heard a word. It was an important letter, asking that the marriage should be brought forward and if the request was granted, it would throw the Palace into some disarray. The tone must be exactly right.

'My apologies, my mind was elsewhere. Please read it through again.'

Why was it so hard to concentrate? As the scribe nodded and began re-reading the letter, Nikolaos found his mind wandering almost immediately. He had much to digest. Princess Theodora seemed convinced that Župan Djuradj was responsible for Peter of Rascia's death. Murder, she had called it. And then Djuradj had apparently demanded her hand in marriage.

Is there more that she is not telling me?

Certainly it appeared that the poor woman had been bullied into hiding. That must be why she had taken so long to come home; that must be why she had resisted meeting Nikolaos for so long. It was possible she feared that he, too, would bully her.

As her face swam into focus in his mind, Nikolaos felt a surge of possessiveness towards her.

Prince Djuradj shall not have her. She is my princess. His Majesty had asked that Nikolaos uphold the arrangement that the previous emperor had made and Nikolaos had agreed. He had had his own reasons for agreeing. The sense of possessiveness was somewhat surprising.

'She is beautiful,' he muttered.

It was only when the scribe looked up from the scroll that Nikolaos realised he had spoken out loud. 'My lord? The letter is acceptable?'

'Let me see.' Taking the parchment, Nikolaos ran his eyes over it. *'"If it is not too great an inconvenience, we ask that Your Majesty agree...."'* He read to the bottom of the scroll, to the place where he had mentioned Prince Djuradj's marriage proposal to the Princess. *'"...Your Majesty, Princess Theodora Doukaina has laboured under some distress concerning actions of the Župan of Zeta, whom she believes responsible for the death of her fiancé, the Župan of Rascia. I cannot say whether this is the truth. However, it has come to my attention that representatives of the Zetan prince have pursued Princess Theodora from Rascia. I personally have reason to know they are in the City, if not the Palace. Further, the Princess has confessed that following the death of the Prince of Rascia, she received a clandestine offer of marriage from the Zetan Prince.*

Prince Djuradj must know that our princesses are rarely given in marriage to foreign princes. Not only is his proposal an insult to the Empire, it

*is a blatant bid for power. Prince Djuradj wishes
to extend his influence in Rascia; it is even possible he is planning to invade there. It seems likely
that Prince Djuradj has convinced himself that
marriage to the woman formerly betrothed to the
Prince Peter would give him credibility in the
eyes of the Rascian aristocracy, not to mention
a spurious sense of legitimacy.*

*The Princess and I have had a private conver-
sation on this subject, and whilst I cannot believe
the Zetan prince presents a real threat either to
Your Majesty or the state, I shall naturally keep
a close watch on any contact the Princess might
make with him.*

*Your Majesty, it is for these reasons that I
would recommend that my marriage with Princess Theodora should take place as soon as possible. I remain, Your Majesty, your most loyal
and obedient subject...'''* Hmm, that all seems
in order. Hand me the quill.'

Nikolaos signed the letter with a flourish.
'Please take it to His Majesty without delay.'

'My lord.' The scribe bowed and went out.

It was then that Nikolaos realised that the Princess's question about his mother had pushed his
cousin, Brother Leo, out of his mind. He had not
been prepared to discuss his mother and had almost snapped at her. *I had to leave before that
happened. She is an Imperial princess, a blood
relation of Empress Irene. I cannot lose my tem-*

per with an Imperial princess. There would be time to ask about Leo after their marriage.

'My lord?'

Elias had come in with the white, silver and gold dress uniform of the General of the Athanatoi Cavalry folded over his arm.

'Is this the uniform you will wear at your wedding, my lord?'

'I am undecided—why?'

'Some braiding on the tunic has come loose, my lord.'

'Have it repaired, I must be worthy of a princess, mustn't I?'

'Yes, my lord.'

Elias went to kneel in front of Niko's travelling chest, then began pulling out more uniforms, muttering under his breath about the need for certain generals to have more respect for their gear. Niko wondered what the Princess would think when she learned about his parentage, his *real* parentage.

'Do you think you might wear the heavy breast armour, my lord?' Elias said. 'I seem to remember the gilding was scratched.'

'Elias, stop obsessing over my uniform, I should like your counsel.' In the past, Nikolaos had discussed many problems with his manservant and he respected his judgement.

Elias leaned back on his heels. 'My lord?'

'It concerns my birth.' Nikolaos felt uneasy, he was going to marry the Princess, but she had yet to learn of his illegitimate birth. Ought he to tell her *before* their marriage? Would the realisation that her husband was illegitimate weigh with her? 'I know you have observed the coolness that has developed between me and my mother.'

'Indeed, my lord, and it saddens me.' Rising, Elias closed the travelling chest.

Nikolaos fixed his whole attention on his manservant's face, alert for the slightest change of expression, the slightest hint of shock at what he was about to say. 'While she lay ill, my mother told me something touching on my birth. She told me—'

'So that's it,' Elias said. 'I wondered if it might be. Lady Verina has told you about your father, my lord, your *blood* father.'

Nikolaos felt his mouth fall open. 'You know? You know that Governor Gregorios was not my father?'

'I have suspected this for many years, my lord.'

'You have?'

'I can see your mother in your features, but I have never been able to see Governor Gregorios. To be sure, you and the Governor both have brown eyes, but the resemblance is ephemeral, your eyes are much darker. And physically, my lord, you are larger and your nose—'

'You always suspected.' Nikolaos rubbed his face with his hands. He felt stunned, utterly stunned that Elias had long suspected that Governor Gregorios was not his father. 'My mother is a grave disappointment, I was profoundly shocked.'

Elias frowned. 'My lord?'

'My father—I am referring to Governor Gregorios—must have been devastated by my mother's betrayal. He adored her. How could she betray him like that?'

'Lady Verina and Governor Gregorios seemed very close,' Elias agreed, rubbing the back of his neck.

'So I thought, until my dear mother's confession.'

'Have you asked Lady Verina how it came about, my lord?'

'I don't want details! I have no wish to speak to her. She betrayed my father, she betrayed me.'

Elias gave Nikolaos a look he had not seen from his manservant in years. Disapproving. Disappointed. 'We all make mistakes, my lord. You should speak to your mother.'

'Don't look so sour.' Nikolaos raked his hair with his hand. 'Elias, be honest—'

'Aren't I always?'

'Yes, my friend, indeed you are,' Nikolaos said drily. 'Except that I thought I knew you, and now you tell me you have long suspected that I am not the son of Governor Gregorios. Tell me, have suspicions over my birth ever weighed with you?'

'Not in the least.'

'Do you know who my father is, my *blood* father?'

'No, my lord. Didn't Lady Verina give you his name?'

'All she would say was that he had been born outside the Empire, she refused to enlarge. Elias, you have seen the Princess...do you think this would affect her acceptance of our marriage?'

'I do not know the Princess well enough to comment, my lord, but I do not believe so, she has already been betrothed to a foreign prince.'

'So my barbarian blood will not trouble her?'

'How could it? Her previous fiancé was Rascian.'

'He was the Župan, the Rascian prince—I am a mere general.'

'You are Duke Nikolaos of Larissa,' Elias said, standing very straight. There was no trace of disappointment in his gaze and the pride in his voice brought a reluctant smile to Nikolaos's lips. 'You have been brought up in the Empire; you are General of the Immortals, Commander-in-Chief of the Tagmata, the most trusted officer in the Emperor's army; you—'

Nikolaos made a chopping gesture with his hands. 'Enough. Elias, I accept you do not believe my foreign blood will make the Princess shy away. One more question. What about my illegitimacy? Do you reckon she will baulk at that?'

Elias looked steadily at him. 'It's true that many people are shocked by illegitimacy, but I do not believe the Princess will be one of them. However, it is as I have said, my lord—I do not know her. You have spoken to her. If you are in any doubt, my lord, why tell her? It is not common knowledge. Governor Gregorios was happy to accept you as his legitimate son. That is how the world sees you.'

'I have yet to tell His Majesty, Elias. You are the only person in whom I have confided.'

Elias bowed his head. 'I am honoured by the trust you place in me, my lord. I shall say nothing of this to anyone.'

Nikolaos gripped his manservant by the shoulder. 'Thank you, Elias.'

Elias bustled out of his quarters, grumbling about the scratched gilding on his heavy armour, and left Nikolaos to his thoughts. His conversation with Elias had gone some way to relieve him.

My barbarian bloodlines alone will not shock the Princess; she was clearly more than fond of Prince Peter. But my illegitimacy... Much as I would prefer to make a clean breast of it before I make my marriage vows, I shall not mention that. Not yet.

Later, if she sees my silence as duplicity, as a means of gaining legitimacy for my illicit birth...

He sighed.

I must be realistic. No marriage is perfect, we are both using each other. Princess Theodora needs protection from the Prince of Zeta; I want to strengthen my position at Court. It is not as though she is getting nothing out of the arrange-

ment. I will protect her...provided she remains a loyal subject of His Majesty.

At the back of his mind was a thought that Nikolaos did not care to examine. There were similarities between Župan Djuradj and himself. Both he and the Prince of Zeta had decided that marriage with Princess Theodora would improve their position in society. Holy hell, what was he thinking? Župan Djuradj was refractory and disloyal. Nikolaos refused even to consider the idea that there might be similarities in attitude between himself and a rebel princeling in faraway Zeta...

Princess Theodora is mine.

What had her life been like in Rascia? In an instant, Nikolaos could see those large brown eyes flashing fire at him. She had been furious when he had restrained her in the Fountain Court. He grinned—the combination of fire and hesitant innocence had been unexpectedly arousing. Had Prince Peter indulged her? It seemed likely. The presence of an Imperial princess at the Rascian Court would have been a great prize, he would not have wished to offend her.

So, Princess Theodora was used to getting her own way, and a princess, particularly one who had been spoiled, was not going to be easy to control.

God alone knew what freedoms she might have enjoyed in Rascia.

Be that as it may, she was back in Constantinople and she was marrying him. He would woo her, he did not want a marriage poisoned by conflict. Yes, he would woo her, but he would also master her. There was no way that his wife would be permitted the freedoms Governor Gregorios had given his mother. Even if she was an Imperial princess.

Chapter Seven

Seven days and nights flew by in a flurry of activity and preparation.

Martina was teething and fretful and far too noisy for a child who ought not to be drawing attention to herself. Theodora flung herself into soothing her, hoping that by doing so she would not have time to dwell on the difficulties involved in her forthcoming marriage, nor indeed on the disturbing incident Duke Nikolaos had mentioned taking place in the street behind the Hippodrome.

She fought a losing battle. News that Boda had accosted the Duke in person had removed any lingering doubt that Župan Djuradj had several men in the City. That his men had warned the Duke off marrying her made her cold with dread. Had the Prince of Zeta discovered her deep secret?

As the days passed and her wedding day drew

nearer, Theodora found herself lost in a labyrinth of circling thoughts, caught up in spiral after spiral of worry. She could find no way out. When Martina wailed and went red in the face, it was a relief to take her in her arms and walk the length of the reception chamber and back, rocking and soothing for all she was worth. Keeping herself busy with her daughter was one distraction from her anxieties.

Surprisingly, Theodora also found respite in dealing with her wedding arrangements. It was a distraction that was far more pleasant than she had expected, though she soon learned that even something as apparently innocuous as thinking about her wedding clothes brought its own challenges...

While she promenaded up and down with Martina, a servant brought in a selection of delicate shoes on a silver salver and offered them up to her.

'I suggest this pair, *despoina*,' Sophia said, indicating a pair of purple slippers.

'Dark purple? Surely that colour is too deep?' Theodora asked, frowning at the slippers as she jiggled Martina.

'Not at all, *despoina*, these are for your wedding day. Empress Irene herself has approved this colour. You are permitted to wear the rich purple on your wedding day.'

Theodora handed Martina to the wet-nurse, Jelena, and picked up a slipper, eyeing it with some misgivings. 'I was not born in the Purple Chamber, Sophia, I do not have the right.'

Deep purple dye was incredibly costly. Everyone in the Empire knew that only princes and princesses born in the special birthing room at the heart of the Boukoleon Palace had a right to wear it.

'My lady, this will be your wedding day,' Sophia insisted. 'The citizens are expecting a show.'

Dear Heaven, the slipper was the deepest, darkest Imperial purple. What would the people think if they knew Theodora was not the impeccable princess they believed her to be? She had lived too long in Rascia. Her sins were such that, even on her wedding day, she was not entitled to such an honour. She replaced the slipper on the salver, and lowered her voice. 'What a sham it all is, Sophia.'

'Sham, my lady?'

'You know the truth.' *Most of it.* 'I am not what everyone believes me to be. I am a disgrace.' Theodora jerked her head at Jelena, who had taken Martina over to one of the tall windows and watched as the nurse waved an ivory rattle in front of her daughter's face. 'Jelena, if you need the coral teething-ring, it is in the small basket by the cradle.'

'Thank you, my lady.'

Sophia retrieved the purple slippers from the salver. 'You ought to wear these. It is no sham and you are not a disgrace.'

'Sophia, you are too loyal.'

'I only give loyalty where loyalty is due, my lady. You have served the Empire well.'

Theodora could not bring herself to respond, guilt held her tongue.

'Princess, you served the Empire ten years ago when you accepted Prince Peter's hand in marriage and went to Rascia; you serve the Empire today by returning to marry the Duke. You have given your life to the Empire.'

Theodora inclined her head in acknowledgement of Sophia's gracious comments, even if she could not agree with them. Only she knew the full truth, she was a disgrace. She was deceiving *everyone*, she had begun doing so even before Peter's death. She had good reason, but that was no excuse. *I am no longer the innocent girl who left Constantinople. And I have come home as an outsider.*

'Truly, I am not entitled to wear the Imperial purple.' She waved the tray away.

'But you will, won't you?'

'Since the Empress has given her instructions, and the people expect it, yes.'

But I shall not feel comfortable, not for a moment. I should not be representing the Imperial House in such a way. I shall have to think of it as a performance. I shall be like an actress in the Hippodrome—yes, my marriage to Duke Nikolaos shall be my greatest performance.

She stiffened her spine. 'Which fabric do you recommend for my gown?'

'Here, my lady.' Thetis gestured a servant-girl forward. She had a shining length of purple silk draped reverently across her arms. 'Unless you would prefer this?' Thetis indicated a bolt of paler cloth lying on a side-table.

'Yet more purple,' Theodora muttered. 'It is all purple.'

'Purple suits you,' Sophia said.

I feel like an imposter. I am an imposter. I am deceiving everyone.

Theodora hoped she would feel better once the ceremony was over. Marriage to the Duke would make her feel less of an outsider. She could not be marrying a better man. Duke Nikolaos had the full confidence of the Emperor; he commanded the Imperial Army, he was honour personified—in short, her betrothed was so much a part of the fabric of the Empire, he was ideal. She needed him far more than he needed her.

The Duke believed she wanted his protection, but that was not the whole of it. She needed him to blot out her sin. She needed him to help her reclaim the land of her birth. *I will be happier when the whole business is over and done with.*

Theodora had been trying not to think about her betrothed, he was yet another of those disturbing things that she was trying not to dwell on. Although it had to be said, thinking about Duke Nikolaos did not disturb her in quite the same way that thinking about Župan Djuradj disturbed her.

Duke Nikolaos of Larissa excited her, he made her nervous. His physicality was impossible to ignore. Not that she wanted to ignore it. Had there been no secrets between them, Theodora would relish the thought of sharing a bed with him. Her awareness of his masculinity and her physical attraction to him was a revelation. Theodora had never thought she might enjoy a man's body. Princesses married for duty, not pleasure. She had grown into womanhood knowing that she would marry Peter. There had been no physical excitement there, only acceptance. Duke Nikolaos made her suspect that, with him, mutual physical enjoyment was a definite possibility.

Or it might be, if she did not have so many secrets. She hated not being open with him. Would there never be an end to it? When Theodora had decided that, come what may, she was going to keep her daughter, she had known it was not going to be easy. But she had had no idea that everything would spiral out of control so wildly. Every day her life was becoming more and more complicated...

She cleared her throat. 'Do we know what Duke Nikolaos will be wearing?'

'My apologies, my lady,' Sophia said, smiling, 'we have just received word on that, I meant to tell you straightaway. The Duke's manservant sent to say that Duke Nikolaos will be wearing the dress uniform of the General of the Immortals.'

'White with silver and gold,' Theodora murmured, remembering the tunic he had worn in the Fountain Court. Would he be wearing full armour? She hoped not. If there was to be any kissing, she did not relish the thought of being swept into the arms of someone in heavy armour. Not that she was thinking about anything as trivial as kissing.

'You are to be carried from the Palace to the church in a palanquin—'

'I am to have a litter?'

'Yes, my lady. And Athanatoi Cavalry officers will form part of your escort.' Sophia waved at the bolts of material. 'Which do you like, my lady?'

Theodora fingered the silk in the maidservant's arms. 'This is heavenly, so smooth. I love the way it shimmers.'

She reminded herself that the people of Constantinople were not the only ones to be expecting a show. She had not forgotten the Duke telling her that he wanted their marriage. He had fought for His Majesty and he expected public acclamation of his service—she was his reward. Theodora stared at the rippling, delicate silk. The Duke had been most accommodating when she had asked that their marriage be hurried along. He wouldn't be getting the virgin that he expected, and at the moment he did not have the faintest notion that she needed him so much more than he needed her. He might cast her off when he learned the truth, but in the meantime she could at least give him this—if Duke Nikolaos wanted a show, then he must have one.

I am a princess. I am an actress. This will be my greatest performance.

'This one, Thetis, the dark purple.'

Thetis beamed.

All week, gifts flooded into the apartment. Duke Nikolaos sent her a delicate gold ring. It had an enamelled front with a secret compartment behind it. On an impulse, Theodora cut off a lock of her daughter's hair and slipped it inside. She put the ring on the middle finger of her right hand, and there the ring stayed, a reminder of her pledge to marry him.

The next day, he sent her a set of polished silver bangles; they were sleek of line, sophisticated. The day after that, a gold set was delivered, they had been made to the same pattern as the silver ones. The gold bangles were accompanied with a note which read, *For my beautiful bride, in the hope that they please her. They are not as heavy as the diadem.*

In the privacy of her bedchamber, Theodora studied the bangles. The clean lines and lack of ornamentation was most appealing. Duke Nikolaos might be one of the most powerful men in the Empire, but even he could not compete with the wealth of an emperor or a prince. She liked it that he hadn't tried, that he had instead attempted to find gifts to suit her temperament. He had remembered their discussion about crowns.

Interleaving the bangles, silver with gold, she slipped them on her arms, smiling as the cool metal warmed to her body temperature. Afterwards, the bracelets jingled with her every movement, reminding her of him—not that she needed any reminder. The Duke's gifts gave her hope that this marriage might one day be more than a matter of expedience. What would life be like if Duke Nikolaos became more to her than simply her protector, her means of coming home? And how would it be if he came to look on their marriage as more than a matter of political expediency?

Duke Nikolaos was not the only one to send gifts to the apartment. From His Majesty and her cousin the Empress, Theodora received an amethyst and pearl studded collar.

The Lord Chamberlain sent her a ruby-encrusted necklace.

'Put these in the strongbox, if you please, Sophia. And please send messages of thanks.'

'Yes, my lady.'

Another courtier sent her an icon that had been painted by the monks on Mount Athos.

'That can go on the east wall in the bedchamber, Thetis. Please convey my thanks to Lord Constantine.'

Princess Theodora received a jewelled reliquary that had come from Ravenna. She received perfumes and gilded oil lamps, enamelled belts and cloak pins; she was given ribbons and flowers, the apartment was awash with flowers.

And petitions. Lord, the petitions...

My lady, I beg you to have words with your cousin the Empress. My fourteen-year-old daughter, Maria, would make the perfect lady-in-waiting. She has been well trained. She is pretty and quiet. And should the Empress not need another lady, perhaps you yourself might consider...

Princess Theodora, I implore you, my son, Demetrios...

Through it all Martina cried, her gums were tender and everyone must know of it.

Oil of cloves was called for; more rattles were found—silver, ebony, they even tried a humble gourd—but Martina was not to be placated. Every indignant wail reminded Theodora that by rights her daughter should be Princess of Rascia. It was as though Martina was intent on letting the world know how much she objected to her present, unsatisfactory status.

On her last official morning as an unmarried woman, Theodora's ladies cloistered her in her bedchamber to clothe her for her wedding. It seemed to take an age. First her underskirts, then her purple robes. There was smoothing, pinning, and last-minute stitchery.

'You have lost weight, my lady.'

'Oh?'

Every time Theodora shifted, the silver and gold bracelets tinkled like bells. Sophia stood behind her, busily coiling her hair into place. Like the rest of her, her hair had been oiled and washed and perfumed. Theodora could feel gentle fingers on her scalp as Sophia worked.

Catching a glimpse of yet more purple, she caught Sophia's hand. 'What's that? What are you doing?'

'It is only a violet, *despoina*. You love their fragrance, so I thought to weave one or two into your hair, it will look very pretty. Unless you object?'

Theodora released Sophia's hand. 'Please continue.'

'Which rings shall you wear, my lady?' Thetis asked.

'No rings save the enamelled one, I thank you. I shall wear the silver and gold bangles, though.'

'Very well. What about the large diadem, Princess?'

Theodora shook her head. 'A simple one will be better, particularly with the violets. We must allow for the wedding crown.'

Thetis nodded and handed her a fringed shawl. Naturally that too was purple. Theodora pushed away the inevitable feeling of guilt. She refused to allow guilt to dominate her today. *This is a show, Today is all for show.*

'Excuse me, my lady?' Jelena came in carrying Martina and, for once, Theodora's noisy daughter was at peace. 'Will Martina be going with you into the new apartment?'

Theodora's stomach tightened with the familiar anxiety. She glanced over her shoulder and exchanged looks with Sophia. In the last week, she had not seen the Duke for more than a few moments, but they had found time to discuss where they might live. They could not keep this apartment because of its location in the women's quarters, but His Majesty had offered them another apartment in the Boukoleon Palace. A set of chambers a couple of floors below this one was free, and the Emperor had said that he would be delighted if Princess Theodora and Duke Nikolaos would move into it after the wedding. The plan was that Theodora's attendants, along with their belongings, would be transferred to the new apartment while the wedding ceremony took place.

'Duke Nikolaos has said that he welcomes all my entourage, Jelena. You and Martina are an important part of my household.'

Theodora had yet to mention Martina or Jelena to the Duke and she was more than a little concerned about this, but it was customary that the husband of a princess should accept her entire household.

Martina gurgled and reached for a bead necklace round Jelena's neck. Absently disengaging her tiny fingers, Jelena looked doubtfully at Theodora. 'Does the Duke know you have an infant in your entourage?'

Theodora struggled to conceal her misgivings, she had not told him because she had been reluctant to draw his attention to Martina. What if he objected? She had hoped to avoid an argument, at least until after the wedding.

'The Duke is expected to welcome everyone, Jelena.'

'Will there be a nursery in the Duke's apartment?'

'There will be when I have informed him of Martina's needs. In the meantime, you may pick out the chamber you think most suitable and use that.'

'Thank you, my lady.' Dipping into a curtsy, Jelena went out.

'I hope I am doing the right thing, Sophia,' Theodora murmured.

'Despoina?' Sophia pushed the final hairpin into place and surveyed her handiwork, a small smile on her lips.

'Will there be difficulties, do you think? Will Duke Nikolaos accept Martina? It may not be easy for a man like the Duke, a warrior who is more at home in the barracks than the Palace, to find himself surrounded by my ladies. Martina may be a step too far.'

Sophia's expression sobered. 'I have given this much thought in the last few days and I have been praying that you would ask for my views. It might be wise to delay the Duke's introduction to Martina. Theodora, with your permission, I should like to tell you my conclusion…'

Theodora's heart sank. Sophia had used Theodora's Christian name, something she rarely did. Few people were privileged to address Theodora so intimately. That Sophia chose to do so today proved she was touching on matters that were deeply personal to her mistress. And deeply important.

'Please, Sophia, continue.'

When Sophia took a deep breath, Theodora knew she was not going to like what Sophia was going to say. 'Thetis, you may leave us.'

'My lady.' Thetis left the bedchamber and softly closed the door.

'Theodora, I do not believe this is the time to pass Martina off as the child of a slave. Especially when the Duke will be—forgive my bluntness—especially when he will be within his rights to bed you in eight days' time. A man of his experience may recognise that you are not a virgin and he is very likely to leap to conclusions about the true identity of Martina's mother.'

Theodora wanted to put her hands over her ears to block out the unwelcome words. 'You have a suggestion, I take it?'

'Send Martina away for a few weeks. Let the Duke get to know you…allow a…a bond to develop between you. Then you may recall Martina.'

'Send Martina away?' Theodora twisted the enamelled ring round on her finger. 'Sophia, that is the one thing I cannot do! I thought you, of all people, understood this.'

'Theodora.' Sophia's gaze was earnest. With a smile she reached up and adjusted Theodora's circlet. 'I urge you to reconsider. The Duke has been agreeable over the altered date for your wedding, but I do not think he will be so agreeable over the presence of a baby in your entourage. Make sure he is in love with you before you tell him.'

Theodora felt her lips curl. 'A man in love will believe anything?'

Sophia smiled. 'No, but he is more likely to *accept* anything.'

'Sophia, he may never love me—'

'There's a convent nearby, Saint Elizabeth's,' Sophia said, ignoring Theodora's objection. 'I am sure that if you gave them a donation, they would be happy to take both Martina and Jelena. Saint Elizabeth's is very close to the Palace, you could visit every day.'

Theodora set her jaw. 'Your suggestion is unacceptable. Martina stays with me.'

'Martina will be quite safe in the convent. And it might not be for long. Theodora, you have already caught the Duke's interest—'

'*No!* Sophia, that is my last word on the subject. I forbid you to raise it again.'

Sophia held her gaze for a moment, before bowing her head. 'As you wish, *despoina.*'

Theodora looked down at her enamelled ring and sighed. 'Bring the hand mirror, if you please. I should like to see if I am fit to go to my wedding.'

Sophia found the mirror and Theodora found herself gazing at a stranger, a gorgeously arrayed stranger. Her gown, in deepest purple as decreed by the Empress, fitted her to perfection. Her slightest movement was accompanied by the rustle of heavy silk. Bracelets chinking, she inspected the intertwining violets sewn on the hem and the sleeves.

'The seamstresses have done well to finish the embroidery in time,' she murmured. 'Was this your idea, Sophia?'

'Yes, my lady.'

Sophia had arranged her hair on the top of her head, shaping it into shining twists and curls. Several long strands were twined about the simple coronet. 'My hair has never looked better and you were right about the violets—they add a touch of lightness. Thank you, Sophia.'

'I am glad you like them, my lady. You look every inch the princess. Quite magnificent.'

Theodora looked dispassionately at her reflection. She didn't feel magnificent. She felt sick with nerves. She was clinging to the thought that she would feel better once the church service was over. The marriage ceremony would wipe away past sins, it would be a new beginning.

What will the people see when I walk into

Hagia Sophia? Will they see a magnificent princess or will they see me, the real me?

They will see what they expect to see—I have been trained.

The golden coronet Theodora was wearing to her wedding might be lighter than the diadem she had worn to her betrothal ceremony, but she was carrying a weight of expectations that was heavier than any diadem. *The City wants a magnificent princess. A perfect princess.*

Theodora tried to see what Sophia saw. Her wedding dress was very grand, the hem trailed across the marble floor, swirling out behind her, yard after extravagant yard of finest silk. Pearl and amethyst earrings swung from her ears; the priceless amethyst and pearl collar that had been a wedding gift from His Majesty glowed about her neck.

She studied her face. The reflection was largely a lie, only her eyes betrayed her real self. Wide brown eyes, *frightened* eyes, stared back from the polished surface of the mirror. Yes, her true self was there, hidden behind kohl and rouge and carefully applied cosmetics. Her true self must remain hidden. *The people must see the image, they must see what Sophia sees. Today I am a perfect princess. I am entirely without sin.*

She could only pray that Duke Nikolaos saw only perfection. She was not ready for him to see the true Theodora.

Pushing her doubts away, she waved the mirror aside. 'The palanquin is ready?'

'Yes, my lady, it awaits below.'

Theodora gave Sophia a calm smile and swept into the reception chamber to accept the good wishes of her other ladies. Two questions went round in her mind. *How long will it take for the Duke to see the real, flawed Theodora? And how will he react when he does?*

It had rained earlier. The steps of the Palace portico were dark with wet. The wind—an easterly—was brisk and chill. As Theodora paused on the top step, goose-bumps formed on her arms.

The palanquin was the largest she had ever seen. And it had been painted in the same exact shade of purple as her gown. It had a domed roof—more purple—flecked with silver stars. As Theodora looked uneasily at it, her heart jumped. *I am deceiving everyone.* A hanging on the side of the palanquin worked loose and snapped in the wind. A slave rushed forward, caught the silver-fringed cloth and briskly tied it back. Other slaves were lined up, waiting to carry the litter. There were several onlookers—ladies, stable boys, eunuchs from the Imperial offices, scribes…

Theodora glanced up. The sky looked restless—a bank of untidy, leaden clouds was being pushed relentlessly to the west. 'I hope that wind doesn't wreck all your work, Sophia,' she said, briefly touching a violet. For once, she was happy not to be riding.

A shawl appeared and was held over her head. 'I am only grateful that Lord Basil insisted on the palanquin,' Sophia said, clucking gently as she ushered Theodora down the last of the damp Palace steps. 'Thetis, lift the train higher.'

Thetis scrambled to deal with the yards of Imperial silk, and although she could have managed without her ladies, Theodora allowed herself to be helped into the palanquin. *The people want a show and I must give it to them.* Her palms felt clammy, but she resisted the impulse to wipe them on her gown.

'You, too, Sophia, I want you to come with me.'

Sophia's face lit up. 'You want me to ride to Hagia Sophia with you?'

'If the bearers can manage us.'

Theodora leaned back against the padded seat and listened to the mutterings as Sophia spoke to the slaves. Then Sophia climbed in, squeezing in next to her.

'Are you sure there is room?'

'I do not wish to ride to the church alone.'

The litter shifted and swayed, and they were on their way. Soon she would be married; soon she would feel as though she belonged again. Theodora shivered.

Naturally, Sophia noticed. 'That wind is very

strong,' she murmured, reaching to close the curtains.

Theodora held out a staying hand, her bangles clinked. 'Leave them, Sophia. The Court expects a show and a show we must give them.'

It was easier than she had imagined, sitting in the gently rocking palanquin as her wedding party wound its slow way to church. Theodora's other ladies processed on foot behind, betraying their presence with the odd muffled squeal as one lady stepped in a puddle; as another got her gown wet; as another slipped on wet paving...

Theodora leaned forward to smile at some women gathered in one of the gardens; she lifted a hand to acknowledge the bowing noblemen by the bronze fountain. Moving inexorably towards her marriage, her smile never faltered, her face felt stiff, but she smiled on. Her heart thudded, her mouth was dry.

The litter-bearers bore the palanquin with scarcely a jolt under the shadow of the Palace gate and out into the square outside Hagia Sophia. More people—the square was crammed.

'Holy Mother, half the City is staring at us,' she murmured.

'The people love you, my lady,' Sophia said.

They do not know what they are looking at. Would they love me if they knew the truth? I doubt it.

If only she did not feel so alien, so distanced from everyone. She reminded herself she would feel more at home after the ceremony. 'They do not know me, Sophia.' *Careful, be careful what you say.*

'My lady?'

'I mean only that I have been out of the Empire so long, how can they love me?'

'They love you.' Sophia's voice rang with sincerity.

Theodora was beginning to feel that her face would crack with the effort of smiling. 'If they knew what they were looking at, they might not be so pleased.' Sophia's eyes became thoughtful and Theodora fell silent—she had said too much.

Outside the Palace grounds, lines of soldiers flanked the way, keeping it clear for the palanquin. The Empire's regiments were out in force for the wedding of their Commander-in-Chief. First there were foot soldiers, she glimpsed the red dress uniform of the Varangian Guard, grey clouds reflected in the blades of their battle-axes. Rank after rank of them. Hoofbeats announced the arrival of the Immortals, a white standard flew from a cavalry officer's lance—silver and gold swirled at the edge of her sight. They must almost be there. Her heart banged against her ribs.

'That's the Duke's regiment.' By now her face—the face with the smile on it—felt as if it was no longer hers.

'Yes, my lady.'

The litter moved gently on. Theodora smiled.

Sprays of flowers were tossed through the doorway—lilies, rosemary, bay. She no longer saw the onlookers; she no longer noticed the regiments forming her guard.

And then it happened.

Her eyes locked on a pair of hard, dead eyes. *Boda!*

Her skin iced over. Boda's smile was cold as a glacier. Something thudded on to the floor, missing a purple slipper by an inch. A stone with a scrap of vellum tied to it. The litter seemed to lurch.

Sophia frowned and made to kick the stone out.

'No. If someone has sent me a message, it is my duty to read it,' Theodora said, amazed that her smile was still in place. She held out her hand.

'Princess, I do not advise...'

Theodora flexed her fingers. 'Sophia, if you please.'

Sophia picked up the stone and handed it over.

Remembering to nod brightly at the passing crowd, Theodora loosed the vellum from the stone and smoothed it out on her purple skirts.

Bold black ink jumped out at her—*We know your secret.*

She swallowed down a gasp. 'Close the curtains!' *Which secret?*

'But, *despoina*, I thought—'

'Close the curtains!' *Which secret?*

Sophia whipped the curtains closed. The light dimmed.

The palanquin rocked, they had come to a halt.

On the right side, a masculine hand reached in and shoved back the curtain. Theodora forgot to breathe. The sleeve was dazzlingly white and edged with gold braiding. Warm dark eyes met hers. Questioning, steady eyes.

'Duke Nikolaos!' Theodora's breath released in a rush, she had never been so relieved to see anyone in her life. *Not Boda, it is the Duke.*

The Duke was on foot, his wide shoulders blocked Hagia Sophia from view. He extended his hand. 'Princess, with your permission, I wish to enter the church at your side.'

For a moment, Theodora could only sit with her hands clasped at her breast, while her heartbeat settled. *Not Boda.* The Duke had such a warm, reassuring gaze. She had seen the warmth before and had no difficulty understanding it—it was the warmth a man felt when he was looking at a woman he desired. The kiss they had shared in the Fountain Court had revealed that. Further, it had revealed that she desired him, she wanted to trust him.

In contrast with his officers, Duke Nikolaos was not wearing heavy armour. He was bareheaded and had come to marry her in a white silk tunic emblazoned with the silver and gold braiding of his regiment.

Slowly, for she felt as though she was crossing an impassable gulf, Theodora gave him her hand.

It wasn't the warmth she had seen that enabled her to take his hand, nor was it the steadiness. Oddly, it was that questioning look. Theodora's past was littered with many mistakes, but she knew her judgement of this man was sound. Duke Nikolaos had the strength one would expect to find in the Commander-in-Chief of the Tagmata. It was a subtle strength she had not thought to look for in a military man. It was most attractive, impossibly compelling. Her hand trembled with a curious mixture of relief and apprehension. And, if she were honest, anticipation…

Soon, we shall be married. This man desires me—ours will not be a marriage in name only.

Sophia hurried to help her from the palanquin. A cheer went up. People began clapping and stamping. The clouds were starting to part and a spear of sunlight gilded Hagia Sophia's domes and the mosaics over the doors. An awning and covered walkway had been rigged up so they would not get wet if the rain returned. Theodora noted these things with part of her mind, the rest was focused on the Duke. He was every inch the warrior in his blindingly white uniform, a tall distinctive officer whose presence filled her mind with dark desires and secret longings that she, as an Imperial princess, had never thought to experience.

A sudden shyness took her and she could no

longer look at him, not properly. Her gaze fixed on the gold braid on his sleeve, on the possessive strength of the hand holding hers. When Sophia had finished arranging her skirts and train, she forced herself to overcome her shyness and shot him a glance from under her lashes.

Her mouth went dry and her belly seemed to turn over. The Commander-in-Chief of the Tagmata was so handsome. It was impossible to ignore the fluttering in her belly...

What will it be like when I bed with this man?

What was the matter with her? Rather than thinking about the marriage bed, she ought to be contemplating the sacred nature of the vows she was about to make. Thank the Lord, she would have eight days to get used to the idea of sharing a bed with him, the fluttery sensation was bound to go away. She had never felt it with Peter, nor had she ever been troubled with such...unseemly thoughts.

Theodora had never really understood the nature of lust—she had assumed it was an affliction only suffered by men. The Duke was giving her reason to doubt this. The thoughts and responses Duke Nikolaos evoked in her were surely sinful. And entirely inappropriate. The Church Fathers knew what they were doing, the decree that married couples should remain chaste for eight days after their wedding was designed to quell troublesome desires.

It would be eight days before she and the Duke

would be permitted to share their bodies with each other.

Eight days…eight days…

Princess Theodora Doukaina was getting ahead of herself.

It was with such inappropriate thoughts in mind that she turned to give the citizens of Constantinople a last, brilliant smile before turning to enter the great domed church.

Chapter Eight

Nikolaos glanced down at his bride, dismayed by the way she had recoiled at first sight of him. When he had opened the curtain of her palanquin, the Princess had shrunk back into the shadows, scowling up him as though he were a monster. If she had tried, she could not have made it more plain—she was being forced into this marriage.

He wished he could fathom her. The marriage had been brought forward at her urging; she had returned his kiss in the Fountain Court—he had not imagined that slender body melting against him. His blood heated at the memory.

And now she was looking…*hunted* was the word that sprang to mind. Princess Theodora looked as though she were being pushed to marry the Minotaur.

Only a few moments ago, as the palanquin had approached the church, she had been smiling.

Playing the part of the beautiful, happy Princess. And she *had* looked happy. That had not been wishful thinking on his part.

She looked happy until she saw me. Then she had her lady whisk back the curtain to shut me out.

Nikolaos kept smiling as she stepped out of the palanquin, it was the best way to hide a welter of confusing thoughts. Lord, she was lovely—he ached to possess her. The simple golden circlet suited her better than the amethyst-encrusted diadem. He liked the simplicity of the violets, too. Princess Theodora's quiet, dark beauty did not need heavy ornament. This woman could command attention without the Imperial robes, without the jewels; she had a glow that was all of her own.

As her lady shook out her purple skirts, a lily fell to the ground; the people had been honouring her with flowers. The people loved her.

'With your permission, Princess,' Nikolaos said, setting her hand firmly on his arm. She was trembling and that clear olive skin was drawn beneath the rouge her ladies had put on her cheeks. He prayed that she was not afraid of him. A cold band tightened about his chest—had she really looked at him as though she loathed him?

She is a virgin—can she be worrying about what will happen when we consummate the marriage?

Princess Theodora had no mother to advise

her on what would happen between her and her husband. Had her ladies advised her? Nikolaos understood that the Princess's closest ladies were unmarried, so that seemed unlikely. Who could say what she knew or did not know? It might be better if he consummated their marriage sooner rather than later, then her fears would not have chance to build. If he could teach her that she had nothing to fear from the marriage bed…if he could teach her that it was safe for her to enjoy her body with him and for him to enjoy his with her…

Cleo had enjoyed his body, but Cleo had been a woman with a tarnished reputation. He was marrying a princess, a shy and innocent princess— a princess might not respond as enthusiastically as Cleo had done.

His officers saluted. A horn sounded. Silver trumpets flashed in the brightening day and a fanfare rang out. More flowers were strewn in their path.

'Princess?'

She swallowed. Her kohl-lined eyes were not fixed on him, but on the mill of people beyond the awning. 'Out there…' she murmured.

The moment she spoke, Nikolaos realised that someone else was at the root of her anxiety, someone in the crowd. The tight band fell away from his chest. *It was not me pushing back the curtain that wiped the smile from her face…it was not me…*

He bent his head towards her, smiling for the crowd, playing the part of the loving bridegroom. If she, a bundle of nerves, could play her part, he would play his. 'You saw Prince Djuradj's man?'

'I saw Boda.' she spoke quickly and quietly. 'Prince Djuradj definitely has men in the City.'

Nikolaos guided her on to the Persian carpet that led under the awning. Her hand was icy—this Boda had scared her half out of her wits. That was what Nikolaos wanted to believe and today, that was what he would believe. Today, he would not listen to the tiny voice inside him, the one constantly urging him to caution. He was not going to wonder whether the Princess might be colluding with Prince Djuradj in some way, and that guilt might be the cause of her unease. Not today. It was their wedding day.

'Boda will not be allowed into Hagia Sophia, Princess, only those who have been invited may enter the church today.'

It was cool inside the church of Hagia Sophia and the air resonated with the chanting of monks. Theodora swallowed and repressed a shiver. The ancient dome and mosaic walls transported the monks' voices and sent otherworldly echoes back to them—it sounded as though choirs of angels were singing up in the galleries.

I do not deserve angels.

As Theodora and her bridegroom made their way across the tiled floor, Theodora focused on the sound of their footsteps, on the rustling of her gown. Simple, everyday sounds which made a soft counterpoint to the unearthly voices.

Hagia Sophia was a vast dusky cavern of a church where countless flickering lights pushed back shadows. It was a palace for God in all His mystery. Gold winked out from a myriad mosaics; it gleamed in the halo of a seraph high in the dome; it dazzled in an Emperor's crown glimpsed behind a marble pillar; it twinkled in an Empress's collar. Glass tesserae fractured and trapped the light—the blue in the Saviour's robe, a green gem in an Empress's ring, the red of a chair…

Theodora and the Duke came to a halt beneath one of a hundred hanging lamps suspended from the dome. Standing at the heart of the Empire, they were handed candles. They bowed their heads before the Bishop of Constantinople—the Patriarch. Silver threads glittered in the Patriarch's vestments and in the robes of the attending priests.

Absurdly conscious of the man standing calmly at her elbow, Theodora focused on the flame of her candle and her coming vows. She would not think about the past. The enormity of what she was doing hovered at the back of her mind. She would not think about Peter; she would not think about Župan Djuradj. *I am marrying Duke Nikolaos of Larissa.* The heat from the candle warmed her face.

She needed this marriage to work, and she would make it work. Župan Peter had not been strong; the Duke, however, was. *Martina and I need this man; this marriage will be a success.*

The ceremony passed in a haze of incense smoke and painstaking ritual. Theodora had forgotten how long the full rites took. The prayers. The speaking of vows and exchanging of rings. Theodora kept her eyes on her candle, watching the yellow flame as it wavered in a draught and strengthened again.

Behind her, someone in the congregation coughed; she heard the shuffling of feet. More prayers were accompanied by several swirls of incense. There was more chanting. The Patriarch blessed the wedding crowns and she felt the weight of hers being set on her head. The Duke's hand was warm.

'Princess?' His voice. The voice of her new husband.

Theodora tore her gaze from the yellow flame. Even though she knew what to expect, it gave her a jolt seeing him in his wedding crown. He was so much the warrior that it had been hard to imagine what he would look like wearing one. He bore it well. That dark head was held high and proud, he was smiling and the gems in the rim of the crown sparkled and flashed. Vine leaves etched into the gold promised fruitfulness; olive leaves promised peace. He looked distinctive. Genuinely happy.

'Princess, with your permission, we should walk round the church,' he murmured.

Theodora smiled her agreement and that strong warrior's hand tightened on hers as they processed round the church in ceremonial ritual. There was more smiling for the benefit of the congregation. Clouds of incense rose into the dome. More chanting. More angelic echoes from the galleries.

She had done it, she was married to the Duke. They had got through the ceremony without any interruptions—there had been no last-minute revelations courtesy of Prince Djuradj. *I am married to the Emperor's Commander-in-Chief. At last I am truly home.*

There were more prayers, some of them for fertility. Theodora felt herself flush. Did the Duke want a fertile bride? Did he worry that she might not be able to conceive? She hated that she had not been able to be frank with him. She hated that she must make her vows to him when he knew so little about her. He had no idea about her child; he had no idea of the guilt she was feeling being married to him. She did not know him well enough to have told him what it had been like being bound to another man.

She pushed Peter from her mind.

Wreaths of incense coiled around them, catching in her nostrils. Was it guilt that made the service seem interminable? There was yet more chanting and more prayers and then the rites were over and they were walking back to the purple palanquin. They would ride in it together back to the Palace.

It was bright outside, and the wind had swept the clouds from the sky. As they stood in the doorway facing the Imperial Gate, a cheer went up.

'Theodora! Nikolaos!'

Flowers flew through the air. The Duke caught a lily and, bowing, handed it to her.

The people went wild. 'A kiss! A kiss!' they shouted.

Theodora gripped the lily and smiled, even as she scoured the crowd for Boda. *Where is he? Is he still there? What might he do?* It was all very well for common sense to tell her that, with the army out in force, Boda and his henchmen could do nothing. The familiar dread was back, a cold lump in the pit of her stomach.

Duke Nikolaos interposed himself between her and the crowd. 'No one will disturb us, my lady,' he murmured. 'Come.'

And then they were sitting alone in the palanquin, he had dismissed Sophia.

'My lord,' Theodora heard herself objecting, as he dealt courteously with yards of purple silk. 'How will Sophia get back to the Palace?'

'She has legs.' He grinned. 'Your other ladies walked, it is not far. My officers will escort her.' Leaning out, he gestured the bearers forward and took his place at her side. The palanquin rocked.

Sprays of leaves and flowers showered through the windows. Theodora could scarcely see the floor for myrtle, bay and lilies. It smelled like spring.

'My lord—'

'Nikolaos.' Strong fingers squeezed hers. 'We are husband and wife and I would prefer that you call me Nikolaos, particularly when we are on our own. Further, with your permission, I should like to address you as Theodora. Do I have your permission, my lady?'

'If that is your wish.' She was trying not to scour the faces of the throng lining the route. The palanquin had almost crossed the square in front of the church and she hadn't seen Boda. Perhaps, having delivered his message, he would leave her alone for a while.

'A kiss! A kiss!' a woman cried, waving a scarf to attract their attention.

Others took up the refrain. 'Kiss her, General! Kiss the Princess!'

Nikolaos looked at her, dark eyes dropping briefly to her mouth. 'With your permission, Princess?'

Theodora gave a jerky nod. 'I thought you were going to call me Theodora.' Her voice sounded croaky.

He smiled and wound an arm round her shoulder as he gently tipped up her chin. 'Relax, Theodora,' he whispered, 'this won't take a moment.'

Nikolaos touched his lips lightly to hers. He

had been burning to kiss Theodora ever since he had realised that she had not been frowning at him. She was heart-wrenchingly lovely, he wanted her with every bone in his body, but the kiss must be brief. His wife was a Princess with impeccable bloodlines and this was a public kiss—he must show respect.

A soft moan caught him off-guard and Nikolaos let his mouth linger on hers for an instant or two longer. Her scent was womanly and exotic; he breathed it in, allowing it to penetrate deep into his memory. *Theodora. My wife.*

The roar of the onlookers became an irrelevance. By some sorcery the crowd was suddenly a thousand miles away. Her lips were warm and sweet and hard to draw away from. The air was rich with scents—the lilies her well-wishers had strewn on the floor of the palanquin, the light scent of violets, bay. He forced himself to raise his head. It would be folly to make the citizens of Constantinople think he was treating an Imperial princess with disrespect. Reluctantly, he released her.

Theodora's eyes were closed, her lips were slightly parted—the look of expectancy was irresistible. Nikolaos kissed her again, taking hold of her shoulders. When he felt her hand sliding round his waist, his stomach rocked. He wanted more, much more. And he did not want to wait eight days for it either. Those eight days of chastity were beginning to look like torment.

The second time Nikolaos raised his head, the crowd's roar surely reached the heavens. The palanquin swayed. It wasn't enough, his blood was heating fast. It didn't help when his wife reached for his shoulder and leaned into him. He felt a light kiss on his neck and gathered her close.

'With your permission, Princess,' he muttered, sliding his hand firmly round the back of her head. Then, heedless of her marriage crown, or his, heedless of her elaborately styled hair, he kissed her in the way that he desired.

Properly. To hell with the crowd.

She shifted nearer.

Deeply. Devil take their expectations.

Her mouth opened under his.

Thoroughly. This was his wife.

Her tongue met his. She pressed her breasts against his chest. When he groaned, he could swear she answered him in kind, but he could not be certain because the hoots and applause from the crowd was deafening.

'Kiss! Kiss! *Kiss!*' they screamed.

'Another! Give us another!'

Nikolaos was only too happy to oblige. And so, it seemed, was his bride.

Silk rustled. The palanquin was full of sighs, the scent of crushed violets and of femininity. *His wife.*

'Theodora.' There wasn't enough air in the palanquin—his pulse throbbed, he ached with want. Her crown was definitely an impediment.

If he didn't push it aside and unpin that shining brown hair, he would surely go up in flames. He itched to tear off the purple robes and...

May the Lord have mercy. Startled at the rush of desire...at the need she evoked in him, a need so powerful it hurt, Nikolaos tore his lips from Theodora's. He was astonished to realise how hard he was breathing. If he were not careful, he would be consummating their marriage in full sight of the entire City.

She, too, was breathless. Her crown had slipped, it was tilted slightly to one side. His heart clenched. On her the wretched thing looked almost endearing. Some of her hair had come undone, a sinuous curl coiled seductively over her shoulder. Violets were scattered everywhere, and the lily she had been holding was bent and squashed.

Theodora stared at her new husband, swallowing hard. She hoped the people could not see the effect he had on her. She was meant to be innocent, a pampered princess who had known protection every day of her life. This man made her forget all that.

'Your crown has slipped,' he said, reaching to straighten it. His eyes—the dancing eyes—were hot and wicked.

Face on fire, Theodora attempted to slide away from him, but there was little room. 'My lo— Nikolaos, we ought to take care, we are in public.'

'As you wish.'

Apparently complaisant, he sank back against the thick upholstery. He gave her another grin. It was not in the least complaisant, it seemed to promise nights filled with endless delight. Retrieving one of her hands, he lifted it to his lips in the acceptable courtly manner. As far as the delighted crowd was concerned, their princess had chastened her passionate husband, he had obeyed her and she was being given a polite, apologetic kiss.

Except she knew it wasn't an apologetic kiss. He nibbled her fingertips, once, twice…making her limbs turn to water, trying to charm her. She snatched her hand away.

He gave a soft laugh. 'Until later, Theodora.'

Dangerous—that charm made him dangerous. Theodora hadn't anticipated charm. She must take care not to allow him through her defences. She hadn't believed it would be possible, not after Peter. It must not be possible—she couldn't grant any man that power. *I am an Imperial princess, I am marrying him for Martina's sake. I am marrying him so that once again I may call the Empire my home.*

Jerking her head, Theodora stared resolutely out of the window.

'Smile, my Princess, you're forgetting to smile.'

His voice was full of warmth and laughter, and something clenched deep within her. *Charm. I have underestimated this man.*

The palanquin left the square and passed through the Palace Gates. Guards snapped to attention. Theodora's breathing and heartbeat returned to normal. Her cheeks cooled.

The way Nikolaos had kissed her...it was as though he had been branding her! Peter hadn't dared to handle her in such a way. Not once. Surreptitiously, Theodora ran her tongue round her lips—she felt almost...bruised.

They were approaching the Boukoleon Palace where a row of maidservants was lined up to greet them. Theodora gave them the obligatory smile. It startled her that this time, the smile felt genuine.

Their wedding day was almost over. In the banqueting hall, under the Imperial standard, Theodora sat very straight in her high-backed, cushioned chair. If she moved, even an inch, she was afraid she might crumble. She had played her part to the point of exhaustion and her most exacting scene was yet to come. Was Nikolaos expecting to sleep with her?

Her husband sat next to her in an identical chair and they looked out over a table crowded with silver candlesticks, gold platters and sparkling Venetian glassware. Theodora was too tired to focus on the faces around the board. Nikolaos had been most supportive as one ritual had been succeeded by another, she could not have wished for a more attentive bridegroom. He had smiled as he waved for her glass to be filled. He had served her himself with the choicest cuts—offering her sturgeon, quail, and stuffed peacock's eggs. He had called for ginger and cinnamon pastries when she mentioned how she relished them. In truth, she ate frugally. It seemed churlish to wish for this, their wedding feast, to be over, but Theodora had had enough. She wanted to know whether Nikolaos was expecting to sleep with her.

'Lord Basil is in his element,' she said, sighing, as one lengthy and particularly boring speech segued seamlessly into the next.

Nikolaos sent her one of his wicked grins. 'I thought he would take exception when we brought the wedding date forward, but he relished the challenge.'

Her husband's tunic was dazzling in the blaze of the candles. With his silver and gold braiding and his jewelled wedding crown, Nikolaos might be taken for a king. Despite her fatigue, his dark face kept drawing her attention. The lines of that strongly-formed nose fascinated her, as did those chiselled cheekbones, the finely shaped mouth, the tiny scar beneath his eye…

Theodora reached blindly for a wine glass, she sipped and tasted nothing, she was too tired.

'Not long now,' Nikolaos said.

Their wedding feast was unusual in that both men and women were present. In the Palace it was more common for the sexes to eat separately.

There had been no sign of the Emperor and Empress. With several days of their penitential fasting left to go, their Imperial Majesties would not be taking part in state banquets for some while.

Thank goodness. Theodora was only too relieved not to be seeing the Emperor. The longer her meeting with His Majesty was delayed, the better. She wanted to make sure of Nikolaos before speaking to the Emperor.

Theodora's aunt was present, further down the board. Theodora smiled at her over the rim of her Venetian glass.

'I was hoping to meet your mother, my lord,' she said. 'Is Lady Verina not here?'

Her husband's expression froze. 'No, my lady, she is not.'

'That is a shame.' She laid her fingers on the back of his hand. 'Is it because we brought the marriage forward? Was there no time to send her a message?'

His hand lay unresponsive under hers. Theodora's spirits sank. She had married a man she had only spoken to a handful of times, but she had believed she could warm to him. The wicked light in his eyes had hinted at pleasures that might be shared; his unexpected charm had touched her heart. That light was gone, so had the charm—he was looking at her with cold, cold eyes. How had she thought she could warm to him? He was a complete stranger. What had happened?

'I sent no message.'

Theodora stared. 'You will send her one, surely?'

Broad shoulders lifted. 'I wasn't planning to.' He paused. 'My lady, even if I had sent a message, Larissa is too far away for my mother to have reached the City in time for the ceremony. I didn't see the point.'

She leaned towards him. 'Your mother will want to know that the marriage has taken place. You will send her a message.'

He drew his head back, studying her. 'Is that a command, Princess?'

Theodora reached for a honey pastry she did not want, hoping he had not noted how his shift of mood had upset her. It would not do to give this man power over her. 'Your mother should be told our wedding has taken place. My lord, you are fortunate to have a mother.'

His lips twisted. 'I am?'

His apparent callousness took her breath away—something was very wrong here. Biting into the pastry, Theodora resolved to discover what lay at the root of his anger against Lady Verina. Their wedding feast, while they were under the eye of half the Palace, was not the place for her to be making intimate enquiries, nor was it any place for an argument.

She swallowed down her pastry. 'Indeed, you are most fortunate,' she said mildly. 'My mother died years ago and I still miss her. The same goes for my father. They died shortly after I was sent to Rascia.'

His mouth softened and the harshness left his expression. 'That must have been hard for a young girl far away from home.'

'Yes.'

'How did it happen? I knew your parents were dead, but I cannot remember being told how they died.'

She stared at a knife on the table. 'My parents were coming to visit me in Rascia. There was a storm off the coast of Corfu and their ship went down. They drowned.'

Shifting his hand under hers, he linked their fingers. 'I am sorry. That is a terrible thing for a young girl to accept. Particularly one sent to live so far from home.'

Theodora nodded and smiled, and turned the subject. The rest of the feast passed without upset. Theodora's husband was once again the attentive bridegroom and Theodora took care to avoid mention of his mother.

Finally, after a succession of toasts presided over by Lord Basil, they made their escape, slipping from the banqueting hall shortly after a luteplayer from Apulia began singing.

On the arm of her husband, Theodora was led to the door of an apartment a few floors below the one she had occupied as an unmarried woman. She nodded at the guards in passing, so occupied with the challenge ahead of her—convincing her husband she was an untouched princess—that she barely noticed the Varangians had been replaced with men from the Athanatoi.

'Goodness,' she said, brightly, as they crossed the threshold. Wall lamps flickered with yellow light. 'This apartment is the twin of my old one.' The reception chamber here had the same tiled floor, the same tall windows overlooking the Sea of Marmara, the same diaphanous purple curtains billowed in the on-shore breeze.

'His Majesty has been most kind,' Nikolaos said. 'This is a world away from my quarters at the barracks.'

Theodora walked the length of the room, past lamp after lamp. She hoped her husband could not read her. She had done it, she was married, but marriage had not eliminated all of her problems. With Prince Djuradj's men in the City, it had become even more important to bind Nikolaos to her. She did not think that conversation alone would win him. Nikolaos was unashamedly physical…so virile…he responded to her lightest touch. Before she met him, it had been easy to imagine she could hold him at bay for a while. She was no longer so certain.

She paused by the brazier at the far end of the reception chamber. The coals glowed red, the heat ran up her arm. As in her previous apartment, the brazier stood outside the door of a room that looked identical to the one Martina had occupied. Thankfully the door was shut, she could hear muffled singing behind it. A lullaby. Dear Heaven, Jelena was singing to Martina. Nikolaos would hear.

She whirled round and found him half a pace behind her.

Oh, no! What if Martina cries?

'Our apartment meets with your approval, my lady?'

Our apartment. Sweet Mother.

'It is lovely, very much like my old one.' Theodora began to babble, anything to cover up the sound of Jelena's lullaby. 'The servants have been working hard, they have moved everything so quickly, my lord. Even the curtains.'

'Nikolaos,' he murmured. 'Call me Nikolaos.'

She snatched at his hand, his lips formed a slow smile. *My touch did that.* Ignoring his smile, she towed him away from the nursery and prayed Martina did not cry until she had found a way to tell him there was a child in her entourage.

Days, Martina will have to be quiet for days.

Theodora came to an abrupt halt outside the bedchamber and dropped his hand as abruptly as she had taken it. 'Good night, my lord.'

He made a sound of regret. 'Pity. You got my hopes up there.'

'My lord!' She gave him a shocked look. 'You cannot have forgotten the eight days of chastity enjoined on us by the Church?'

Dark eyes stared into hers, his mouth lifted into a smile. 'You believe in that nonsense?'

'I...I...*yes*!'

'Hmm. We shall see.' He looked at her mouth, before slowly running his gaze up and down her body.

She felt it like a caress. A caress that left her feeling...extremely unsettled. It left her wanting. *Dear Heaven, what is this man doing to me?*

'I shall give you some time with your ladies, Princess, but I shall be back later. We will share a bed tonight.'

Bowing, he strode from the apartment.

We will share a bed tonight...tonight...

The doors shut behind him. With her husband's words echoing in her ears, Theodora flew down the length of the reception chamber and into the small room at the end. Jelena was nursing Martina, smiling as she stroked the soft baby hair. A tiny starfish-shaped hand was splayed out across Jelena's breast. Squashing down a pang of what she was horribly afraid was jealousy, Theodora looked at the wet-nurse.

'I can see Martina is well, Jelena. You have everything you need?'

'Thank you, *despoina*, we have everything.'

'I will see her in the morning,' Theodora said, softly. She stared longingly at her daughter for a few precious seconds, then quietly closed the door.

Tonight...tonight...

In the bedchamber, Sophia had lit more lamps and was waiting to attend her. The great mulberry-coloured bed was waiting, too, with its swags of drapery and tasselled cushions. Theodora felt her pulse jump, it was all over the place.

'The servants have been busy. I was not sure they would manage to shift the bed downstairs,' Theodora said, lifting a foot for her slipper to be removed. A brazier stood to one side of the bed. She frowned. 'Sophia, I did not ask for a brazier.'

'The chamber was chilled.'

'Please have it removed.'

'My lady?'

'It gives off too much light. I don't want light, not tonight. And put out the lamps, will you? Save for the one by the bed.'

'Very well, my lady.'

Theodora was so consumed with her thoughts that she did not see Sophia calling for servants, she did not see them carefully removing the brazier, nor did she see Sophia turning down the lamps. *I have married a man who believes me to be a virgin and I am anything but virginal. I want there to be truth between us, but if I tell him about Martina tonight, the moment he learns I am no virgin, he will suspect she is my daughter. He may force me to give her up.*

'Sophia, should I tell him?'

'About what, my lady?'

'Martina.'

'You will say she is yours?'

'As we discussed, I had planned to say she is an orphan I have adopted. It is going to be impossible for me to hide the fact that there is a child in my entourage for long. A few moment ago he almost stumbled across her. I had hoped to wait until…later to tell him.'

'I think it would be wise to wait, my lady,' Sophia said, taking Theodora's shawl from her and loosening her gown. 'Please lift up your arms.'

Theodora raised her arms and spoke through the silk as it was eased over her head. 'What if she cries?'

'She will not cry, Jelena is with her. And if she does, the nursery is at the far end of the apartment. The door will remain closed all night.'

Sophia's smile was reassuring, but Theodora was not reassured. As she readied herself for bed—washing, quickly redressing her hair before replacing the wedding crown—the worries circled.

Martina was teething, and for a child so small she had a large voice. *I cannot give her up.*

'Do you think he will consummate the marriage tonight, Sophia?' she asked. Her cheeks heated at the thought.

Sophia shrugged. 'Who can say? A man like the Duke may do anything.'

The door latch clicked—it was the Duke.

Chapter Nine

'Thank you, Lady Sophia,' Nikolaos said. 'That will be all.' He had changed out of the dress uniform of the Athanatoi and had put on a long green tunic that was belted at the waist. He was still wearing his wedding crown.

Theodora stood in the darkened bedchamber, a bundle of conflicting hopes and desires. *He has not removed the wedding crown. Does that mean he is going to honour the tradition of the eight days of chastity?* She did not want him to consummate their marriage. *He might turn against me if he realises I am not innocent.* At the same time, she was honest enough to accept that part of her was looking forward to the consummation. *I desire this man.*

Sliding the bolt across after Sophia had closed the door, her husband walked towards her. A gentle finger stroked her cheek. His hand lifted, teasing a tendril of hair out from under her crown. As a violet fell to the floor, his lips curved. A small tug brought her chest to chest with him and she forgot to breathe.

She cleared her throat. 'My lord—'

'Nikolaos, please.' He grinned. 'Or Niko, if you prefer.'

'Nikolaos—'

'So formal,' he murmured, leaning forward and pressing a kiss to her cheek. 'So beguiling, my little princess bride.'

Theodora's cheek warmed where his lips had been. That swooping sensation was back in her belly and she knew it was not entirely caused by nervousness. She desired this handsome general who had become her husband. She didn't feel ready to allow him to know her fully, but she could not deny that she was drawn to him.

'Don't be afraid,' he murmured.

'I am not afraid.' She reached for his shoulders. Nikolaos was taller than Peter, she had to reach higher than she was used to. Her new husband also had shoulders that were wider and more muscled. He was all warrior, so very…male. Boldly, Theodora slid her hands across his chest. The green tunic could not hide the power in his frame, he had muscles everywhere. What would it be like to be swept up in his arms? He would be gentle with her, she hoped. He would be capable of tenderness…

Cleo. She knew the name of his mistress and

for some reason it jumped to the front of her mind. She frowned.

He drew back. 'What is it? Theodora?' Large hands rested on her waist, his thumbs gently stroking just below her ribs.

'Nothing.' She studied his face—the characterful line of that Roman nose, the curve of his mouth. She didn't love him, she liked and respected him, but she didn't want to lose him to anyone else. He was her husband and she intended to keep him. Closing the space between them, she noted both the flare of interest in his eyes and the answering ache in her belly. *I want you.*

'I have to say I agree with you about crowns,' he said, bending to kiss the side of her face.

'Inconvenient, aren't they?'

'Mmm.' He kissed her ear. 'I should like you to remove mine.'

Theodora let her fingers move up and down on the side of his neck. She told herself it was so subtle a movement, he probably would not notice. 'And the eight days of chastity?'

He groaned and her fingers froze. She heard a soft laugh.

'I think we are both in agreement that chastity is not for us, my princess. With your permission, we shall consummate our marriage tonight.' His dark head lowered and he nuzzled her neck, giving her earlobe a soft bite. 'My crown, if you please.'

Lifting the crown from him, she placed it on a table.

Slowly, as though he were afraid of startling her, he did the same for her. Then he was back, close enough for her to enjoy his body heat, guiding her hands to his belt. 'With your permission, my princess, I should like you to help me.'

His decisiveness—*We shall consummate our marriage tonight!*—overrode some, if not all, of Theodora's qualms. 'Very well, my lord.'

If she allowed him this, it would help bond him to her more fully, as Sophia had suggested. He might accept her secrets more easily. She prayed that would be the case. Against the odds, he was winning her trust. In truth, she could easily see herself becoming fond of him. *Sweet Mother, let him come to feel affection for me, too.* Nikolaos would honour his obligations to her, she was sure, but she wanted more than the honouring of obligations. And then there was Cleo—Theodora really didn't want to lose him to anyone else.

Her fingers fumbled at the buckle, she could not undo it. Her hand fell away.

Dark eyes smiled into hers. 'Come, it is time my princess was unveiled.' Deft fingers worked at her belt and it fell to the floor with a small clatter. Catching her hands, he set them on his waist. 'With your permission, Theodora, I really would like your assistance.'

Theodora was no virgin, but there had only been one other man she had touched in such a way. Her pulse jumped, secret inner muscles tightened. 'You truly wish to bed me tonight?'

He lowered his head and nuzzled her neck. 'I burn for you, Theodora.'

She had to fight down a sudden rush of panic; she was taking a lot on trust and her fears were never far away. She was desperate to believe Nikolaos was so honourable that he would accept her, flawed as she was. Had she judged him correctly? She could be mistaken, there were no guarantees. *What will he do when he discovers the truth?* 'But, Nikolaos, the traditions...the formalities...the Patriarch? The Patriarch will be most disappointed—'

'Who's to tell him? I certainly won't. This is between you and me.' A teasing light entered his eyes. 'The eight days of chastity are not for us, my princess. You have shown commendable maidenly modesty by objecting, but that is quite enough. We shall consummate our marriage tonight. Here...' He guided her hand back to his belt buckle. 'Try again—help me, if you please.'

This time, Theodora managed the buckle and she could not help notice that he was already very much aroused. Somewhat shakily, she put the belt on a side-table.

He pulled her to the side of the huge, silk-draped bed and flung the mulberry-coloured coverlet aside. Sitting on the edge of the mattress, he drew her on to his lap.

Taken by shyness, Theodora leaned into him

and buried her head in his neck. *We have not doused the light! We must douse the light...there are faint marks on my breasts and stomach, he must not see them. If he does, he will know I have had a child.*

She forced her head up, thankful she had had the foresight to have the brazier removed. However, it would be to no effect if the lamp was not put out. 'The light, Nikolaos, I do not like the light—' A teasing mouth cut her off and his tongue began exploring. She was surrounded by the musky scent of aroused male. He nibbled her lip, he licked it in the most gentle but determined of seductions. Her mouth opened.

As their tongues met, a delicious weakness spread through every limb. Kissing this man was intensely pleasurable. Theodora had no notion a woman could feel so eager. Her breasts tightened. She felt a shameless impulse to rub herself against him—the power of the impulse shocked her. *What is happening to me?* She gripped his shoulders and forced herself to look into his eyes.

'Nikolaos, the light...'

'Mmm?'

'The lamp—' He was kissing her ear as she waved vaguely at the soft glow by the bedside.

'So shy,' he murmured.

It was true, she did feel shy. That at least was no lie. 'Please, Nikolaos, I hardly know you.'

Dark eyes looked into hers; his nose nudged her cheek; he nibbled her earlobe.

'As you wish.' Leaning over, he reached to turn down the lamp. Night crept in on them. The dark was not complete though, she could see his dim outline, a powerful masculine shadow. 'Better?'

'Thank you.'

Sheets rustled as the shadow that was her husband moved quietly in the dark. His warrior's body was warm and filled her with longing. Theodora had never imagined that she would want any man other than Peter; news of her betrothal to Duke Nikolaos had been a shock. But the Duke was, she was learning, a good man. A strong and honourable man. And he had, she was beginning to suspect, a possessive nature.

He will protect me. More importantly, he will protect Martina, particularly if I please him.

'With your permission, Princess?'

Theodora allowed him to push her back into the mulberry-coloured pillows and sent up a swift, if muddled, prayer. Tonight she must give the performance of her life. She must pretend that she was a virgin and that this was the first time she had lain with a man. She must also—God help her—please him.

Were these two aims compatible?

Leaning over his innocent, princess bride, Nikolaos swept Theodora's silk bed gown up over her thighs. The gown was soft, her skin was softer. Like velvet. The air smelled of violets. Of her. 'If I may, Princess...' He set his hand on her hip and ignored the small gasp. 'Lift up a little.'

Silk whispered over sweetly perfumed flesh. The mattress dipped as she did as he asked. Dragging the gown clear, he dropped it on the floor. Her body was naked beneath the gown and she lay, trembling slightly, against him. She felt warm, delightful. Pure. He ached to see her.

Nikolaos enjoyed looking at his women; in his experience, the act of love was greatly enhanced by looking. It wasn't simply that he found the beauty of a female body arousing and pleasurable, it was also that he found it was easier to judge a woman's response if he watched her. Nikolaos liked his lovers to enjoy him. He suppressed a sigh. If his princess wanted darkness, he was not going to force her into the light. Not tonight.

Setting an elbow on a pillow, he found her cheek and kissed it. She murmured something he could not catch, he was too distracted. The desire to see her was burning in him, he pushed it to the side. In the days to come, perhaps, when she had become accustomed to him...

As he drew her fully into his arms, his mouth went dry. Her nipples were pressing into his chest through the fabric of his tunic, a realisation that set a heavy, sensual pulse throbbing in his loins. Her response might be caused by fear or cold. Or desire. Nikolaos did not think she was afraid of him; he hoped she desired him, but he could not be certain. If there was just a little more light, if the servants had but lit the brazier as he had asked...

He frowned. Odd. He could not recall seeing a brazier in the bedchamber and he distinctly remembered ordering one. Of course, the moment he had set foot across the threshold, he had had other thoughts on his mind...

'Theodora, are you cold?'

'No.'

She desires me. She is also untouched. I must take care.

'There is no rush, Theodora, the whole night is before us.'

Nikolaos was careful where on her body he put his hands in those first few moments. *I must not alarm her. She is a princess with impeccable bloodlines and this is her first time.*

It was a pity about the lamp, a pity about the brazier. In the dark he could not follow her expression, which made judging her reactions to his touch something of a challenge. He was certainly fully aroused. He was achingly hard, ready. His innocent princess did that to him with remarkable ease.

Deciding to keep his clothes on until he was certain she was completely willing, Nikolaos set about wooing his wife.

He stroked her hair, weaving his fingers in and out of strands that were silky and fragrant with the lingering scent of violets. He found her mouth and kissed her, and kept it gentle until she moved and gave another throaty little murmur. Her small breasts shifted against him. A groan escaped him. More. He drew closer, he needed more, he wanted to cup her breasts in his palms, he wanted to learn the shape of her with lips and tongue...holding back was not easy.

'Theodora.' His voice was choked.

Small hands framed his face and brought his mouth back to hers. She gave a breathy moan and her mouth opened.

His tongue touched hers, subtle, questioning. *Do you like this, my princess?*

Another slight moan came out of the darkness, and she pressed closer. It felt almost as though... as though... Yes, it was a deliberate movement, she was rubbing her chest against him and it was no accident.

Leaning into her, Nikolaos deepened the kiss. After a moment he withdrew slightly and when those small hands held him to her, he smiled. His tunic was fast becoming an impediment. 'Remove my tunic, little one. Please.'

'Very well.'

Her voice was a sensual murmur, it shook a little. And—or was this his imagination?—she sounded slightly startled.

Fabric pulled as he hurried to help her, dragging the tunic over his head. He hesitated and, so she would be aware of what he was doing, he carried her fingers with his to the ties of his chausses. 'And, if I may...?' She was a princess, an innocent princess, he had to ask. Desire was like a fever in him, never had he felt it so strongly. He must not alarm her.

'Of course.'

Flinging the rest of his clothes aside, Nikolaos pulled her fully against him. The feel of hot silken skin against his robbed him of thought. He was weak with hunger. Burning with need. She was breathing very fast, her slight body trembled against him. And there was no way he could hide how much she had aroused him.

'Princess? You are alarmed?' He felt her shake her head.

'Not alarmed, only…' there was a slight pause '…rather surprised. I had not expected to feel so…so…' Theodora slid her fingers into his hair and brought his mouth back to hers.

Her kiss was searing. Heady with lust, in a vain attempt to regain control, Nikolaos tried to keep his mind on the individual sensations—on her tongue searching his; on her teeth biting his lower lip; on her hands stroking fire down his ribs and side; on her hands reaching his buttocks and pulling him firmly against her.

He was more than ready for her. He was pressed against her thigh, and she could be in no doubt of how ready he was, yet still he held back. One simply did not tumble a princess of the Empire even if she was… She was sliding her palms over his chest; she was wriggling that sinuous body as she pressed it against him; she was caressing his back, gripping him by the waist...

He gritted his teeth and she pulled her mouth away.

'Princess.' Nikolaos was suffocating with want, breathless. He was the one with experience and his virgin princess was reducing him to a quivering mass of needs. 'I want to get this right,' he managed. 'I do not want to rush at you and...upset you.'

A soft laugh sounded in the darkness. 'I do not think that will happen, my l— Nikolaos. My body enjoys your touch.'

My body enjoys your touch. They were startling words from a woman, even from a princess who had more freedom to speak her mind than most. They did not, however, displease him. On the contrary, they were exactly the encouragement he wanted.

'Does your body like this?' He slid his hand down her shoulder and fitted it over one of her breasts. She gave one of those little wriggles and pressed it more fully into his palm. Perfect, the shape of her was perfect. His blood pounded, desire burned in every vein.

'Oh, yes.'

'And this?' Lowering his head, he found her other breast with his mouth and took the nipple into his mouth. When he sucked, her whole body bucked and she gasped. 'Oh, yes. Nikolaos...'

Smiling against the perfumed satin of her

skin, he worked his way across, planting a trail of kisses to the other breast. His hand moved lower. Lower. Down over a smooth belly, down past the curls, down…

'And this?'

'Oh!' Her legs opened, she writhed and pushed against his hand. He felt her fingers running through his hair. 'Oh, yes.'

He could wait no longer.

Theodora breathed in her new husband's scent. It was dark and spicy—like him, it was utterly male. This man made her feel safe in a way that Peter never had. He made her body react in a way that Peter never had. Caught between shock and delight, she sucked in a lungful of air, hardly daring to believe the aching sense of need his clever fingers were drawing from her. She pressed her lips against a satisfyingly wide shoulder and covered it with kisses. She took the tang of salt on to her tongue. *Delicious, this man even tastes delicious.* And she was melting with desire. Theodora didn't delude herself that it was love that was making her feel this way, but, Lord, she had never felt like this with Peter…

Her new husband's groan was soft in the dark. It welcomed her, his whole body welcomed her as hers welcomed him.

I cannot wait. The urgency of the need overrode all else. She wanted to let go, to surrender utterly to him and yet…

I hardly know him! He is a stranger! Part of her, the wise part, the part that must remember who and what she was, held back. *I am a virgin in his eyes. I must play the innocent.*

The rest of her was finding that increasingly impossible and control was becoming a distant dream; she was being seduced by light touches and tender kisses. And by his extraordinary ability to rouse her body into a frenzy. Fleetingly, it crossed Theodora's mind that she had made something of an error, that she should have known Nikolaos would have this effect on her. Except—how could she have known when until this moment her only experience had been with Peter? When it came to seducing a woman, Peter and Nikolaos had nothing in common. This man, her new husband…

I cannot wait.

'My princess…' warm breath caressed her ear '…my beautiful princess.'

Her heart ached. When his lips fastened on her neck, the spark ran down her body all the way to her toes.

She wrapped a leg round his and was caressing his calf with her foot before she realised what she was about. Clearly, the sensible part of her, the wise part, was rapidly losing its command of her will. And when she felt the slight abrasion of masculine hair, another spark settled in her belly. She was on fire with want.

This is no way to prove my innocence! She dragged her foot away.

It didn't help when a large hand tugged at her thigh, replacing her foot exactly where it had been a moment ago. 'Mmm.' Nikolaos shifted so he lay over her and that dark, spicy scent surrounded her. That didn't help either.

I am a virgin. I must play the virgin. The thought became weaker with his every touch, until, no match against the clamour of her body's needs and desires, it became the merest whisper...

'With your permission, Princess...'

He entered her smoothly. Sweetly. So sweetly that he had done no more than rock once, twice, thrice...and a wave of pleasure swept through her. Her body clenched around his. 'Nikolaos!'

'Princess?'

His breath was loud in the midnight-black of the bedchamber. Startled? She could not say. He rocked in and out, in and out, and then froze and shuddered into her.

'Theodora,' he muttered.

'Lord.' So dazed she could barely move, Theodora stroked his hair and kissed his cheek. Her heart ached. If only she could have been completely honest with this man...he deserved complete honesty. The least she could do was confess how he made her feel. 'That was...that was... wonderful.'

She stared blindly into the dark. *What will he*

think of me? He thought he was marrying a virgin and one touch from him and all sense flies from my head. There is no way that he will believe I was a virgin after that. I can only hope I satisfied him.

Nikolaos laughed, it probably sounded cynical and he did not care. He had misread her from the first. She had not been nervous about meeting him, she had been hiding a guilty conscience. Still, he should have known better than to expect a woman to deal honourably with him. If his lady mother had taught anything, it was that women were not by nature honourable.

Nevertheless, he could not deny he and Theodora were physically compatible. And she was a princess, even if she had misled him.

His lips covered hers, and he ran his fingertips briefly over her hair before allowing them to come to rest on a breast. 'Wonderful indeed. You are beautifully responsive, Princess. Next time, we shall try a slower pace.'

Nikolaos rolled to his side, the coolness of the sheets made an intriguing contrast with the warmth of his wife's skin. *She was not a virgin.* He was not sure how to react, and was honest enough to recognise that his wife's lack of virginity had brought him, and her, much pleasure. He hadn't dared hope that the little princess would throw herself into his arms with such abandon and he hadn't been looking forward to initiating her for one reason only…he had never liked the idea that a woman's first time might be marred by pain. It was a relief not to have to tutor a nervous girl. And she did have a liking for the physical act of love, which was refreshing and unexpected in a princess.

In short, it had been a pleasant surprise to discover her so eager, even though it meant she had not been a virgin. He smoothed her hair, while his discovery sank in. Her hair was so soft, a joy to touch. Like the rest of her.

He cleared his throat. 'You have done this before,' he said, quietly.

Her breath stopped, an oppressive silence held the bedchamber. Then 'Yes.'

'Prince Peter?' He heard her swallow and kept on stroking.

'Yes.'

So, there were to be no denials, no pretence. Nikolaos liked that. It had to be hard for her, a princess of the Empire, to confess that she had not been innocent when she had come to her marriage bed. He respected her honesty, even though it left him with a bitter taste in his mouth. *She must have loved Prince Peter very much to have given her virginity to him out of wedlock.*

'Thank you for your honesty.' Nikolaos could not think why the idea of Theodora loving Prince Peter was so unpalatable. Theodora had spent several years in Rascia, she would have had time to get to know her prince. And it was clearly important to her to know a man, he thought, recalling one of her objections. *'I hardly know you.'*

He cupped her face with his palm. 'You are renowned as being something of a horsewoman,' he said. 'You could have claimed to have lost your virginity that way.'

There was another brief silence. Her hand was lying on his waist, and she gave him a gentle squeeze.

'I…I thought about it. I intended to try to deceive you.' She gave a light laugh. 'You know how it is, I am expected to be…untouched. However, I find I do not want our marriage to be founded on lies.'

'You loved him—I recall you telling me.' Settling on his back, Nikolaos drew her to his side, reaching down to arrange her leg so it lay over his. He liked the feel of that slight weight against him. He liked the way she had come trustingly into his arms, surrendering utterly.

'In case you need reassurance, I will respect your secret. It will be *our* secret,' he said. 'No one shall know you anticipated your vows with Prince Peter.'

Our secret.

'I thank you. Nikolaos?'

'Mmm?' His hand went on moving up and down, touching her skin, her hair. He was unable to stop caressing her.

'I did love Peter, very much. But he…I…' She inhaled deeply. 'Despite the fact that you and I barely know each other, despite the fact that we should not have touched each other for eight days, I would have you know that I enjoyed…what we did. Very much.'

Her breast was pressing against his side. Her hand lay on his chest. She was stroking him in much the same way that he was stroking her, as though she could not lift her hand from his skin if she tried. His blood stirred. *She desires me as much as I desire her.*

Lifting his head from the pillow, he shifted to face her. He could not see her in the heavy darkness, but the scent of violets was all about them. Her skin was like velvet against his. And he heard a definite warmth in her voice. It had not been there when he had first stepped into the bedchamber. He wasn't sure what he had expected from his wedding night—a shy virgin, pain, possibly even tears. Whilst this wedding night was not ideal, it did hold much promise…

Running his fingertips down her side, he pulled her hips to his, so she could feel him straining towards her and understand that his need for her had yet to be slaked.

'I enjoyed our consummation, Princess.'

'So did I,' came the soft answer.

'Enough to try again?'

She eased back, and a small hand closed firmly around him.

Lord. His blood heated. 'We shall take it a little more slowly this time.'

He felt a kiss land on his nose.

'Then, again, with your permission, Princess…'

Nikolaos had one last thought, before coherence fled. *Thank God she hadn't been a virgin.*

Afterwards, Theodora lay awake, staring blindly towards the bed canopy. Her husband had satisfied her physically *four* times—and each time the ache in her heart had intensified. She had admitted the truth too soon what had she been thinking?

The man at her side—now sleeping—was affecting her reason. She wanted there to be truth between them, but that had been no reason to admit to her lack of virginity.

I have put Martina at risk. Because Nikolaos knows I was no virgin, the moment he sees a child in my entourage, he is bound to suspect she is mine. Sophia was in the right. Martina must be sent away. I was a stubborn fool not to have accepted this from the first.

If she could have brought herself to lie to Nikolaos, it might have been possible to keep Martina in the apartment. But the urge to give him a piece of the truth had been overwhelming. She liked him, she hated lying to him. Regret coiled inside her, cold and insidious as a serpent.

I couldn't bear to tell him any more lies, and now Martina will have to be sent away! I cannot send her to a convent, she must be kept close, so that I may see her. Is there somewhere in the Pal-

ace? No, that will not be possible, word would get out.

Where? Where can I send her? Somewhere in the City?

No, no, I want her near. There must be somewhere...

In the quiet, grey reaches of the night, shortly before dawn, Theodora stirred and came slowly awake. While she was asleep, Nikolaos must have tucked her against him, she was lying in his arms. Even as her troubles flooded back, she found room to enjoy the sensation of being held so close. If it had not been for her fears, for the guilt she felt at continuing to deceive him, she might enjoy being married to this man.

A faint series of cries reached her, like those of a gull floating on the morning breeze.

Martina! Awake and crying. Dear Heaven...

Theodora eased out of her husband's arms and fumbled for her gown. The marble was cool on her bare feet as she wound a shawl round her shoulders and slipped into the reception chamber. Martina was crying her heart out. Hurrying to the small chamber at the end of the apartment, Theodora pushed open the door.

'Jelena?' She took care to close the door behind her.

Lamp at her elbow, Jelena was holding Martina against her shoulder, rubbing her back. 'Another tooth is on its way, *despoina.*'

Lifting her daughter out of the nurse's arms, Theodora kissed Martina's forehead. It was very hot. 'Poor thing. Come, Martina, be at peace,' she crooned. 'Hush, Martina, please.'

What if Nikolaos wakes? Martina's cheeks were flushed, her face was angry and her crying was surely loud enough to be heard in the Hippodrome.

'Hush, my dove, hush.' Rocking her daughter for all she was worth, Theodora glanced desperately at the nurse. 'You have tried oil of cloves?'

'Yes, my lady.'

Nikolaos woke with a start. The sheets were cool on the other half of the bed and a faint light was leaking under the door. She had flung back the covers and crept out. Apart from him, the bedchamber was empty.

Their wedding crowns lay on the side-table, gold gleaming quietly in the early morning light. By rights, Theodora should not have left the bedchamber without hers. Uncertain whether his bride wanted her ladies to know they had already taken their pleasure of each other, Nikolaos rolled out of bed and pulled on his tunic. Ramming on his crown, he scooped up Theodora's and strode into the reception chamber.

'Theodora?'

Purple curtains rippled in the morning breeze; at the opposite end of the chamber, dying embers glowed in a brazier. He heard rustling. Coals shifting in the brazier? He couldn't be sure. In the harbour below, the seagulls were crying.

'Theodora?'

A door opened and Theodora stepped into view, faintly outlined by a wedge of light. 'Nikolaos!' She came swiftly towards him, eyes huge and full of concern. 'I hope I did not wake you.'

'I missed you,' he said simply, and held out her crown. 'You forgot this.'

Hooking her arm through her crown, she glanced briefly up at him and nodded. 'Thank you, I had forgotten.'

'The Patriarch would not approve,' he added, teasingly.

'Indeed he would not, although I do feel that while we are in our apartment we should be allowed some respite from the protocols.' Tucking her arm into his, an unexpected intimacy that warmed him deep inside, she drew him firmly past the chamber where he knew her ladies were sleeping in the direction of their own bedchamber. 'Don't you agree?'

Nikolaos halted. Her eyes had fixed on his mouth, her fingers were shifting gently on his arm in what could only be described as a caress. Yet something was out of place here...her voice was too bright. It sounded slightly forced.

'What were you doing? Are you unwell? Do you need me to waken one of your ladies?'

She gave him a direct look. 'That will not be necessary. I...I was looking for my shawl.'

It was a long shawl with a deep fringe that seemed to float out as she walked. Nikolaos could swear he had seen it last night, lying at the foot of their bed. 'You were looking for your shawl?'

Her head lifted. 'Yes, Nikolaos, my shawl.'

She is lying. Nikolaos held the door of their bedchamber open for her and said nothing as the warm feeling evaporated and his wife sailed back into their bedchamber with her wedding crown fast in her hand.

She is lying.

Chapter Ten

Nikolaos heeled the door of their bedchamber shut and folded his arms across his chest. The light was strengthening, which was a blessing—he needed to watch Theodora's expression. Something was making her jumpy and, as he had so pleasurably discovered, wedding nerves were not at the root of it. His bride had not been a shy virgin.

She replaced her wedding crown on the table and sent a furtive glance his way; he caught another as she sat down on the edge of the bed and gave a pretty yawn.

'You are tired, Princess?'

They had not slept much last night. Last night Nikolaos had given himself up to pleasure. This morning in the cold dawn light he wondered that he could have been so easily distracted. She had deliberately deceived him over the matter of her virginity, and it followed that she might not be above using her body to lull him into complacency. Was she somehow involved with Župan Djuradj? Nikolaos had assumed that once their marriage had taken place, Prince Djuradj's threats would stop. Djuradj must know that Nikolaos would not permit his wife to be bullied. There was another possibility…but, no… Theodora would never collaborate with the Župan of Zeta. Whenever his name had crossed her lips, her tone had been scathing.

'Am I tired?' She smiled, he could see it cost effort. 'A little.'

Another of those uneasy glances had Nikolaos rolling his shoulders. Removing his wedding crown, he dropped it next to hers on the table, thinking ruefully that whatever she was hiding from him, at least she had not lied about the wearing of crowns. They did give one a headache. Thoughtfully, he turned towards her. He might not trust her, but she was an Imperial princess. Much as he might want to, he could hardly interrogate her in the same way that he would question a soldier, subtlety was needed. She tipped her head back and watched him approach. So wary.

'What is it, Theodora?' Gently, he lifted her hand from her lap. 'Something is troubling you.'

She shook her head, far too quickly for his liking, and several dark skeins of hair tumbled about her. His gut clenched, Lord, she was pretty. Even when she was lying—something *was* troubling her—she quickened his blood. Nikolaos found himself looking at her mouth, watching as her tongue moistened her lips. Another nervous gesture. One that ignited a distracting response in him—he wanted to kiss her. Ruthlessly, he squashed any thought of kissing, he must keep his mind clear, he needed to think.

'Is it Župan Djuradj?'

'No.' Her hair rippled about her.

Another lie. He could tell it was a lie because she was so vehement. She was afraid of Prince Djuradj. Why?

'He will not harm you now you are my wife.'

Theodora is not a liar by nature. Nikolaos was coming to know her and—his spirits rose—she did not want to lie to him. After they had bedded, she had confessed her lack of innocence readily enough, in circumstance when most women would have lied. Further, she had seemed happy to trust him with that particular secret.

What else is she hiding? Sensing that blunt questions would get him nowhere, Nikolaos decided that an oblique approach might lead him to a place where he might find his answers.

Smiling in a companionable manner, he seated himself at her side on the bed and ignored the flare of surprise in those beautiful brown eyes. 'Princess, there is something I have been meaning to ask you—about a relative in Rascia.'

Her expression remained wary, her dark eyelashes lowered. 'You have relatives in Rascia, Nikolaos?'

'A cousin. You should know him, he was confessor to your prince.' When her face went grey, his blood chilled.

'You are Brother Leo's cousin?'

'Good, you do know him.' Nikolaos spoke cheerfully, to mask his increasing concern. 'I thought you would. Is he in good health? My cousin must have taken Župan Peter's death hard—I know from the messages he sent my mother that he had a high regard for him.'

Theodora's eyes had gone very wide, her breath was flurried. Tearing her gaze from his, she stared at her toes. 'Prince Peter and Brother Leo were very close,' she murmured.

'And...? How is my cousin? My mother mentioned that it has been some time since she heard from him.'

Her foot moved, she was peculiarly intent on her toes. Nikolaos received the distinct impression she was choosing her words with care.

'I...I have not seen Brother Leo since shortly after Peter's death. I am afraid I could not say.'

Ice shivered down his spine—she was prevaricating. Saint Giorgos, help him, what was she hiding? It went against the grain to suspect an Imperial princess of involvement in anything that might jeopardise the security of the state, but he had to find some way of dragging the truth from her. And soon.

She married me for protection. It had been an unexpected delight to discover that he and his wife were a match in their marriage bed, but Nikolaos was not going to make the mistake of deluding himself that it was anything more than that. Princess Theodora, like Cleo, had accepted him into her bed because she needed him.

Women want protection.

Those slight shoulders were drooping; there was sadness in her bearing and it gave him pause. She was grieving, she had married him because she had needed protection. The gift of her body had been part of the arrangement between them, their unspoken arrangement. Yet she had, he was confident, had her joy of him.

She is attracted to me.

There was much that confused him. Most worrying was Theodora's connection to the Prince of Zeta. She had seen the man who frightened her on her way to Hagia Sophia, and had said his name was Boda. Did Boda have some kind of hold over her? Why would she not explain? Why could she not be open with him? She was a mystery.

Finally, when Nikolaos had given up all hope of learning any more about his cousin or her fears, her chest heaved. Small fingers squeezed his. 'Prince Peter trusted your cousin, Nikolaos. As did I. That is all I can say. I am sorry...'

With a pang, Nikolaos realised he should not have reminded her of Prince Peter. Her mouth had gone down at the corners, misery was coming off her in waves. It was no way for a bride to be on the morning after her wedding. 'Princess, I can see you are unhappy, it would help if you could see your way to telling me what it is you need.'

She went a shade paler. 'I thank you, Nikolaos, there is nothing I need.'

Nikolaos stared at her, willing her to enlarge, and though she gave him a quiet smile, she said nothing more. *She is grieving for her dead Prince.*

Nikolaos had opened his mouth, intending to tell her that he would do his best to ensure her happiness, when there was a sharp rapping on the door.

'*Despoina?* Lord Nikolaos? I have brought water, water and refreshments.'

Lady Sophia. Water. Refreshments. Hell. Further questions would have to wait. Nikolaos shoved his hand through his hair and rose. 'Come in.'

Looking meaningfully at his bride, he gestured at the crowns on the side-table. 'It is time to face the world again. We will have to wear those wretched things outside the apartment.' *And while we are in public, I will have little chance of encouraging you to open up to me.* Somehow, he must teach her to trust him.

Straightening her shoulders, she nodded. 'It is customary.'

Her lady-in-waiting entered at the head of a small train of servants bearing water and trays and, judging by the light pouring in from the reception chamber, it was time Nikolaos was elsewhere. He had a meeting to attend.

'My apologies, Theodora, I must leave you this morning,' he said, bowing over her hand. His eyes locked with hers. 'I have had my fill of eating in public, so with your permission, Princess, I shall return to our apartment this evening so we may share our evening meal in peace and quiet.'

Theodora gave him a startled look. 'Am I not expected to dine in the hall in the women's quarters?'

'Naturally, it is for you to decide, but I should like to get to know you better. And if you are dining in the women's quarters…' he grimaced. 'Hang the conventions. I would rather you dined in here. With me.'

'Very well. I shall look forward to it, my lord.'

Theodora watched her husband stride out of the bedchamber with mixed feelings. Her evasiveness had disappointed him. Regret sliced through her, like a blade. He mistrusted her. From the first, Duke Nikolaos had struck her as a man of deep loyalty and uncompromising integrity. Why else would the Emperor trust him at the head of his army?

So straightforward a man would never understand the complex set of circumstances that forced her to deceive him. Such a man could never imagine what she had been forced to do in order to guard Martina. When he learned the extent of her deceptions, she would lose any chance of a happy marriage. And that mattered—suddenly, alarmingly, that mattered very much. She wanted their marriage to succeed.

Nevertheless her noble, upright husband had managed to shock her this morning. *He is cousin to Brother Leo!* In his capacity as confessor to Peter of Rascia, Theodora had come to know Brother Leo well. She had made many a confession to Brother Leo; she had attended many a service at which he had officiated—mass, evensong, weddings…

She and Peter had often talked long into the night and when she had been younger Brother Leo had acted as her guardian. More than that, he had become a dear friend. It had been Brother Leo who had suggested that should anything happen to Peter, Duke Nikolaos of Larissa would be best placed to take care of her. However, not once during any of their discussions could Theodora remember Brother Leo mentioning that the Duke was related to him.

'Which gown this morning, my lady?' Sophia asked, breaking into her thoughts.

'The blue one with the stars on the skirts,' Theodora said, absently.

In all honour I ought to tell Nikolaos about his cousin's death. Yet if I do tell him, he will have more questions. And I will have to give him more half-truths, more evasions…and every half-truth and every evasion will put more strain on our marriage. He will be pushed further and further away.

Theodora held out her arms for the blue gown to be slipped on. She submitted to Sophia dressing her hair and setting the wedding crown in place. With every moment her heart grew heavier. Tears pricked at the back of her eyes. *Martina will have to be sent away. I cannot take the risk of keeping her here.*

Twice she opened her mouth to tell Sophia as much. Twice she closed it again.

Sophia pinned and tweaked, and tweaked and pinned. Finally, her gown and wedding crown were in place and the silver and gold bangles were jingling at her wrists. Theodora sank on to the mulberry-coloured bedcovers with a sigh. She had not even broken her fast and already she was worn-out. A ball of misery sat tight in her guts.

Soon the servants would make up the bed, they would tidy the pillows that lay askew from her night with her new husband, the fading violets would be thrown away. A lump rose in her throat. Physically she and Nikolaos had been so close. The wedding night—and the man—had far exceeded her expectations, so much so that for a few happy moments she had deluded herself into thinking she could trust him with everything. Nevertheless, here she was the next morning and the gulf between them was wider than the Hellespont.

Her eyes stung. *Martina!* She covered her face with her hands.

'My lady! Whatever is the matter?' Sophia asked, gently peeling her hands from her face. Dimly Theodora was aware of Sophia dismissing servants, of the bedchamber door closing. 'Did the Duke hurt you?'

Sophia's face was lost in a haze of tears. 'No, he didn't hurt me. Far from it.'

'What is it then?' Sophia drew back. 'You are thinking of Prince Peter?'

'No, no, it's not that, it's...' Theodora's voice broke on a sob. Blindly, she grasped Sophia's hand and fought for control. This wasn't like her—Princess Theodora *never* cried. She dashed her tears away. 'It seems I must cede to your wisdom, Sophia.'

'My lady?'

'You were right about Martina, she cannot stay here.'

'I wondered when you would realise.'

Rising, Theodora began pacing up and down. 'You were right and I was wrong. The Duke is too intelligent to be deceived for long, particularly with Martina right under his nose. And last night...' she felt a flush rise '...the Duke realised I was not innocent.'

'He was angry?'

'Thankfully not.' *He spared me his anger because we are a match in bed.* 'However, if we were to feed him the tale that I have adopted the child of a slave, he would be quick to make connections. He would know Martina is my child and then... Sophia, that must not happen!'

Thoughtfully, Sophia tapped her teeth with a nail. 'I wonder...'

'Martina must leave this apartment. Where can she go? She must be close by—I shall need to see her as much as possible.'

'There's that nearby convent—'

'No. A convent is far too... There are too many unknowns. Martina must be with people we can trust.' Abruptly, Theodora stopped pacing. 'I have it! I shall send her to Katerina—Commander Ashfirth has the house under guard at all times. There are young children in Katerina's household already—Martina will not be out of place.'

'What about Commander Ashfirth? Will he object?'

'He's a reasonable man, he adores Katerina and he knows she loves children. I shall pay them a visit shortly to explain. Hopefully it won't be for long.'

'Princess, much as it pains me to say this, it might be for some time.'

'It won't be for long,' Theodora said firmly. If she spoke with enough determination, she might come to believe it. 'Just until I can think of a way of having Martina close that will not rouse the Duke's suspicions.'

'That won't be easy.'

'Sophia—' Theodora put steel in her voice '—I shall think of something.'

'My lady, you say the Duke accepted your lack of innocence without difficulty—do you not think it possible he might accept Martina too?'

Theodora stiffened. 'It is too soon to tell him about Martina.'

Sophia gave her a puzzled look. 'The Duke seems direct and realistic, my lady. A man of the world—he has accepted you…'

Theodora took a deep breath and willed herself to speak calmly. 'I can't risk telling him about Martina.'

'As you say, *despoina*. But I do think the Duke could support you. Martina may be illegitimate, but she is still a princess of Rascia. Her welfare is important, he will see that.'

Forcing a smile, Theodora pushed her secrets to the back of her mind. 'One day I may tell him, but for the present it is best if Martina goes to Katerina. I trust Katerina, and if Martina is at her house I can see her every day.'

'Yes, my lady.'

'Tell Jelena to pack for herself and for Martina. And please explain where she is going.' She reached for the door latch. 'Thetis can summon my escort, I shall ride on ahead to alert Katerina. It is only courteous that I speak to her first.'

'Katerina appreciates your past generosity—I am sure she will not refuse.'

'Nevertheless, I should like to speak to her. As

soon as Jelena and Martina are ready, you may bring them to Katerina's. And, Sophia…'

'My lady?'

Theodora held herself very straight. 'It is most fortunate that the Duke has accepted my lack of innocence. It would be a great pity if he came to hear that a baby was smuggled out of our chambers. Be *very* discreet.'

On returning that evening to the quarters he shared with his wife, Nikolaos found her in the reception chamber. She had her back to the door and was staring out at a sky that was bright as a furnace; it burned with crimson and gold, molten colours which had spread over the Sea of Marmara as though poured from a vast crucible. The water looked like beaten copper.

'Good evening, Theodora.'

He thought he heard her sniff. She didn't answer, merely gave a slight nod and continued looking out over the sea. Like him, she was wearing her wedding crown. When she continued staring through the window, Nikolaos slipped his arm round her waist and pulled her firmly against him. She neither accepted nor rejected the embrace, remaining immobile at his side.

'It is so beautiful,' she murmured. 'I had forgotten.'

Nikolaos felt a flash of anger—she hadn't bothered to look at him, she was almost ignoring his presence. Was this how it was going to be? Not only was she avoiding his questions about his cousin, now she was barely acknowledging him. Reaching out, he turned her to face him. 'Princess?'

She was crying, her brown eyes were awash with tears. 'Princess?' His anger evaporated, his chest felt tight.

Flushing, she dashed her tears away. 'It is nothing. As I said...' her voice was choked as she waved vaguely at the sea '...the beauty here... I had forgotten...it overwhelmed me for a moment.'

Blinking rapidly, she looked at him through damp eyelashes and a delicate finger lifted to touch his crown. 'Good evening, Nikolaos. I had not thought to see you still wearing this.'

She gave him a wobbly smile. There were tear-tracks on her cheeks, it was obvious she had been crying for some time. Nikolaos doubted very much that his wife had been moved by the sunset—she was grieving for Prince Peter. Helpless in the face of such misery, Nikolaos bent and kissed a tearstained cheek. 'Good evening, wife.'

Clearly, this was not the night to interrogate her, he would have to bide his time before questioning her further. A few hours could not make much difference—he could ask her about her involvement with Prince Djuradj on the morrow. And his questions concerning the welfare of his cousin? They, too, could wait.

* * *

Theodora's husband had left the apartment the following morning, muttering about a polo match he was organising to honour the Emperor's accession. Theodora had only half heard him, her mind was on Martina. *Has she settled in at Katerina's house? I must find out.* She dressed for riding in a leaf-green gown and was soon ready.

She and Sophia were in the reception chamber, on the point of heading for the stables with their escort when an officer of the Athanatoi Cavalry came in.

'Princess—' the officer bowed '—a lady has brought you a message.'

The messenger turned out to be one Lady Anthousa, a senior lady-in-waiting to Empress Irene. Theodora had no clear recollection of Lady Anthousa, only a vague memory of her being close to her mother. Notwithstanding this, etiquette required that Lady Anthousa be offered refreshments. Under normal circumstances, if Theodora were not in such a fever to see Martina, she would be eager to talk with an old friend of her mother's.

So it was that, instead of hurrying straight to her daughter as she had hoped, Theodora found herself exchanging courtesies with Lady Anthousa.

'Welcome back, Princess,' Lady Anthousa said, wrapping her in a scented embrace. 'I expect it is a relief to be home.'

'Naturally I am pleased to see the City once

more,' Theodora said, 'though I deeply regret the loss of Prince Peter.'

'Of course, of course.' The older woman's gaze lingered on Theodora's wedding crown. 'May I offer my best wishes on your marriage?'

'Thank you.'

'I knew your mother well.'

Theodora studied Lady Anthousa. She was a matronly woman and a long-forgotten incident came back to her. 'I believe I remember playing with your daughter, Camilla. Is she well?'

Lady Anthousa's eyes brightened. 'Indeed she is—she is married herself, with three children.'

'Three? How lovely.'

'I have seven grandchildren altogether. Oh, my lady, I was not sure you would recall us, you were away so long.' She leaned closer. 'My dear, your mother would be delighted at this marriage. She was so anxious when you left, she fought against your betrothal to Prince Peter.'

'She did?' Theodora seized on Lady Anthousa's words, greedy for insight into her mother's mind. Never in her presence had her mother raised objections about her betrothal to Prince Peter. She had spoken much of duty, of the honour being done to her, of the need to uphold the dignity of the Empire and the necessity of remembering at all times that she was a princess. But raise objections? Never in Theodora's presence.

Lady Anthousa nodded. 'Your mother knew your betrothal to Prince Peter was expedient, a political necessity, but that did not mean she was happy about it. She fought like a lion to stop you being sent away.'

'I never knew,' Theodora murmured.

Lady Anthousa patted her hand. 'I thought you might not.' She smiled and glanced at the wedding crown. 'Your mother would much have preferred this alliance, she would be so relieved you have come home. You are happy?'

What could she say? 'Yes.'

'It is too soon, but I pray you are as blessed with children as I was…'

Lady Anthousa chatted on. She was pleased about the regime change; she loved being a lady-in-waiting to Theodora's cousin, Empress Irene; she was pleased the weather was at last turning warm; she was pleased there was a new cook in the Palace…

Theodora's mind began to wander. Her foot tapped. She liked Lady Anthousa, but, delighted though she was to be talking to a friend of her mother's, this was not the best of times. Martina! She cleared her throat. 'Excuse me, my lady, I believe you had a message for me?'

'Oh! My apologies, my dear, in the excitement of finally seeing you, I quite forgot. A celebratory feast is taking place in the women's dining hall tonight. The Empress wishes you to attend.'

'A celebratory feast?' Theodora did not conceal her surprise. The Emperor was known to be doing penance for seizing the throne and many courtiers were keen to show their loyalty by following his lead. Why, even she and Nikolaos had had to have a special dispensation to be married early. This was largely why the banquet after their wedding had been kept small. 'What about the forty days of sackcloth and ashes? What about the fasting? I thought it was to continue until Ascentiontide.'

'The fasting is all but done and this is not really a feast. It's for Lady Euphemia of Thera.' With a covert glance at the guards by the doors, Lady Anthousa lowered her voice. 'She believed herself to be barren, but has recently been brought to bed with a son. Will you attend?'

'I shall be delighted, except...' Theodora hesitated. Nikolaos had expressed a wish that they dine on their own in the apartment again. Last night Nikolaos had been quiet, conversation had been slow. It was only when they had taken to their bed that matters had improved...thankfully there was one area where communication did not seem to present any problems. One touch and the man reduced her to a bundle of needs, she liked to imagine that he felt the same. Maybe he did not at the moment, but with time...

With a wrench, Theodora brought herself back to the present. Lady Anthousa was waiting for her reply. Nikolaos would have to understand, she could hardly refuse the Empress.

'I shall be delighted. Please convey my thanks

to Her Majesty. I look forward to seeing her to-night.'

No sooner had Lady Anthousa drifted out, than Theodora linked arms with Sophia and hurried to the great doors. Their escort jumped to attention.

'We are ready,' she said. 'Did you send to the stables? Are the horses ready?'

The Athanatoi officer bowed. 'Yes, *despoina*, the horses are waiting.'

Duke Nikolaos was not on the polo field as his wife believed. Nor was he in his barracks, or closeted with his Emperor. He was in an anteroom in the Boukoleon Palace, attempting to persuade a fellow general that reform of the army was more than a good idea, it was a necessity.

'His Majesty must see the need for change,' Nikolaos said, leaning against a frescoed wall bearing a lurid depiction of Andromeda chained to her rock. 'Particularly after his mercenaries ran wild on entering the City. That cannot be allowed to happen again.'

'You want rid of the mercenaries?'

'Ideally, yes.'

As the discussion progressed, Nikolaos caught his mind wandering as he wondered what his wife was doing. He could hardly keep Princess Theodora imprisoned in the apartment. It was a delicate situation. He had asked Elias to keep an eye on her that morning. If Elias came to say she had left the Palace, he would have little choice but to have her followed. Until he knew precisely where her loyalties lay, he would keep her close.

'You're saying we need to return to the more traditional regiments?' General Isaac was saying, stroking his beard.

'I'm saying we need soldiers with ties to the land; we need men who care about more than money and plunder, and carrying off women.'

'It's all very well being idealistic, Niko, but the old regiments are weak—there aren't enough men. Without mercenaries we are not at full strength.'

Nikolaos nodded. 'That's true at the moment. We need them because the Empire has been managed by out-of-condition courtiers who wouldn't know a lance from a pike. The army has been run down and revenues that might have been used on good men have been wasted on useless vulgarities such as this.' His lip curled as he gestured at the wall-painting behind him. 'We need training, discipline, order.'

'Excuse me, my lord?' Elias rapped on the doorframe.

Nikolaos took one look at his manservant and his heart dropped to his boots. 'The Princess has left the apartment?'

'She is going riding in the City, my lord. She and Lady Sophia are on their way to the stables.'

'I trust they are taking an escort?'

'Of course, my lord.'

What is she doing? If only he could believe she was simply reacquainting herself with the City. Last night his questions had once again been deflected. First there had been those tears. Nikolaos had not had the heart to interrogate Theodora whilst they had been eating. And later, in their bedchamber, she had distracted him by other means.

Shamefully easily.

And then, before he had known it, the morning light had crept on to their bed, and Lady Sophia's appearance with a bevy of servants had signalled that the time for private conversation was over.

At least she is taking an escort. Whatever she is doing, it must be aboveboard if she has my men with her. And they will protect her. Nevertheless…what is she doing? His mind would not be at ease until he knew.

'Tell Paul to saddle Hercules,' he said. 'No, not Hercules, he's too conspicuous, I'll take Hermes. I won't be a moment.'

'Very good, my lord.'

Elias went out and Nikolaos moved to follow him, boots ringing loud on the mosaic floor. He glanced back at his fellow general. 'Think about it, Isaac. I am making no secret of my intentions. Our army needs to be sharpened up. Major changes. I intend to convince His Majesty of the need for urgent action. I would value your support. Your ideas.'

General Isaac held out his hand. 'My support

you have already. And as for ideas, there are one or two I have been saving for just such a moment.'

They shook hands and parted on the steps of the Boukoleon. From there, Nikolaos went straight to the Imperial Stables.

Nikolaos reined in, bemused. Elias had brought him to one of the more prosperous residential streets, just off the Mese. Here, grand houses were hedged about by high walls and not visible from the street. Nevertheless, Nikolaos knew exactly whose house lay behind that wall— he had been here many times.

'This is Commander Ashfirth's house.'

'Yes, my lord.'

'And the Princess went inside? You are sure?'

'Yes, my lord.'

Cut into the wall was a solid door and a wide gate, both were closed. The gate led straight to the stables. For a foot soldier, Commander Ashfirth had an uncommon liking for horses. As did Princess Theodora. Somehow, Nikolaos doubted that his wife had come to share her interest in horses with the Commander.

Why the hell is she here?

'Knock for admittance, Elias. I will be joining my wife for a time.'

Chapter Eleven

Katerina's courtyard was warm and sheltered; high walls warded off the wind and the sun had climbed high enough to play in the budding branches of a plane tree.

Surrounded by ladies, by shawls and cushions, Theodora sat on a stone bench with her green skirts tucked neatly about her and Martina firmly on her lap. The shadows of unfurling leaves shifted on the paving at Theodora's feet. Another infant was being cradled by one of the servants, a small child was rolling a ball the length of the courtyard, and the air was filled with the sounds of chattering ladies and of cooing doves.

Theodora smiled as Martina gurgled up at her. Small, chubby fingers reached for her earrings.

'No, you don't, my dove,' Theodora murmured, delving into the pile of shawls for the distraction of a silver rattle. 'It is a relief to see she has stopped teething, Jelena. Did she wake you in the night?'

'No more than can be expected, *despoina*.'

'She is settling in well, my lady,' Katerina said. 'You need have no fears for her here.'

'I know that.' Theodora's heart clenched. There was no point reminding everyone how hard it was not having her daughter near her, her ladies understood how she felt. If it had been painful having to stop feeding Martina, this separation was agonising.

The smart clip of hoofs coming from the direction of the stables had her looking sharply at Katerina. 'Are you expecting visitors?'

'Not that I am aware of.' Katerina gestured at a maidservant. 'Lucia, please go and see who it is. We do not wish to be disturbed. If they insist on seeing me, take them into the house and offer them refreshments. I will join them shortly.'

Theodora bent over her daughter and pressed the silver rattle into her hand. Martina smiled and cooed and waved, and the tinkling of tiny bells drowned out the sound of the ladies and the doves in the tree.

Without warning, silence fell over the courtyard.

Theodora glanced up and the courtyard seemed to tilt. Nikolaos! He was striding towards them with the confidence of a man who appeared very much at home in Commander Ashfirth's house. If the maidservant had told him Katerina did not wish to be disturbed, she doubted he had heard her.

Katerina went to greet him as Theodora, mind in a tangle, leaped to her feet. Martina's rattle was suddenly very loud.

Vaguely, Theodora was aware of her husband bowing to Katerina and introducing himself. His wedding crown glinted in the sunlight. 'I assume you are Katerina. My apologies for bursting in like this. My name is Nikolaos of Larissa, I am a friend of your husband's.'

'Good day, my lord,' Katerina said. 'You are most welcome, but I am afraid you are too late to see Ashfirth, he is escorting His Majesty—'

'It is my wife I have come to see,' Nikolaos replied.

Avoiding his eyes, Theodora thrust Martina at Jelena and something about the movement—its jerkiness, her sudden tension—startled a whimper from her daughter. 'I thank you for letting me hold her,' Theodora said, as Martina, who had been content on her mother's lap and resented being bundled about, dropped the rattle and let out a full-throated wail. Gesturing to include the other baby, and the child playing with the ball, Theodora smiled at Katerina. 'You have done well to save these children, Katerina. I fear I do not have your knack with them.'

Nikolaos watched his wife like a hawk as she

hastened towards him, green skirts whispering across the stone flags.

'Nikolaos.' When she offered him her hand, he noted she was wearing the ring he had given her, he also noted a slight tremor in her fingers. 'I thought you were practising on the polo ground this morning.'

'That's this afternoon. I had a conference this morning, but I have postponed it.' Nikolaos had been brought up short when he had first entered the courtyard. The delight on Theodora's face as she had gazed down at that baby had, quite simply, taken his breath away. She had looked so beautiful, as she watched the little one with such longing, with such adoration. In that moment, she had put him in mind of the Madonna.

She wants a child, I will give her one. It was a startling thought. Except that when she had looked up and seen him, all delight had been wiped from her face, she had frozen with obvious fear. *She fears me? How in hell has that happened? Her change of expression when she saw me...*

What had happened to the woman he had walked with in the Palace gardens, the mysterious, engaging woman who brought his protective instincts to the fore and had convinced him that their marriage would work? Did he dream her up? And where was the sensuous woman who shared his bed? Could this frightened, suspicious woman be one and the same?

I told her that marriage to me would keep Prince Djuradj at bay. She is safe now—I thought she understood that. Why is she still so fearful?

As Nikolaos looked down into his wife's beautiful, long-lashed eyes, eyes that he was learning held many secrets, he realised Katerina was addressing him. He gave her a distracted glance. Like his wife, Katerina was small and dark and very pretty, though Katerina would never hold a candle to Theodora's breathtaking beauty.

'Would you care for wine, my lord?' Katerina was saying. 'Ashfirth has bought part of a consignment recently shipped in from Crete. It is worth trying. We also have mead, if you prefer.'

'No, thank you, Katerina, I—' Nikolaos broke off, his gaze sharpening.

Katerina's eyes were uncannily similar to his wife's, they even had the same little green flecks. In truth, when the two women stood side by side, they might be taken for twins. The resemblance—height, build, colouring—it was extraordinary. He took Katerina's arm and urged her closer to Theodora. 'Stand there, if you please. Be still. Good Lord, has anyone ever commented on the resemblance between you and the Princess?'

Both women flushed and the resemblance was, if anything, strengthened.

'Good Lord,' Nikolaos repeated, staring.

'It is a coincidence,' Theodora murmured, breaking the spell. In a swirl of silk, she embraced Katerina. 'Thank you for letting me see the children. I shall visit again, if I may.'

'You are welcome any time, *despoina*.'

'Thank you, thank you.' Theodora hurried to the woman holding the baby and dropped a swift kiss on the child's forehead. She looked over her shoulder at Nikolaos. 'Will you escort me back to the Palace, my lord?'

'Assuredly.' Somewhat bemused at her rush to leave—it seemed she couldn't get away quickly enough—Nikolaos let her take his arm and allowed her to hustle him out of the courtyard.

On the ride back to the Imperial Stables, Theodora couldn't seem to stop talking, so he let her tell him about Katerina's plans for the children. Apparently they were slaves she had bought at the market. Her words washed over him, while on another level of his mind his thoughts ran on. There were two images in his head and he was unable to reconcile them. One was Theodora sitting peacefully on the bench with the baby, the other was her sudden rush to leave. *She was quite content, until I arrived. And my remark on the similarity between herself and Katerina made matters worse. What is going on?*

Nikolaos should have had enough of women and their secrets—his mother's behaviour ought to have ensured it. But with every day that went by, he was becoming more and more entangled with his mysterious wife. He liked her. He could not stop thinking about her. *She cannot be a threat to the Empire.* He would take his oath on a fragment of the True Cross that Theodora would die rather than ally herself in any way with the Zetan Prince.

There were moments when unravelling the mysteries surrounding his wife seemed more important than his ambitions for reforming the Imperial army!

As they rode through the Palace gates and received the salutes of the guard, he shot her a sideways glance. The bond of affection between her and Commander Ashfirth's wife had been clear. And despite what she had said in the courtyard, Theodora was good with children; the swift kiss she had pressed to the baby's forehead had looked like a blessing.

Secrets. He sighed as they trotted into the stable yard. The devil of it was that he wanted this woman, his princess, to share her secrets with him. He didn't want her to mistrust him any more than he wanted to mistrust her.

Nikolaos was frowning as he helped his wife dismount. He was past caring that his mother had let years pass before sharing her secret with him. Indeed, it might have been better if his mother had never made her confession, if she had kept her sordid secret to herself.

Theodora, on the other hand—he offered her his arm and together they took the path that led to the Boukoleon—Theodora had such a way with her, he wanted to know everything about her. He wanted her to confide in him, he wanted her trust. Nikolaos couldn't think why this was becoming so important. He didn't love her. Perhaps it was important simply because he didn't want their marriage to become the sham that his mother's had become. Lord Gregorios had been a fine man—he had deserved better than to be betrayed.

There was a bitter taste in his mouth. *Lord Gregorios was not my real father.* He clenched his jaw. *Did he know? Did Lord Gregorios know that Mother had been unfaithful?*

The small banquet in the Great Hall of the women's quarters passed quickly, but not quickly enough. Even a relatively informal meal had enough ceremony and protocol to make time drag. As was customary, Theodora arrived in the reception chamber before the Empress. She was to sit with her cousin at the head of the table, in the place of honour.

While Theodora and the other ladies waited for Empress Irene to arrive, she stifled her impatience for the whole business to be over. It wasn't that she was eager to return to her apartment, where she was in no doubt that her bridegroom awaited her, but the thought of hours of tedious ritual and ceremony was frankly alarming. If she made a false step, she would cause a scandal. She must smile at every lady who caught her eye. She must try to remember everyone's names, a task that was impossible, given that apart from her waiting women, she had not seen these people for years. She must...

'Good evening, Lady Anthousa. How lovely to see you again. Good evening, Lady Euphemia.'

A trumpet sounded and a flurry in the doorway announced the arrival of a young woman. Empress Irene! Quiet dropped over the hall; ladies sank into deep curtsies.

Little more than a girl, the Empress was wearing a rich purple gown, an ornate jewel-studded diadem and a golden collar of great magnificence. As if that wasn't enough to announce her status, the train of ladies following in her wake removed all doubt.

Theodora remembered the etiquette—her rank dictated she must be the first to greet her cousin. 'Good evening, Empress.'

'Princess Theodora?' The Empress caught her hands. 'How lovely to see you! You will sit at my side, we have much to talk about.'

'It will be my pleasure, Your Majesty.'

Theodora and the Empress took their seats at the head of the table and the Empress signalled for the others to take their places.

Fish soup was served in silver platters; it was cold and over-salted, but Theodora praised it, as was expected. Platters of roast boar were brought in and a glazed boar's head, having been paraded around the hall—yet more ceremony—was placed directly in front of the Empress. Theodora watched the young Empress pick at her food and remembered her penitential fasting was not over until Ascentiontide.

The boar was well cooked—it had been flavoured with thyme and rosemary—but, like the fish soup, it was cold. There was roast swan and fish sauce. Fish sauce was an acquired taste Theodora knew was inherited from Roman times. Tangy and highly salted, one could eat it with anything. There was goat in a rich sauce with pine nuts and raisins…

She felt sorry for the Empress and, more than once, saw her casting longing looks at the spiced breads and honey pastries, at the dried fruits and nuts…

At last the feast had come to a close and Theodora found herself back in her bedchamber with Sophia assisting her to disrobe.

'The Empress is so young,' Sophia said, chattily. 'I knew, of course, but even so it came as a surprise.'

'I believe she is fifteen.' Theodora handed Sophia her bracelets and rings to put in the strongbox and was moving to the ewer when she noticed Martina's coral teething-ring lying on the bed. She picked it up as Sophia emerged from the dressing chamber.

'Sophia, did you put this here?'

'No, my lady, I have no idea how that got there.

Most of Martina's things are already at Katerina's, this must have got left behind. I am sorry.'

Uneasy, Theodora turned the teething-ring over. It came to her that someone had deliberately placed it on the bed, but she could not think why that should be.

'Princess, look…'

Sophia had found a scrap of vellum. Theodora's breath caught, she had seen a similar piece before; one very like it had been flung into the palanquin on her wedding day.

'Is that a message? Let me see.' Bracing herself, Theodora took the vellum and began to read, *We know about the baby. Be warned. We want her and we shall find her, wherever she is. She does not belong to you.*

For a moment, Theodora was rocked with nausea. 'Sweet Mother, Boda's been in the apartment!'

'But how? He could not have got past the sentries. I shall go and ask them if they noticed anything unusual.' Sophia started for the door.

Theodora caught her arm. 'Wait! Think. Boda must have slipped in and out without their knowledge.'

'Princess, that cannot be possible—let me speak to the men.'

'No. Our questions are bound to get back to the Duke.' *Boda has been in the apartment, looking for Martina.* 'We got her away just in time.'

Boots clicked on the marble floor behind her,

the footfall was familiar. 'Got who away?' Nikolaos said, coming towards her.

Theodora's heart leaped to her throat, there was no way she could hide the teething-ring. Dark eyes rested curiously on it.

'What's this?'

Theodora said the first thing that came into her mind. 'It…it's a gift for Katerina. For the baby. I found it at the market.'

Long fingers took the teething-ring from her, he did not seem to have noticed the vellum. 'Pretty,' he said, softly. 'Which market? When did you find time to buy it?' He tossed it casually on to the bed. His eyes were cold as glass and Theodora wondered how much of their conversation he had heard. 'Between visiting your friends and attending the Empress in the dining hall, I should think you have had scant time for markets and coral teething-rings.'

He knows I am lying. Theodora's throat constricted. 'I…I…'

Nikolaos raised a brow at Sophia. 'Thank you, my lady, you are not required tonight.'

Sophia fled.

Theodora knew she was in deep trouble. Suspicion sat large in her husband's eyes, and when he put his hands on his hips and said, 'Well,' she knew that evasion would no longer suffice. The time for truth was finally upon her. Or as much of it as she dared tell him. Behind her back, she dropped the vellum on the floor. It was too dangerous to tell him *everything*.

'There are to be no more delaying tactics, my lady,' he murmured. 'I have had enough of them.'

Theodora put her head up. 'You are quite right, I shall tell you as much as I may.' She gave him a candid look. 'I hardly know where to start.'

'It begins in Rascia, does it not?'

She nodded.

'Then start with my cousin, Leo. He's dead, isn't he?'

She stared. 'You know?'

'You would have told me if he were alive,' Nikolaos said, moving closer. He took her hand and guided her to the bed. To her horror, she could see the parchment sticking out from under it; heart jumping, she kicked it out of sight.

'Theodora?'

'Brother Leo spent much time with Prince Peter, so it was no surprise that he was present the night that Peter was assassinated. I do not know exactly how they died—it happened at one of the border outposts and reports were…unclear. I understand they put up some resistance. Their bodies were much cut about…' she bit her lip '…I was not permitted to see them, you understand, but I do know their murderers took the coward's way.'

'My cousin—a monk—would not have been armed. You are saying that Prince Peter was also unarmed?'

'No, but most of his wounds—there were several—were in his back.'

Warm fingers caressed hers, his eyes lost their glassy hardness. 'I am sorry, this is painful for you.'

'I understand you have to know. Brother Leo was your cousin.' Briefly, she stared at the calloused, masculine hand covering hers. 'Are his parents living?'

'No, but my mother holds him dear, in memory of her sister. With your permission, I shall tell her.'

Theodora nodded.

'And you hold that Prince Djuradj of Zeta is responsible.'

'I *know* he is responsible.'

'Proof?'

There is no proof that I can give you. All I know is that Prince Djuradj must know my deep secret if his men are hunting for my daughter... and I cannot speak of that. Fear for Martina's life held her silent on that score. Boda was here, he had tracked Martina to the apartment and the placing of her teething-ring on the bed was a signal of some dark intent. Kidnap? Murder? The Župan of Zeta was capable of anything.

'Nikolaos, the outpost where it happened was close to the Zetan border, but other than that there is no proof.'

'Pity.' Nikolaos played with her fingers. 'What

connection is there between you and Commander Ashfirth's wife, Katerina?'

'We are not related, the resemblance between us is purely coincidental.' Theodora paused. She was wondering whether it would be safe to tell him about Katerina's part in helping to delay her return. *I do not want to lie any more than I have to.* She took a deep breath. 'Katerina was my maidservant. I confess I asked her to impersonate me…before…before my return to the Palace.'

Nikolaos released her hand, his gaze speculative. She could almost see him wrestling with himself, he wanted to believe her. At least, she hoped he wanted to believe her…

'Nikolaos, I am sorry I misled you.'

'You were grieving for Prince Peter and you didn't want to marry anyone else, so you ordered a maidservant to take your place?'

Theodora lowered her eyes. 'Yes.' She wished she could tell him more; however, the full enormity of her sin was such that she could only confess it to Emperor Alexios. She dreaded that day.

'Who else knows about this? Your ladies?'

She nodded. 'Lady Anna of Heraklea was of particular help.'

'I should like to speak to her.'

'Why?' Glancing up, Theodora saw that the small scar beneath his eye had become more prominent, he suspected there was more. 'Lady Anna has left the City.'

'How very convenient. Where did she go? Heraklea?'

Theodora lifted her chin, there was an edge to his tone she did not like. 'No, Anna went to Apulia.'

'*Apulia?* Theodora, what is going on?'

'Anna is to marry an Apulian knight.' Theodora laid a hand on her husband's arm. When he made no move to accept or reject the gesture, her heart sank. 'Nikolaos, believe me, Anna left the city to marry, she helped Katerina to play her part, that is all. There is no great conspiracy. I was not ready to come home.' His dark face had become so grim, she withdrew her hand.

'No great conspiracy? You had better be telling the truth. Let me get this straight—I am expected to believe that you were so set against marrying anyone but Prince Peter, that you inveigled your ladies, *all* your ladies, into a scheme to delay coming home?' His eyes were watchful, calculating. 'That day I first saw you in the apartment, you had just returned. I see it now, that's how you did it. You were never ill, admit it.'

'I admit it, I was never ill.'

'So Katerina took your place and you hid yourself away. It was the old Emperor who agreed to our marriage—wouldn't it have been easier to inform him you had no wish to marry me?'

'I tried that. I was not presented with any choice in the matter and one does not argue with an Emperor, even an old one. And then the coup complicated everything… Nikolaos, I would have you know that I am not displeased with my husband.'

He went on studying her, a slight frown between his brows. Suspicion was in his very bearing—he looked stiff and unyielding—but she thought he was trying to believe her.

'You still have secrets.'

She turned away. 'I admit there are…difficulties. The secret is not entirely mine. Nikolaos, I want to trust you—'

'I want to trust *you*.' With a sigh of exasperation, he tossed his wedding crown aside and shoved his hand through his hair. 'My loyalty lies with the Emperor. I never thought to find myself asking this of you, an Imperial princess, but where do your loyalties lie?'

'Where do my loyalties lie?' Aghast, she sat very straight. 'How dare you!'

'It is my duty to dare, my lady.' A muscle jumped in his jaw. 'You have already confessed that the Prince of Zeta sued for your hand after Peter of Rascia's death. Prince Djuradj's men are here in the City, and you yourself have admitted you have had dealings with him in the past.' He spread his hands. 'On the face of it, Princess, there is much to give me pause.'

In a trice, Theodora was on her feet, looking down her nose at him. 'My lord, I think you had better leave before either of us says something we might later regret.'

Rising, he gave her a jerky bow. 'As you wish, Princess.'

Gritting her teeth—*how dare he impugn me? How dare he question my loyalty?*—Theodora watched him snatch his crown from the bed and jam it on his head.

'My lady, you should know that the polo match is to be held tomorrow afternoon. Most of the Court is expected to attend.'

Theodora lifted a brow and said nothing.

'Both the Emperor and the Empress will be there, I believe they expect you to join them. Until then, my lady, I strongly advise you to remain in this apartment. You will be safe here. So, until tomorrow afternoon...' He gave her another curt bow and was gone.

Theodora glared after him. How dare he! Not only did he suspect her of colluding with Prince Djuradj in some way, but now he was ordering her to keep to the apartment.

Sophia appeared. 'The Duke is not sleeping here tonight?'

Theodora gritted her teeth. 'He most certainly is not.'

'Women!' Back in the barracks, Nikolaos hurled his wedding crown on to his pallet and stared bleakly at it.

'You have been speaking to your mother, my lord?' Elias asked. Retrieving the crown, he polished it with his sleeve.

'My mother? Lord, no, I am talking about my wife. When I met the Princess I thought there was a chance that she might prove exceptional, that she might not share women's love of secrets, of deceit. It seems I am wrong.'

'I am sorry to hear it, my lord.'

'She…oh, never mind.' Nikolaos gave his man-servant a rueful grin—what could he say? He wanted to trust someone who was not prepared to trust him. 'I am a madman, Elias.'

'Yes, my lord. My lord, about your mother…'

Nikolaos felt his frown deepen. 'What about my mother? I am telling you, Elias, I am in no mood to hear you singing my mother's praises.'

Slowly, Elias shook his head. 'I wouldn't dare—you are like a bear with a sore head to-night. No, my lord, I simply wanted to ask if you were aware that your mother has arrived? She has been asking after you.'

'My mother's in the Palace? You expect me to speak to her?'

'Not tonight, of course not,' Elias murmured. 'Perhaps tomorrow?'

Nikolaos let the question go unanswered—he did not want to talk about his mother. He would have to speak to her soon, though. *Leo is dead, God rest him. The news will knock Mother back, I hope her illness does not rear its head again.* His mother's confession about his parentage had appalled him—even so he did not wish more un-happiness on her. Lady Verina had not been the same since the death of her husband Governor Gregorios. It was odd how the loss of the man she had betrayed should affect her so powerfully. Women! Another woman walked into his mind's eye—a delicate, passionate beauty who by some miracle he had married. Why in Hades hadn't Theodora mentioned Leo's death before now?

Unbuckling his belt, he tossed it at Elias. 'Before I bed down, send in Captain Markos, will you? I am doubling the guard on my wife's apartment.'

'Your wife's apartment?' Elias looked keenly at him. 'Princess Theodora has dismissed you?'

'Who said the Princess has dismissed me?'

Wisely, Elias did not answer.

Chapter Twelve

'Is this wise, my lady?' Sophia whispered as she and the Princess glided towards the sentries at the apartment entrance. Theodora had told her that Nikolaos expected her to remain in their chambers that morning.

Theodora gave Sophia a quelling look and was opening her mouth to tell her exactly what she thought of her husband's suggestion, when she noticed four guards had been posted at the doors, rather than two. Her jaw tightened. 'One moment, Sophia—something is out of place here. Officer!'

The men saluted and their officer stepped forward. He was wearing a white tunic beneath silver and gold breast armour—the distinctive uniform of one of her husband's Immortals. *'Despoina?'*

'You are a cavalry officer, are you not? From my husband's regiment?'

'Yes, my lady.'

'What is your name?'

'Captain Markos, my lady.'

'Captain, I meant to ask this after my wedding—what happened to the Varangians who were formerly posted outside the apartment?'

'They have been redeployed, my lady. I understand the Emperor has need of them.'

Theodora held the Captain's eyes. 'Who ordered the change?'

'General Nikolaos, my lady.'

'And the doubling of the guard—did the General order that, too?'

There was the slightest hesitation. 'Yes, my lady.'

How dare he! He is having me watched.

Clenching her hands in her skirts, Theodora attempted to cover her rising anger with a serene smile and wondered if Captain Markos had noticed her displeasure. 'Thank you, Captain. Be at ease.'

She proceeded to the head of the stairs. 'Captain?'

'My lady?'

'I shall shortly be leaving the Palace. Will men from the Athanatoi be escorting me today?'

'Yes, my lady.'

'On the orders of my husband?'

'Why, yes, my lady.'

There was no doubt of it—he was having her watched. Theodora gave a heavy sigh, half-hoping to discomfort the Captain. Nikolaos had chosen well, though; if Captain Markos noticed her irritation, he hid it. Would he report her reaction back to Nikolaos? 'Captain, I should like you to arrange for an immediate escort. And should my husband enquire after me, you may tell him I am going riding.'

'Where will we be going, my lady?' The question was posed courteously, but in her view it should not have been asked.

Theodora gave the Captain a haughty look. 'You are impudent, Captain.'

Captain Markos didn't reply. He was probably following specific instructions. Theodora supposed she ought to be grateful that Nikolaos had not ordered her to be physically constrained. She might be a princess, but even a princess was subject to the will of her husband. Unfortunately, that was the way of things here.

Nikolaos has ordered me watched—his men will be following my every move. She understood his reasons—he mistrusted her connection, tenuous though it was, with Prince Djuradj. Her throat ached. With something of a jolt, she realised that she was not simply irritated and angry, she was also feeling regret. Regret and anger. Her insides writhed, it was a poisonous combination. She had hoped for better from Nikolaos.

'I am undecided where I am going,' she said, in a deliberately lofty tone. 'Rest assured, though,

I shall be back in time for my husband's polo match.'

'Very well, my lady. I will lead your escort.'

Theodora gave Captain Markos a sickly smile. 'How kind.'

Surrounded by an Athanatoi cavalry escort in pristine white tunics and silver and gold breastplates, Princess Theodora and Lady Sophia rode out of the Great Palace. Leaving the Senate behind them, they were soon clattering across the Augustaion—the main square—towards the Mese. As she rode, Theodora was struggling with emotions that were as unexpected as they were unsettling. *How could he? How could he order me watched like this?* It was humiliating. Of course, as a loyal soldier of the Empire he would feel he had no choice. And she could hardly leave the Imperial Palace without an escort. Nevertheless… *I thought he liked me, he must know I would never do anything to jeopardise the security of the Empire.*

She had been naïve. The Duke was attracted to her physically. It did not follow that he understood her, it did not mean that he had insight into either her soul or her character. He liked the look of her and he enjoyed bedding her—it was as simple and as basic as that.

He is a man. He knows I have been deceiving him and this is my punishment.

They trotted on to the Mese, Middle Street, approaching the area where Katerina lived.

Catching Sophia's eye, Theodora picked her words with care. Captain Markos and the men were crowding them, she knew they were listening. 'I had hoped to visit Katerina this morning, Sophia, but I have changed my mind.'

Sophia sent her a sympathetic look, she understood how much she wanted to see Martina. She would also understand her reluctance to do so whilst under the eye of the Athanatoi.

'Where are we going, my lady?'

'To the other side of the City. I intend to visit my parents' grave.'

Sophia's eyes widened. 'Is there time, my lady? The graveyard lies some way outside the City walls and you are expected to attend the polo tournament.'

Theodora lifted her chin. She did not care if Captain Markos thought her unreasonable to choose to visit her parents' grave today. She was counting on him telling Nikolaos about her defiance, she wanted to prove she had a will of her own. She also needed the exercise, she would feel calmer after the ride. 'There's time. I have waited years to pay my respects at my parents' grave.' She put scorn in her voice. 'No polo tournament is going to stop me.'

This time, the long ride did nothing to calm her. Standing by her parents' grave upset her far more than she had anticipated. Years had passed since their bones had been returned to the City and the gravestone was mottled with lichen. Theodora lay flowers and stayed to say prayers with tears blurring her vision. She could still hear the catch in her mother's voice as she told her that she had been greatly honoured to be chosen to be Prince Peter's bride. She could see the sorrow in her mother's eyes as she had explained that Theodora must leave Constantinople and go and live with her betrothed in faraway Rascia.

That must never happen to Martina.

By the time Theodora returned to the Palace, her nerves were stretched to the breaking point. As she and her ladies were walking towards the polo ground, she found herself jumping almost out of her skin every time anyone approached. It would not do. She knew why she was so anxious—she had to see Martina, and she had to see her today.

Martina will surely be safe at the tournament. There will be guards everywhere...

'Sophia?' She caught her lady-in-waiting's sleeve, murmuring, 'Do you think Katerina is attending the tournament?'

'I do not know, my lady. It's possible. The Varangian Guard are fielding a team and I hear Commander Ashfirth is to be their captain.'

Theodora blinked. 'The Varangians are fielding a team? They are foot soldiers.'

'Commander Ashfirth is a keen horseman—don't you recall the stables at his house, my lady?'

'I remember them being quite extensive. Send a message to Katerina, would you? Find out if she's planning to come, I should like her to join my party. And tell her to bring the children. I am sure they will enjoy watching the horses.'

Sophia raised a brow. 'Are you sure? The children are very young, my lady.'

'Sophia, that was not a suggestion.'

'My lady, I know you are anxious to see Martina, but are you certain?'

'Martina will be but one child among three. She will be quite safe with so many soldiers about. We have our escort—' she jerked her head towards the ever-watchful Captain Markos '—and there will be Immortals and Varangians on the field.'

'They will not be on guard, my lady. This is an entertainment.'

'When the Emperor arrives, he will bring armed Varangian Guardsmen with him. Sophia, please…'

'My apologies, my lady, I shall see to it at once.'

Slaves, servants and noblewomen curtsied as Theodora led her women through the latticed gate. The crowd heading to the field by the sea wall parted respectfully to let their newly married princess through. Captain Markos and his men accompanied them, close as shadows.

Several wooden stands had sprung up around the polo ground. 'Goodness, impressive,' Theodora said, pausing to take stock at the edge of the field.

It was as though a sorcerer had been at work overnight. There were two raised platforms on either side of the field. Purple awnings and Imperial standards over the stand on the northern side marked it out as reserved for His Majesty's relatives and favoured members of his household. There was no sign of the Imperial family yet, but it could not be long before the Emperor arrived.

It was a relief to see dozens of armed Varangians already in place—their red uniforms formed a bright line in front of the Imperial stand. Others were posted at regular intervals around the ground. The Court was gathering. A faint drumroll floated across the grass from a band of musicians, she heard the fluting of a pipe.

'Which stand shall we choose?' Thetis asked. 'Will you join the Imperial party?'

'Mmm?' Theodora only half-heard the question. Her attention had been drawn to the horses tethered behind a rope by the sea wall; she was searching the grooms and riders for a particularly tall, dark man in the white uniform of the Athanatoi. There he was, laughing with one of the grooms. Even at a distance, Nikolaos made a compelling figure. He stood head and shoulders above the others, wedding crown glinting in the afternoon light. Her chest ached. Theodora was surprised to see the crown, particularly after their disagreement yesterday evening. Surely he wasn't planning on wearing it when he and his team rode onto the field?

'Are you joining the Imperial party, my lady?'

'Not today,' Theodora spoke firmly. She was not ready to do anything that might put her in the position of having to lie to Emperor Alexios. If His Majesty engaged her in conversation... if questions were asked... 'We shall watch the match from the southern stand, near the sea wall.'

'What are those people doing near the ropes? Should they be so close to the horses?' Thetis asked.

'They are likely studying their form, deciding whether the Varangians or the Athanatoi are likely to win.'

'They will place bets?'

'I wouldn't be surprised.'

Theodora knew which horse—he was more of a pony, really, the animal was no battle-scarred heavyweight—belonged to Nikolaos and she recognised the groom holding the reins. The horse's mane and tail were decorated with ribbons in the regimental colours—white, silver, gold. He stamped his foot, as though impatient for the match to begin. Other horses nearby were also bearing the colours of the Immortals. It was possible they, too, belonged to Nikolaos—a change of horses mid-game was not uncommon. Theodora ran a knowledgeable eye over them. The horse the groom was holding was brown and sturdily built, the more muscular of the three. There was a more slightly built black pony with a white hock and a dappled pony with a plaited mane. Strength and speed, she thought.

A woman stepped out of the huddle of people by the rope and waved. 'Nikolaos!' The woman's voice carried clearly to where Theodora was standing at the edge of the field. The dappled pony tossed its head and several grooms jumped to shift the rope and allow the woman through.

'Who is that?' Thetis asked.

'I have no idea.' Theodora stared unashamedly at the woman, wishing they were nearer, so she could see more clearly. She was not a young woman—her neatly coiled hair was streaked with grey. Her clothing signalled her noble status; the breeze was playing with the tassels of an apricot-coloured shawl, rippling them in the way that only silk could ripple, and she was wearing heavy court damask and an impressive gold bracelet that looked as though it had come straight from the Imperial Treasury.

Theodora found herself holding her breath, waiting for Nikolaos to notice the woman. The moment he did, his laughter stopped and he went very still. The grey-haired woman made as if to embrace him and he drew his head sharply back. Giving the woman a brusque nod, he turned back to the groom.

Theodora narrowed her gaze. There was no

doubt that Nikolaos did not wish to speak to the woman, who held out her hand, as though pleading, but since he had turned his back on her, he could not see. The woman's mouth moved, she was definitely speaking to him. Nikolaos made no sign that he heard, but there was an awkwardness in his bearing that had not been there before. Theodora realised he was conscious, painfully conscious, of the woman behind him.

Squaring her shoulders, the noblewoman turned back to the rope and signalled to a servant to let her pass. Slowly and with great dignity, she moved away from the horses.

A gull mewed as it flew over the sea wall and Theodora realised who the woman was. *That is his mother, Lady Verina. And Nikolaos has rebuffed her in public.*

She felt sympathy—poor woman! She felt curiosity—what had come between them? 'Thetis, we shall be taking our place on the stand in front of the sea wall. Please see to it that my husband's mother is invited to join us.'

'That is Lady Verina, *despoina*?'

'I believe so. And when you have done that, find rugs for when the children arrive. There's plenty of room for them and their nursemaids to sit on the grass at the side of the stand.'

'Yes, my lady.'

Theodora allowed herself to be helped on to the stand. She chose a seat at the end of the front row, from where it would be easy to watch both the polo match and her daughter. When the Emperor and Empress arrived, they would take the stand on the other side of the ground.

Boards creaked as her ladies joined her, skirts hushed across wooden planking. Captain Markos and the rest of her husband's watchdogs clattered into position—they had not let her out of their sight for a moment. She gritted her teeth. She understood that Nikolaos was doing his duty as he saw it, but having half the Athanatoi breathing down her neck rankled somewhat.

Lady Verina was approaching with Thetis. As she drew near, Theodora struggled to set her anger with Nikolaos aside. Nikolaos knew she had not been frank with him. Given his position as Commander-in-Chief of His Majesty's army, he had little choice but to take precautions. *He can take no risks where the security of the Empire is concerned.*

'Princess?' Lady Verina sank into a deep curtsy. Deliberately unclenching her jaw, Theodora held out both hands in welcome and smiled. 'Lady Verina, I am happy to meet you. I am honoured.'

'The honour is mine, Princess.'

'I hear that illness has kept you from Court, Lady Verina. I hope you are fully recovered?'

'I thank you, yes.'

Hazel eyes searched hers, red-rimmed hazel eyes. With a painful twisting in her chest, Theodora saw that Lady Verina had been crying. It was immediately clear that Nikolaos had inherited his strong features from his mother. That Roman nose was most distinctive, as were the high cheekbones, the clear brow... However, there the resemblance ended. Nikolaos was tall, his mother was short; Nikolaos was all hard muscle, his mother was plump and curvy; Nikolaos had dark, dark eyes...

And Nikolaos had made the poor woman cry—the man had a heart of stone.

'Please sit, my lady.' Theodora indicated the seat next to her.

'My thanks.' Deftly arranging her skirts, Lady Verina folded her hands on her lap and stared straight ahead of her. 'I shall be frank, I wasn't sure that you would want to acknowledge me. I am so glad my concern was unfounded.'

'You have had a disagreement with your son.'

'I am afraid so.' Lady Verina's voice wavered, but she maintained her poise, staring straight ahead of her. 'It concerns something that happened years ago. I have been trying to explain the full circumstances to Nikolaos, but he has only heard the half of it and refuses to hear the rest.'

'That I can well believe. I have not known your son long, my lady, and whilst I already hold him in high regard, it has become clear he has a... stubborn streak.'

'That is true.'

In unison, Theodora and Lady Verina turned to look at Nikolaos. He was dragging a bleached leather gambeson over his white tunic. The Immortals would not be wearing their heavy armour here and Theodora was glad to see the gambeson; it would offer some protection—polo was fast and dangerous. A battle in all but name, especially when played by cavalry officers, polo could be brutal. *And a helmet? Please, Nikolaos, wear a helmet.* Men had been killed playing polo.

When the groom handed Nikolaos a helmet, she gave a slight nod. *God be praised.* Despite their disagreement and her resentment at his attempt to confine her to the apartment, she did not wish him ill. He was simply doing his duty, as he saw it. *Already I am fond of him.* Lady Verina's smile as Nikolaos strapped on his helmet was proof that his mother was equally concerned for his well-being.

'I should like to help you reconcile with him, if I can,' Theodora said. 'Could you not tell me what has come between you?'

Lady Verina met her gaze. 'You are very kind, my dear, but I fear I cannot do that. My son feels I have let him down. Badly. Sometimes I fear he will never forgive me.'

'You must be mistaken.' What could this gentle woman have done to so offend her son? Whatever it was, Theodora felt sure Nikolaos could not be so cruel as to keep his mother at arm's length for long.

Her gaze travelled back to the horses, then pulled back to the imposing figure of her husband. They had only known each other for a few weeks—could she hope to understand him in so short a time? Nikolaos fascinated her and it was more than the fascination a bride felt when coming to know her new husband. He was running his hand over his horse's flanks, checking the girth. How gentle those hands could be when he wanted, his touch had made their joining easy. No, not easy, wondrous.

Theodora frowned, the direction of her thoughts—so carnal—made her feel like a stranger, a stranger who would like nothing better than to sit in this box and admire the astonishingly athletic figure of her husband. How could this be? She was angry with him for storming out of their apartment; she resented his setting his men over her like watchdogs; she deeply regretted the way he treated his mother and yet… even with his mother at her side she found herself admiring his form. And what a form it was. The memory of that perfect masculine body moving against hers in the silk-draped bed was ever in her mind. It was a torment, it was a delight. As she watched Nikolaos checking his horse's harness, it was easy to recall the strength she had felt in those wide shoulders and in the rippling muscles of the torso now hidden beneath white linen and padded leather…

She swallowed. It was somewhat galling to learn that one could lust after someone when there was so much unresolved between them.

With a start, Theodora realised Lady Verina was speaking.

'Perhaps I might enlist your help in a small way, Princess?'

'Of course.' *Nikolaos is fortunate to have a mother—he must be made to appreciate her.*

'If I wrote another letter to my son, could you undertake to see that it reaches him and that he reads it?'

'You have written to him recently?'

'Many times. I suspect he has destroyed the letters.'

'I will ensure he reads your new one.' Theodora touched Lady Verina's sleeve. 'Will you not confide in me?'

'When he is ready, Nikolaos will tell you himself, I am sure. I hope for both your sake's that time is not far off.'

'What do you mean?'

Lady Verina's smile was sad. 'It means, my dear, that I should like my son's marriage to be happy, as mine was. There should be no secrets between man and wife.'

A lump of ice formed where Theodora's heart should be. *No secrets. What would Lady Verina say if she knew what I was keeping from Nikolaos? I may never be able to tell him the whole truth. A happy marriage for us is likely to remain an impossible dream.*

'Nikolaos hates secrets, he hates deception of any kind,' Lady Verina added, unknowingly rubbing salt into the wound. 'He has always been the same, so he will tell you all in due course, I am sure. I misled him, that was my mistake. My son is a straightforward man, if at time a little uncompromising—'

'He should not have dismissed you so rudely.'

'He believes he has reason.'

'Because you misled him?' The lump of ice in her chest seemed to shift—Theodora was finding it hard to breathe. If this is how Nikolaos treated his mother, a mother who gave every appearance of loving and caring for him, how would he react when he learned about Martina?

He must never know Martina is mine. And as to my deep secret, that must never come to light.

'Nikolaos will confide in you, I am sure, and when he does, I pray that you, too, will see your way to forgiving me.'

This last remark was so startling that Theodora could only stare. 'I cannot think you have done anything that will require my forgiveness.'

Theodora had an instinctive liking for Lady Verina, it upset her to see Nikolaos treating her so harshly. *He does not realise how fortunate he is to still have his mother! He should cherish her and try to understand her. He should certainly not walk away from her when she is trying to speak to him.*

Aloud she said, 'I wonder where His Majesty is.'

'I do not think he will be long. Look, there's Lord Basil...'

The conversation turned to lighter matters, to the nature of the refreshments that had been arranged for later in the tournament and, after Theodora had admired Lady Verina's gown, to the quality of the latest damasks and twills coming out of the Palace workshops.

A small flurry to the side of the stands announced the arrival of Katerina with a bevy of maidservants. Jelena was holding Martina close to her breast.

Theodora greeted Katerina and watched her daughter hungrily out of the corner of her eye. Martina was wrapped in a wine-coloured shawl, and was deep asleep. Jelena settled with her on the nearby rug, amid the other nursemaids and the children Katerina had adopted. Theodora longed to go and pick her daughter up, but today that was impossible; she would have to be content with looking at her from a distance. Martina's cheeks were plump, slightly pink from teething, but she was clearly thriving.

Sophia and Katerina entered the stand and the other ladies made room for them.

Theodora hoped her interest in the children on the rug and her daughter in particular was not too obvious, but Lady Verina must have followed the direction of her gaze for she said, 'You have a fondness for children, Princess?'

Flushing, Theodora tore her gaze from her sleeping daughter. 'Very much.'

Trumpets sounded. Around them conversation faded—Emperor Alexios and Empress Irene had arrived.

'Not long now,' Lady Verina murmured, as His Majesty's entourage disposed themselves about the Imperial box. Catching Theodora's hand, she pointed at the sky over the Imperial standard. 'Look, the swifts have returned, that is a good omen. The Immortals will win.'

Sure enough, there were the swifts, darting back and forth around a thin curl of smoke from a bakehouse. 'I hope that they do,' Theodora murmured.

The players were ready, Immortals in white, Varangians in red. Nikolaos vaulted gracefully into the saddle, his team mates and opponents did the same.

A man was walking between the horses' enclosure and the sea wall. He looked out of place, furtive. Theodora's gaze homed in on him. He was wearing a helmet and riding boots, but his tunic was grey, he was not in regimental colours. He passed behind the ropes and the grooms to where some spare horses were tethered.

Theodora shivered and touched Lady Verina's arm. 'What do you suppose that man is doing by the sea wall?'

Lady Verina shrugged. 'Perhaps he is in reserve.'

'I do not believe reserves are allowed today.'

A chill of foreboding ran through her. Dimly, Theodora was aware that a peacock had wandered on to the field, she heard hooting and laughter. A groom hastened to shoo the peacock away, she only had eyes for the man in the helmet. She saw him untie a grey horse, mount it and begin riding round the back of the horses. It came to her that he was waiting for something. And he definitely did not want to be noticed, his helmet had a broad nose-guard which masked his features.

Her skin prickled. *Holy Mother, is that Boda?*

Martina! A swift glance should have reassured her—Martina lay among the nursemaids, sleepily chewing a fist. A pulse throbbed in Theodora's temple.

If that man were not so far away, she might be able to see his face. If only he were not wearing that helmet...

The peacock had been chased away. As in a dream, Theodora heard a horn signal the beginning of the game. The ball was thrown into the field. Horses thundered on to the turf, clods of earth shot skywards. White and red clashed, they separated and clashed again, they became a blur. There were whistles and catcalls; there was stamping and applause.

Theodora was blind and deaf to it all—she was fixed on the man on the grey. Could it be Boda? What reason would a player, a *genuine* player, have to skirt the field in so furtive a manner? The helmeted head turned, he was searching the crowd. Theodora's heart stopped as his gaze appeared to rest briefly on her before moving on to the children islanded on the rug. For one chilling moment Theodora was certain, *certain*, he focused on Martina.

Theodora thought the man smiled, but that, of course, was her imagination—she could not see that far. She did see the flash of spurs as he dug them into the grey's flanks. The horse surged forward and everything became a whirl of speed and confusion.

Someone yelled. 'Watch your backs!'

'What the hell are you doing, man?'

Grey horse and rider pounded on to the eastern end of the field, which was clear of play. Athanatoi and Varangians were fighting it out at the western end. The grey ripped across the empty grass, heading straight as an arrow to the children's rug. Someone barked an order and a couple of Palace Guards ran on to the field. Foot soldiers could not hope to catch a man on a horse, the grey raced on.

Theodora jumped to her feet.

Lady Verina touched her arm. 'My dear, you are chalk-white—are you ill?'

Terror was a stone in Theodora's throat—she could not speak, she could not move.

The polo field and the stands snapped into a focus that was agonisingly sharp. Never had the double-headed eagle on the Imperial standard looked so fierce, never had the Imperial purple seemed so bright, or the golden pennants so brash. The smoke hanging over the Imperial box was black as soot, and sounds hit like hammer blows—the thundering of hoofs, the hooting, the cries.

She heard herself screaming. She couldn't help herself. 'Nikolaos! *Niko!*'

The players were dangerously bunched together, sticks flailing as they jostled to get the ball. Nikolaos's heart thudded. He lost sight of the ball, glimpsed it again amidst a tangled blur of horses' legs, lunged with his mallet and managed to get a passing shot through to an Immortal on the fringe of the mêlée.

In one of the boxes, someone was screaming.

Eyes glued to the ball, Nikolaos watched with satisfaction as his team-mate passed the ball between the legs of a Varangian's mount and one of his Immortals struck it. The ball flew on and, as if by magic, the knot of horses fell apart. Giving Hermes his head, Nikolaos galloped down the field towards the eastern end.

That woman's scream—Lord!—it cut like a knife. Nikolaos rarely lost his concentration, but something impelled him to look in the direction the scream was coming from.

Theodora! She was gripping the handrail of one of the stands and everyone was staring at her. Theodora? Screaming? What in Hades?

There was an interloper on the polo ground. A man on a grey was hurtling straight for her stand. Hauling on the reins, Nikolaos brought Hermes to a standstill. Team-mates and opponents rushed past him, leaving him behind as the mêlée swirled round the interloper, moving inexorably past him towards the goal.

'Nikolaos, help! *Please!*' Theodora waved wildly at a rug laid out on the grass next to her box. Nikolaos glimpsed nursemaids, babies…

The interloper whipped the grey into a gallop. An uncanny quiet held the crowd. Smoke! Smoke was gushing out from behind the Imperial box…

'Fire!' The attention shifted from Theodora, and in an instant chaos descended on the polo ground. 'Fire!' Servants rushed this way and that. The Emperor's Guard moved smartly to surround Emperor Alexios, leading him and his Empress quickly out of their box. Sergeants were bellowing orders. 'Bring water! We need a bucket chain. *Move!*'

'*Niko!*' Theodora's scream cut through the uproar. Her eyes were wide, her skin was pale, never had he seen her so discomposed. Vaguely, he noticed his mother standing at her side.

'*Niko!*'

The nursemaids scattered, squealing as though the man on the grey was their nemesis. As well he might be. Nikolaos could not believe his eyes when the man spurred on, towards them. Damn it all, there were children. Babies.

Babies. Time froze. *Babies.*

The horseman seemed to have picked out one

nursemaid in particular, the child in her arms was swathed in something wine-coloured. The girl backed frantically. Nikolaos did not miss the desperate, revealing glance she flung at Theodora.

The skin on Theodora's face was stretched tight. Nikolaos had seen that look many times on the battlefield. Total fear. Blank terror. The truth flashed in on him with blinding, lightning force.

That baby is hers! There was no doubt in his mind. *That baby is Theodora's.*

How odd, he felt nothing. Not anger, not disappointment…nothing. There was no time for thought. Even as Nikolaos gave Hermes his head, the man on the grey reached the nursemaid. Nikolaos could only watch as he leaned out of the saddle, snatched the baby from the girl's arms, and swept on and away.

'Niko!'

With Theodora's cry ringing in his ears, Nikolaos turned Hermes on to the path and spurred after the grey.

Chapter Thirteen

⟨⟨⟨⟨⟨⟨

Black clouds gusted from the back of the Imperial box, dense drifts obscured the paths and courtyards. *A diversion.* In front of Nikolaos, the grey horse and rider took on a ghostly appearance before the smoke swallowed them.

Riding blind, Nikolaos urged Hermes on, down the path to where the smoke was at its thickest. He was determined not to lose his bearings. *This path leads directly to the Palace Gate.* His eyes were stinging. Somewhere ahead was the man on the grey and he strained to pin down the precise direction. Beneath him he could feel his horse's unease—Hermes was responsive to commands, but if the smoke did not clear soon, that was likely to change. Horses feared fire.

Servants loomed out of the smoke, heaving pails of water. 'Which way, General?'

Pulling Hermes aside to avoid running them

down, Nikolaos gestured behind him. 'The back of the Imperial stand is alight. Form a chain.'

'Yes, my lord.' The servants plunged into the smoke.

Nikolaos urged Hermes on. There were hoof-beats ahead, he was gaining. Instinct told him they had almost reached the Palace Gate.

Stray thoughts intruded, interfering with his focus. The baby had to be Theodora's! It would explain so much. Theodora was not a threat to the Empire—she had been hiding an illegitimate child. Several incidents shot through his mind— at the time they had not made sense, now they did. The image of Theodora sitting on the bench in Katerina's garden was clearest of all. Theodora had looked so at peace in that courtyard. She had been holding the child so lovingly but had almost jumped out of her skin when she had noticed him. A horrified reaction that had led him to fear that she misliked him. His spirits rose. That might not be the case. *Theodora was terrified that I would discover her secret, she was afraid I would reject her child.*

Then there had been that coral teething-ring in their bedchamber. A gift for Katerina's baby, she had said. A gift for her own baby, more like. *Theodora has a child, an illegitimate child.*

Nikolaos did not care that the child was illegitimate—who was he to cavil at that? Rather, he was determined to remove any obstacle that might come between them. *I want Theodora's goodwill. I want our marriage to be based on truth.* It was a fierce desire and, until this moment, he had doubted he was going to achieve it—Theodora's evasiveness had not boded well. Thankfully, her reaction at the polo ground explained everything. At last he had the truth. He would save her child, he would prove worthy of her trust, and in time Theodora must see that he was as deserving of her love as Prince Peter had been.

I want her love. I love her. God help me, I love her. Nikolaos had not expected to find love in his marriage, love complicated everything. He felt relief—Theodora was no threat to the Empire; he felt anxiety—the infant must be saved; oddly he felt no surprise. However, this was no time for analysis.

The smoke was thinning. The rump of the grey horse came into focus first, then the arch of the gate. Startled sentries looked his way.

'Stop that man!' Nikolaos cried. The sentries braced their spears.

Hoofs struck sparks as the grey shuddered to a standstill. The rider turned; one arm lifted as he held aloft a squirming bundle in a wine-coloured shawl. A tiny hand clutched the air.

Nikolaos saw the cold glitter of steel and his stomach cramped. The devil, to threaten a baby. He must be one of Prince Djuradj's men—Theodora had mentioned a name. Boda. *Boda.*

The guards formed a barricade under the arch,

their spears formed a fan. The grey side-stepped; Boda was controlling it with his knees, making stabbing motions at the child. The threat was clear—he would kill the baby to ensure his escape.

Nikolaos gritted his teeth, almost floored by the cowardice that would lead a man to use an infant as a shield. He made a chopping motion with his hand. 'Guards, stand aside!' The fan of spears lifted as sentries scrambled out of the way. The man on the grey lowered his arms, looped the ends of the shawl around his pommel and gave his horse its head. The animal leaped forward, clattering into the city with a wine-coloured bundle swinging precariously from the saddle.

Nikolaos was halfway through the gate when he heard more hoofbeats.

'Niko!' Theodora materialised through the smoke. She was astride one of the spare horses and was charging at the gate like a Fury, hair flying.

Focus, Niko. The grey was careering round a corner, entering the Augustaion.

'Sergeant!' Niko yelled. 'Send for Captain Markos.' Markos might already be following, but reinforcements would be needed. He dug in his heels and shot after the grey. Moments later, he was on its tail in the square.

Sunlight bounced off Boda's steel helmet. The wine-coloured bundle bounced at the horse's shoulder, a baby's wail cut off sharply. Was it a girl? A boy? It was irrelevant—all that mattered was that the child must be saved. Nikolaos thundered on at a teeth-rattling gallop. Into one alley, down another. Through a market where astonished citizens dived this way and that like a shoal of fish before sharks. A stall tottered, a pile of clay cooking pots wobbled and crashed on to the paving.

Theodora galloped after him. Nikolaos spurred Hermes on, he would save her child. The poor mite was being jounced about with reckless disregard for its welfare. Why should Prince Djuradj go out of his way to snatch Prince Peter's illegitimate child? The illegitimate child of a prince had little political value. The chilling thought would not leave him. *Boda is only hanging on to the child for protection. I must take great care, one false step and the child is dead.*

Boda was quite the rider, urging the grey on, not sparing the whip. Bowing low over the saddle, Nikolaos refused to contemplate losing Theodora's baby. When a thin, terrified cry reached him, he felt as though a cold spear had turned in his guts.

Was Boda intending to kill the child? Had that been the plan from the beginning? Why kill an innocent child? Nikolaos was grappling with one chilling thought after another, none of them made sense. Ransom was a possibility, but it beggared belief that Župan Djuradj would send a man to Constantinople to kidnap a baby. Besides, if Boda wanted to ransom the child, if he wanted coin for its safe return, he would surely consider the child's welfare. Dead children won no ransoms. No, the child was never intended to be ransomed; it was in the hands of a murderer.

Think, Niko, think. Boda has an escape route planned—where is he going? The layout of the City was as clear as a map in his mind. They had pounded down the length of a street to the east of the Mese and were approaching Valens Aqueduct...

The aqueduct!

Clever. Nikolaos felt a sense of grudging respect. The aqueduct brought fresh water into Constantinople; to all intents and purposes it was a man-made river, a waterway carried by row on row of tall Roman arches. For those with a head for heights, steps led up to the flowing channel at the top. *He plans to abandon the horse and escape over our heads. He will come down wherever he thinks it safest. Clever.*

In front of Theodora, Nikolaos was riding fast as the wind, his horse had wings. Twice, she almost lost him. When Theodora lost sight of him a third time, sheer desperation drove her on.

The aqueduct lay ahead, past a grove of cypress trees and myrtle bushes. Theodora's lungs burned, her heart thudded. Spots were dancing in front of her eyes, she blinked in a vain effort to clear them. Both Nikolaos and Boda had vanished.

The aqueduct towered over her, tier upon tier of arches, diminishing as they ran into the distance. Drawing rein, Theodora took great gulps of air and shielded her eyes against the sinking sun. *Where are they? I cannot have lost them, I cannot!*

The aqueduct cast a dark, distorted shadow on to the street. A child was sitting on the steps of a tenement house, a dog was gnawing on a bone in the gutter. A horse whinnied.

The grey! It was trotting past the cypresses, reins trailing. Two boys, arms outstretched, were herding it towards a third boy, hoping to catch it. She saw no sign of Nikolaos or his horse.

'Where's the rider?' she asked.

The boys stared.

'Man in a helmet, where did he go?'

The larger of the boys pointed towards the aqueduct. 'Up there—they went up the steps.'

They?

Skin icing over, Theodora tipped her head back and looked up. Boda had reached the halfway mark, a wine-coloured bundle dangled from one hand. Nikolaos was not far behind him.

Boda turned and gave the bundle a careless wave. 'Take care, General. I might lose my grip.'

Theodora felt faint. Black mist swirled at the edge of her vision, the world had narrowed down to the wine-coloured shawl that contained her baby.

'*Martina!*' She did not realise that she had cried out until Boda's gaze shifted in her direction. Then she could only watch in horror as he opened his hand and released the bundle.

He's dropped the baby!

Theodora's child seemed to fall for ever. The shawl was unravelling, the world was unravelling. It wasn't Nikolaos thinking these thoughts, he couldn't be, he was too busy preparing to hurl himself off the steps and into the air, wishing he had wings, wishing he could catch Theodora's child and place it safely in her arms.

Like a madman, he leaped sideways, snatched at the bundle and folded himself about it. Trees rushed to meet him.

Icarus, he thought, as he fell. He, too, was a fool. Then everything exploded and went black.

Nikolaos lay curled on the ground on his side, the myrtle bush that had broken his fall crushed flat beneath him. He did not move. Frozen by a numbing mixture of dread and shock, Theodora could only stare as his helmet rolled in an arc across the ground, coming to a stop at the foot of another myrtle. The neck strap had snapped.

Martina's whimper broke the spell. Clumsy with fear, Theodora scrambled off the horse.

He caught her! He saved her!

Snatching Martina out of his arms, feverishly pushing the shawl aside, Theodora checked her, feeling every limb. No broken bones. Save for some minor scratches on her forehead and cheek, her daughter seemed miraculously unharmed. Yelling her head off, as usual.

Ignoring Martina's fury, Theodora laid her gently on the ground.

'Nikolaos?' Lightly, she touched his chest and prayed for a second miracle. He was breathing, thank God, and his colour was blessedly normal. 'Nikolaos?'

He did not look as though he had broken anything. Those strong limbs lay naturally, they were not bent at sickening angles. To be certain, she ran her hands over his arms and legs. Nothing seemed out of place. Another miracle. She breathed again. *God be praised.*

'Nikolaos?'

He coughed and groaned. Dark eyelashes lifted. 'The baby?'

'Safe.' Her eyes burned, blindly she found his hand and kissed it. 'Thank you, thank you!'

With a grunt, he shifted. The myrtle rustled as he rolled off it.

'Niko, are you all right?'

'I'm fine. The gambeson saved me.'

'And that poor myrtle.'

'Yes.' He coughed and flinched, rubbing the side of his chest. 'Might have bruised a rib or two.' He gave her an abstracted smile and squinted up at the top of the aqueduct. Boda had gone. 'Take the child back to the apartment. I'll see you later.'

And then, to Theodora's astonishment, he sprinted to the steps at the bottom of the aqueduct and began to climb.

'Niko, your ribs! Be careful.'

'Later.'

In the reception chamber in the Boukoleon Palace, reflections from the wall lamps flickered on the polished marble floor, and the purple curtains wafted softly in the evening breeze. Theodora had taken a seat close to the gentle heat of the brazier and Martina was snug in her arms, sucking her thumb. As Theodora stroked her daughter's cheek, the fringe of her shawl stirred and her bracelets jingled. Jelena was humming in the small bedchamber, where she was unpacking the cradle and rearranging Martina's linens.

Martina had emerged unscathed from her afternoon's adventure—well, almost unscathed. Courtesy of the myrtle bush, there were those scratches. Gently, Theodora touched the thin line on her daughter's forehead. She had anointed the scratches with salve, they would fade. Martina gurgled and waved her hand.

The apartment door opened and closed, and Theodora looked up to see Nikolaos striding towards her, face unreadable. He had not stopped to tidy himself and looked distinctly unkempt with that dark hair tangled and out of place. He looked very male. Theodora stopped breathing. *What does he know? What does he think of me?*

'My lady.' Politely, he bowed. 'I trust the child took no hurt?'

'She is fine, thank you.'

'She…so your child is a girl.'

Your child. Theodora bit her lip. 'Yes, her name is Martina.' Her husband's formality was completely at variance with his dishevelled appearance. Was he using formality to hide his anger? Or was he hiding something else? Nikolaos was not invincible, doubtless he had trained himself to hide any weakness. He looked weary. She could see rings under his eyes. Perhaps she was not the only one who had lain awake after their disagreement last night. His cheeks were dark with stubble; his tunic was stained, a sleeve torn. And he must be bruised after that fall. Theodora was painfully aware they had much to resolve, but this was not the night. 'One moment, Nikolaos.'

Rising, Theodora went to the door of Martina's bedchamber. 'Jelena?'

'My lady?'

'Here is Martina. I shall see her in the morning.'

When she went back into the reception chamber, Nikolaos was standing where she had left him, staring blankly at the brazier. She received another formal bow. 'Princess.'

He is more than weary, he is exhausted. What happened with Boda?

'Come, Nikolaos.' Taking his hand, she twined her fingers with his. 'We are going to the bath-house.'

A dark brow raised, a small smile lifted some of the weariness from his expression. He looked down at their linked hands. 'We are?'

'You are bound to be bruised. A thorough soak will do you good.'

He must more than ache, he must be in agony—it's a wonder he can move. As Nikolaos lowered himself gingerly into a warm bath, Theodora reached for some soap and stared in horror at her husband's chest. It was all very well for him to say that his gambeson had helped break his fall, but the left side of that perfect male torso was a mass of splotchy bruises, the dark discolouration was deeply disturbing.

'Lean forward, Niko, let me see your back.'

Grimacing, he did as she asked. Holy Mother, there were bruises everywhere. Martina might have emerged almost unscathed, but Niko was suffering.

'Come.' Gently she pushed at one broad shoulder. 'Wet your hair, I am going to wash it.'

'You?' His voice was startled. 'Surely a servant—'

'Hush.' She pressed on his shoulder again. 'Let me do this for you.'

'Theodora—'

'Hush.' She pushed again and this time he slid under the water. While she washed his hair with rosemary-scented soap, she began to talk. 'You will probably regret allowing me this intimacy. I have never done this office for anyone.'

'I am not surprised. Not every bathhouse has an Imperial princess in attendance.'

'I want to do this for you. You saved Martina,' she murmured, massaging his scalp. The scent of the rosemary filled the air. 'You didn't hesitate, not for a moment.'

'Hesitate? Why should I do that?'

Theodora smiled at the back of his head. 'A man who resented his wife for keeping secrets from him might hesitate.'

He shifted to look at her and water sploshed over the side. 'I could not leave a child to that man's mercy.' He shrugged. 'In any event, you did not come to me a virgin. When I heard you scream for me, it was no great leap from there to realise the child was yours. And no great shock.' He caught hold of a lock of hair and tugged, bringing her mouth close. He gave her a brief kiss and released her. 'I sensed you had been keeping things from me and I did not like it. I much prefer to know. Besides, who am I to take exception to your illegitimate daughter? I myself am illegitimate.'

Theodora stared. 'I thought Lord Gregorios was your fa—'

His face closed. 'No. My mother deceived my father. She deceived everyone. I am illegitimate.'

Nikolaos was illegitimate. Theodora lowered her eyes while she absorbed it. *He is illegitimate.* Had he only recently discovered this? If so, it must be a shock. Illegitimacy was no bar to advancement in the Imperial Court, but it must be disturbing to live one's life secure in the knowledge that one's father was the Governor of Larissa. To have that suddenly snatched away would make even the strongest man question his identity.

Theodora went cold. *That was why he wanted me. Did he see marriage to an Imperial princess as a way of redefining himself?* He was no longer the son of the Governor of Larissa so he married into the Imperial family to bolster his position at Court. It was foolish to let this upset her, but she could not help it. *Our marriage was from the first a marriage of convenience, I should not expect more.* Love was making her unreasonable; it was making her yearn for his affection, if not his love.

'Nikolaos, Lady Verina—'

'I do not wish to speak about my mother.'

'Very well,' Theodora said, reaching for a jug and holding it under a warm-water spigot. She wanted nothing more than to help him reconcile with his mother, but she would not force him to discuss her tonight. A man who had covered himself in bruises for Martina's sake had earned the right to some peace.

'Close your eyes, Niko, I will rinse your hair.'

He faced forward, murmuring. 'I like it when you call me Niko.'

'Captain Markos found your horse, by the way,' she said, tipping the water on to his hair.

'So I've been told.'

'Did Boda get away?'

'Almost, but I got him. His idea of using the aqueduct as an avenue of escape was ingenious, but flawed.'

'Oh?'

'It's like a watch point up at the top, you can see for miles. I ran along and soon spotted him on the ground, heading for the docks. Caught up with him at the Lantern Gate. He's in custody and is being questioned. A small…incident took place before I met you and it has been weighing on my mind. It turns out that Boda was responsible for it.'

'An incident?'

'He browbeat one of the City's best saddlers into producing shoddy work. The girth of my saddle…well, never mind, it's been settled now. After Boda's confession today, I went back to the saddler and stressed that if he is ever threatened again, he must report the threats at once.'

She tugged at his shoulder. 'Your saddle was tampered with?'

'Faulty girth. It did no harm, we found it in time. Theodora, the matter is over. All you need to know is that we have Boda. His accomplices have fled the City; you have no more to fear from any of them.'

Theodora opened her mouth and closed it again. *If only that were true.* She rinsed his hair and, mindful of his bruises, started washing his back. Her thoughts ran on. The habit of secrecy was hard to set aside. In Rascia, after news had come that her parents had been killed, she had learned to be self-reliant; a Princess in a foreign land had to keep her own counsel. And shortly before Peter's death she had discovered sometimes it was vital not to be entirely open with one's friends, even those as close to her as Lady Sophia, Lady Anna and Katerina.

There was one deep secret she had not told a soul.

It was a secret she hardly dared think about— she had the ridiculous, superstitious fear that someone might read her thoughts. Only Peter and Brother Leo had known the truth. And now they were dead.

She rinsed soap from her husband's bruised back, running her hands across his shoulders and down the sharply defined muscles of his arms. Beautiful, his body was beautiful. Impulsively she pressed a kiss to his shoulder. She had been affronted when he had set his men to watching her, but that had paled into insignificance when he had hurled himself off the steps of the aqueduct to catch Martina. She would be grateful for ever. Instinct had made her cry to Nikolaos for help, he had not let her down.

'Mmm,' he said, reaching behind for her hand and pulling her alongside him. He took her lips with his. Slowly, carefully, his tongue eased inside her mouth. He felt warm and unshaven; he smelled of rosemary and tasted slightly of soap…

As they kissed, Theodora was conscious of a tightness in her chest, it bordered on pain. It was pain. *I want to tell him the truth.* It was hard to open up to someone even when you loved him. And she did love him. The realisation was unlooked for, but it was not unwelcome. Nikolaos was kind and generous. He had not chastised her for her lack of innocence; he was not chastising her for keeping her daughter's existence from him; he had put himself in harm's way for her…

Theodora felt confused—love had caught her off-guard. *This man is a good man, you might tell him everything.* But could she? Dare she? Nikolaos made her want to throw herself into his keeping and forget all she had so painfully learned. The idea that he might help her solve her problems was—like the man himself—disturbingly compelling. However, self-reliance had been her watchword for so long, she doubted she could change, even for Nikolaos. And there was another important consideration.

Every day, Theodora prayed the truth about Martina's status would never come to light. If the worst happened, though, if the truth did come to light, it would be best that Nikolaos remained ignorant. *If I tell him my deep secret, he will have two choices—he can either betray my sin to the Emperor or, if he does not betray me, he becomes complicit. I cannot put him in that position.*

While Theodora had been waiting for Nikolaos to return that evening, she had done much thinking. *Prince Djuradj has discovered the truth, he knows who Martina really is!* God alone knew how Prince Djuradj had found out, but she must face it, he knew the truth. The unspeakable, unthinkable truth.

She pulled out of the kiss.

'Boda would have killed her.'

Nikolaos sighed and eased his shoulders. 'It seems possible.' He looked warily at her. The front of her gown was dark where water had splashed on it, her hair was disordered, and her lips were red from their kiss. She looked adorable. 'I was not going to say it, I did not wish to cause you undue alarm, but I had come to the conclusion that the Prince of Zeta wishes your—our—daughter dead.'

'*Our* daughter?' Her eyes glistened. She swallowed. 'Oh, Niko, I do love you.'

An unexpected warmth stole through him. The last thing Nikolaos expected from her was a profession of love. He reminded himself that she had likely made it because she was grateful—hell, she probably thought she ought to say it. Uncertain how to respond, he curled his hand round her neck. Heedless of dripping more water on to her, he kissed her again. Her mouth was warm and trembled beneath his. Nikolaos forgot his bruises. Her hands came up and took his shoulders. Nikolaos forgot his aches. Opening his eyes to watch her as they kissed, he saw a tear slide slowly down her cheek.

'*Our* daughter,' he repeated, manfully ignoring the way she quickened his blood and sent hot pulses throbbing in his loins. 'I will protect her as I would protect you. That is my vow.'

He drew back. Theodora made him breathless with want. She filled his vision and his thoughts. Since they had bedded, he desired her more each day; he burned for her now despite the aches in his chest and ribs. However, one simply could not drag an Imperial princess into one's bath and have one's way with her. Even if she was his wife. Later, when he had cleared his mind on one or two points, he would take her upstairs and pray his ribs did not protest.

'Theodora, why is Župan Djuradj interested in your daughter?'

She fixed her gaze on a washcloth in the water. 'I…I am not sure.'

A knot formed in his belly. *She knows. She is lying.* The warmth evoked by her declaration of love was gone. 'No?'

'The Prince of Zeta hates me,' she murmured, picking up a bottle of almond oil. She began toying with the stopper.

'On the grounds that you were betrothed to his rival?'

'I...I have already explained that Prince Djuradj asked me to marry him after Peter's death. He took the rejection badly. Djuradj is the most vengeful of men, he has sworn to hurt me.'

'He sent his men a long way to kill one small child.'

Theodora gave a jerky nod. She was entirely focused on the bottle of oil, twisting the stopper round and round. 'He hates me.'

'There's more to it than that, there has to be,' Nikolaos said, thinking aloud. *Why will she not look at me?* A cold draught was playing over the back of his neck, it was as though the bath water had chilled in an instant. *There is more, there is something else she is not telling me, and it is no triviality...*

'Theodora?'

'Mmm?' She went on playing with the stopper.

'Look at me. What else are you not telling me?'

Brown eyes lifted; her expression was haunted, she was definitely hiding something...

'Nothing, there's nothing.' Her chest heaved. She gave him a smile. It was clearly forced. 'Nikolaos, did I tell you I have at last met your mother?'

'I saw you speaking to her.' He drew back, deciding to allow her the change of subject. It was a crude attempt to distract him and his suspicions were far from allayed, she was not being open with him.

With a sigh, she set the bottle aside. 'Lady Verina is saddened by the rift between you.'

'She should have thought about that before she deceived me.'

'Niko, she would like to speak with you, to explain.'

He shook his head. 'I have had all the explanations I need. My dear lady mother deceived my father. She deceived me, she deceived the entire Court. I have no wish to speak to her.'

Dark brown eyes gazed steadily at him, a small hand reached into the water and took his. 'It is possible you might have misjudged her.'

He stiffened. 'What did she tell you?'

'Only that you will not speak to her. Niko, your mother loves you and that is a great blessing. It does not…it does not become you that you spurn her in public. A mother should be honoured, a mother should be respected.'

He pulled his hand free and, taking a washcloth, vigorously soaped his chest. 'My mother deserves neither honour nor respect. My moth—'

'Your mother loves you.' Reaching out, Theodora ignored the scowl he flung at her and took the washcloth. She dipped it in the water, soaped it and continued where he had left off.

'You are fortunate to have a mother,' she said softly. 'She strikes me as a loving, honest woman.

I do not believe you would regret seeing her and listening to what she has to say.'

Nikolaos caught her wrist and pulled her towards him until her mouth was inches from his. Long, dark hair trailed in the water like a ribbon of weed; her scent—violets, musk and woman— teased him. 'Loving? Honest? Theodora, didn't you hear me? I am illegitimate.' She struggled to pull back, he tightened his hold.

'I heard you, Nikolaos, but I do not see why you are set on spurning her. And publicly. That was shameful, Lady Verina gave you life.'

Her response was so unexpected Nikolaos relaxed his hold, allowing her to rock back on the stool. Wearily, he rubbed his face. He should be glad, he told himself, that Theodora had not rejected him. When he had first learned of his illegitimacy, he had braced himself for her scorn. She had come back to Constantinople to marry a general of one of the most upstanding families in the Empire and instead she found herself married to him—a man whose father might be anyone.

'My father never was Governor of Larissa. I am illegitimate.' A small crease formed in her brow. Nikolaos ached to smooth it away, but he held himself in check.

'Yes, you mentioned that earlier. Nikolaos, I am not sure what you expect me to say.'

'I thought you might resent our marriage.'

Her brow cleared and her cheeks went as bright as a poppy. 'Your mother had a lover, Nikolaos, many women do. And there are many great men, *illegitimate* men, who have served the Empire well. Illegitimacy is no bar to advancement.'

He swallowed and nodded, unable for some reason to form words. She spoke the truth. Nikolaos was aware that some women would react badly on learning their husband had been born out of wedlock. An Imperial princess might have more reason that most to express shock and revulsion. She was showing neither.

Martina. Her child, Martina, was responsible for that. A princess who had given birth to an illegitimate child, a princess who clearly adored that child, was less likely to judge others for their mistakes. His mood lightened. Nikolaos deeply regretted that she was keeping things from him, but all was not lost. Their marriage had much to commend it. On their wedding night the passion that had flared between them had been a delight. Now it would seem that he and Princess Theodora were compatible in more ways than one. *My illegitimacy does not repel her. Her lack of innocence has in truth turned out to be a blessing. I can surely build on that...I shall win her trust.*

'You have only recently discovered about your birth?' she asked, eyes alight with interest and sympathy.

He nodded. 'Apparently others had guessed— my manservant Elias, for one—but I had no idea. I keep wondering whether my father—Governor

Gregorios, that is—I wonder whether he knew and, if so, what he would have thought.'

'It's possible he knew.'

'I cannot shift the thought that the man I think of as my father, the former Governor of Larissa, is not my father at all. He taught me everything, *everything.*'

'Nikolaos, the man who raised you *was* in many ways your father.' Her rings caught the light as she gripped the bathtub. 'I can see this has come as a terrible shock, but I really think you must speak to your mother and hear what she has to say. She might surprise you.'

Nikolaos frowned, he did not wish to speak to his mother. Picking up her hand, he stared pointedly at her mouth. 'With your permission, Princess?' His question brought the pretty flush back to her cheeks.

'My permission?'

She looked delightfully uncertain, the tremble in her mouth was pure temptation. When she moistened her lips, he knew she was remembering their time together in the silk-draped bed. He put her hand on his shoulders and captured her other hand. 'With your permission, Princess?'

She raised a brow. 'I shall change your mind, you know. You only have one mother and you ought to speak to her.'

But she was looking at his mouth and she was smiling.

'With your permission, Princess?'

Dark eyelashes lowered, she gave the tiniest nod. It was exactly the encouragement he was waiting for. Nikolaos shifted to lift her with him into the bath, gown and all, and with much giggling and laughter he went on to discover that when one had the permission of an Imperial princess, one could do almost anything, even join with her in one's bath.

'With your permission, Princess?' Impatient with lacings and ties, he pulled her gown up over gently rounded hips. 'With your permission?'

Chapter Fourteen

Theodora woke with a smile in her heart. Unwilling to move from the great bed quite yet, she adjusted a mulberry-coloured pillow, content simply to gaze at her husband. He was yet to wake. He hadn't said the words, but Theodora felt thoroughly, deeply loved. *I belong with this man.*

His easy acceptance of Martina had taken her breath away. He was a good man, honourable, loyal, brusque at times…but a good man. If she had his love, she could, she realised with an unsettling lurch in her belly, be blissfully happy. Happiness was a blessing Theodora had never thought to look for in marriage. Contentment, yes, if she was lucky; happiness was another matter. Princesses were not taught to expect happiness; a princess learned early on to devote her life to the well-being of the Empire.

If Nikolaos loved me, I might achieve happi-

ness... It was a tantalising thought, undoubtedly born of weakness. As she studied him, she set it aside, happiness was not her right. Particularly in view of what she had done. She was not worthy of the title 'Princess'.

Theodora's smile faded, and the old guilt welled up as she stared with painful longing at her husband. His hair was thick and lustrous, it was puzzling how much she longed to stroke it. Equally puzzling was the thought that she would never tire of staring at him. The curve of his eyelashes…that distinctive nose…the strong shoulders…even the shape of his hand as it lay relaxed in sleep on the pillow.

She was blessed indeed that he had accepted Martina, it was clear he felt compassion for her. Nikolaos resented discovering that he was illegitimate, but that fact had enabled him to accept Martina, Theodora was sure of it. *He thinks that he and Martina are in a similar situation.*

Which in a sense makes matters worse.

What am I to do?

Out in the Palace grounds, a peacock shrieked. Nikolaos stirred and relaxed back into the pillow and a lock of dark hair flopped over his eyes. Taking care not to wake him, Theodora smoothed it back. She had been wrong to think she could keep her secret from him. If they were to have any sort of a future together, she must be open with him.

I love him. I must tell him everything.

It was painful looking at the enormity of what she had done. After months of training herself *not* to look at it, it went very much against the grain. Many times, Theodora had found herself thinking quite irrationally—worrying that if she so much as thought about how selfish she had been, someone would see into her mind, they would drag the truth out of her and then...

She sighed. Not facing her sin had become her habit. It was a habit she must break, and this was the moment to break it. It was time for the stark truth, for her secret to be revealed.

Nikolaos is not my first husband. I was married to Peter in secret, and Martina is his daughter. Martina is the legitimate Princess of Rascia.

In marrying Župan Peter early, Theodora had flouted convention, but in keeping Martina's identity hidden from the world, she had done far worse. She had turned her back on years of training and committed a grievous sin against both the Empire and Rascia. She was, for her own selfish ends, keeping the Princess of Rascia from her people.

Theodora bit her lip. Nikolaos had accepted Martina with such grace, and he had done so because he thought he and Martina were kindred spirits. When he learned that Martina was the legitimate Princess of Rascia, would he feel the same compassion?

Would he, as Theodora feared, come to hate her for keeping so large a secret from him? Would he feel betrayed? Used? Her husband was the most loyal of generals. He was honourable. Scrupulous. He would find her motives incomprehensible. If she told him everything, would he find it in his heart to understand? Would he be able to forgive so large a transgression? Or would the knowledge drive a wedge between them? Her only hope was to make Nikolaos understand why she had kept Martina's identity hidden.

All my life I have felt like so much merchandise, being shipped hither and yon for the benefit of the Empire. I did not want this for Martina. I will not have it for Martina.

Theodora was passionate about this. In order to keep her daughter at her side, she had been prepared to accept the stigma of a fallen woman. In order to ensure Martina was never sent away, she had been prepared to deny Martina her rights as the legitimate Princess of Rascia. Never mind that the Prince of Zeta was an ever-present danger; never mind that Martina was a helpless babe-in-arms and the Rascian Court was so chaotic it could never offer her protection.

What she had done was unforgivable—no emperor would condone her actions. There was simply no excuse.

I am a wicked, selfish woman to have deceived the world in such a way. It is time for the truth. My sin has consequences and I must face them, I must tell Nikolaos what I have done.

Theodora sank back against her pillow and

stared up at the mulberry-coloured bed-hangings. Her heart twisted. She felt at home with Nikolaos and after so many years of exile, she felt as though she had finally come to a safe harbour. It was ironic that finally, *finally*, she felt as though she belonged and she must put her newfound peace in jeopardy by telling him the truth.

He is a good man, he deserves no less.

Outside the peacock shrieked and this time she watched Nikolaos come fully awake.

Soft brown eyes smiled into his. Pulling his wife towards him, Nikolaos kissed her. Theodora's response was warm enough to have desire thrumming in his veins, yet he sensed some reserve in her. Sliding a hand round the curve of her buttock, he eased her closer. He wanted her to know he was hot for her and wondered what it might take to make her set aside her reserve.

'How early is it?' He nibbled her ear and inhaled the subtle scent of violets. 'Do we have time?'

She drew back, still smiling, and shook her head. 'We overslept. Sophia will be in any moment.'

Nikolaos grimaced and scrubbed his face, even as he heard the familiar knocking on the door.

'Come in,' he called, reaching for a long, silken strand of hair. Coiling it round his finger, he used it to bring Theodora back to him. 'The bathhouse,' he murmured. 'In an hour?'

Under cover of the bedclothes, a small hand stroked his flank. 'That is a good idea. There is something important I need to discuss with you.'

'My lady? My lord?' Sophia came up to the bed. 'Excuse me, but you must know the Emperor has summoned the Princess to meet him in the small throne room. At once.'

'His Majesty wants to see me?'

Theodora's face emptied of colour. She had emerged from their kiss flushed and relaxed. Sophia's announcement had her eyes filling with shadows. That old hunted look was back, the one he thought he had chased away...

'Yes, my lady.' Sophia hurried to the dressing chamber, as she went under the arch her voice became muffled. 'May I recommend the beaded violet gown with the amethyst diadem?'

Theodora sat next to him in the bed, sheets clutched to her chin. She looked as though she had turned to stone. Her throat worked. *She is terrified.* If she had looked on the Medusa, she could not have looked more frightened.

With a sense of foreboding, Nikolaos covered her hand with his. 'What is it? Theodora?' It seemed incredible that the thought of meeting the Emperor should so distress her. It occurred to him that this was not the first time his wife had been reluctant to speak to the Emperor. At the polo match she had avoided the Imperial box, though as cousin to the Empress she would have been within her rights to join the Imperial party.

He had assumed she had been keeping her distance because of the shame of bearing a child out of wedlock. It could not be more. It was up to him to demonstrate her husband would be her ally. 'Theodora?'

She turned her head, the look in her eyes chilled him to the bone. 'Why does he want to see me?'

Nikolaos kept his voice light. Easy. 'It is likely he saw something of what happened yesterday at the polo match…you screaming…Boda…the fire…'

'He wants to question me about Martina.'

Nikolaos shrugged. 'It would seem so.' He squeezed her hand in a gesture of reassurance. 'It's a wonder he did not summon us before—' he grinned '—though I have to say I am thankful for his forbearance.'

She made no response, simply watched Sophia emerge from the dressing chamber with a long violet gown. 'His Majesty summoned *me*, Niko, just me.' Her voice was flat, her natural vitality seemed to have left her and she was staring at the violet gown as though she loathed it. 'Not that one, Sophia! Not violet.'

'My lady?'

'I cannot wear that to meet the Emperor. Bring me the green damask with the pearl collar.'

'As you wish, my lady.'

Nikolaos took Theodora's chin and forced her to meet his eyes. 'You are not going alone. I can see you are anxious, but I want you to know that you need feel no shame about Martina. You need fear nothing. I am coming with you and I shall support you. Hear this: I will permit no one, not even His Majesty, to chastise you. Martina became my daughter the day we married; she will bear no stigma because you bore her out of wedlock, and neither will you.'

Her eyes filled. Her fingers gripped his. 'Niko—'

To his consternation, she burst noisily into tears. Nikolaos drew her into his arms and over her head his eyes met Lady Sophia's. 'Lady Sophia?'

'My lord?'

'I shall be accompanying the Princess to meet the Emperor.'

'Very well, my lord.'

With Sophia's assistance, Theodora dressed swiftly. All too soon, she had her hand on her husband's arm and was walking down the marble staircase towards the small throne room. She nodded absently at some ladies as they passed them. *What does the Emperor know?*

'Good morning, Princess.'

'Good morning, ladies.'

The corridor leading to the throne room appeared empty, save for the statues lining the walls like guards. They hurried on. They were passing a statue of the first Emperor Constantine, when

Lady Verina stepped into their path and swept into a deep curtsy.

'Lady Verina, good morning.' Theodora smiled and pushed her anxiety to the back of her mind.

'Good morning, Princess.' Rising from her curtsy, Lady Verina gazed up at her son, eyes taking in his wedding crown. Her mouth trembled. 'Nikolaos.'

'Mother.' Giving Lady Verina a cold nod, Nikolaos walked on.

Hearing a stifled sob, Theodora's heart twisted in sympathy and she dug in her heels. 'You must excuse us, Lady Verina, the Emperor has summoned us.' As Lady Verina fled down the corridor, Theodora lowered her voice. 'That was inexcusable, my lord. Your mother deserves your respect.'

'If my mother wanted my respect, she should have thought twice before she broke faith with my father.'

There was no time for more, the Varangians flanking the gilded doors of the throne room were within earshot. The Emperor's Guard saluted as Theodora and Nikolaos passed through. Two more Varangians stood either side of the canopied throne, their presence a clear indication that the Emperor would arrive at any moment. The purple canopy seemed to dwarf the room; the double-headed eagle on the Imperial standard seemed to glower.

The corridor rang with quick footsteps. The guards stood stiffly to attention and Theodora was taken by the desire to pick up her skirts and run for her life. The strain of standing her ground was such that she began to tremble.

Nikolaos threaded his fingers through hers. 'It is all right, my princess. There will be no recriminations.'

'I can't do this! I am not fit to be a princess.'

'That is the most ridiculous thing I have ever heard. Of course you are.'

'Niko, you don't understand—'

'Theodora, calm yourself. Try and remember, *you are not alone.*'

Her throat closed and Niko's dark features were lost behind a rush of tears. Outside, she heard the chink of arms as the Guard saluted their Emperor. 'Nikolaos, I haven't told you everything.'

Dark eyes gazed steadily at her. 'Oh?'

'I was going to tell you this morning, before the summons came.' Would the guards detain her if she took to her heels? When a laugh escaped her, Theodora recognised that hysteria was a heartbeat away. 'What is the penalty for deceiving an Emperor?'

Nikolaos went very still. 'I beg your pardon?'

She swallowed. 'Niko, I must speak to you— get me out of here.'

Nikolaos tightened his lips and shook his head.

'It is best to face fears head-on. There will be no more evasions. We face this together, and we face it now.'

Emperor Alexios strode into the throne room, the heels of his riding boots clicking sharply on the floor. Theodora struggled not to flinch with his every footstep. Gems glittered on a magnificent belt. Other than the belt, the Emperor was dressed informally. A short black tunic concealed the hair shirt he was rumoured to be wearing until his forty days of penance was over. Theodora knew Alexios Komnenos to be about the same age as her husband, but knowledge that he was Emperor had made her envisage an older man. He was dark and bearded, much younger than her imagination had painted him. His youthfulness did nothing to relieve her—he was still the Emperor. He was holding a document which looked like a letter.

This is the Emperor. I cannot lie to an Emperor. But I am ashamed to tell him the truth. I am a disgrace.

She gave the Emperor her best curtsy. He made an impatient sound. 'Enough of that. At last I meet my wife's cousin. Princess, it has not escaped notice that you have been somewhat elusive since returning to Court.' The Emperor frowned at the document. 'Doubtless you have been hoping to avoid chastisement.'

Theodora's heart lurched, she kept her gaze

down. Her heart gave a few more desperate heart-beats and, when the Emperor said nothing more, it became painfully obvious that he required a response. She lifted her head and looked imploringly at him. 'Your Majesty, it…I…' What did that document contain? In a sense it no longer mattered. The time for secrets was over and Theodora knew that as far as the Emperor was concerned there would be no excuse what she had done. She swallowed. 'I did great wrong.'

'Yes, Princess, you did.' The Emperor tossed the letter on to the throne and looked dispassionately at her. 'You should not have married him so soon.'

Nikolaos stirred. 'So soon, Your Majesty? Forgive me, but you gave your permission for us to bring the marriage forward.'

Emperor Alexios shook his head. 'I was not referring to your marriage to the Princess, General, but to Princess Theodora's first marriage.'

The mosaic walls seemed to close in on her.

Nikolaos gave her a startled frown. 'Her *first* marriage?'

Theodora could not bring herself to look at her husband. She gazed at the Emperor's riding boots—they were dyed Imperial purple—and wished she could sink through the floor. *I should have warned Nikolaos, I should have warned him…*

'Her *first* marriage? Excuse me, Your Majesty.' Taking Theodora by the arms, Nikolaos placed himself directly in front of her and searched her face. It was unsettling to be the subject of such an intense scrutiny. 'You were *married* to Prince Peter?'

'I...I...yes.' As his fingers bit into her, a thousand questions jostled for precedence in Theodora's mind. *How has the Emperor found out? Who wrote that letter?* Lady Verina's words echoed like a death knell at the back of her mind. *My son is a straightforward man...he hates deception of any kind.* One thought clarified and took precedence over the rest. *Nikolaos must hate me, he will feel I have betrayed him.*

Her belly tightened. Her husband's face was closed, implacable; his dark eyes were hard as jet—Nikolaos would look like this when pronouncing sentence on a soldier who needed disciplining. *He has judged me and found me wanting.*

'Niko—'

Abruptly, he released her and stalked to the throne. He reached for the letter. 'May I, Your Majesty?'

'Assuredly—it was written by your cousin.'

Theodora held her breath while Nikolaos began to read.

With a face as inscrutable as that of the Sphinx, he glanced coldly at her. 'As His Majesty has just said, Leo wrote this.'

The Emperor rested a hand on his hip. 'It was sent to my predecessor. In the chaos after my... accession...it was mislaid. After what I saw yesterday at the polo tournament, I ordered a search. It came to light this morning.'

Nikolaos allowed the letter to curl back into a scroll, dropped it on a tasselled cushion and stepped towards her. 'My cousin writes to explain why he sanctioned your marriage, your *first* marriage. He was concerned for your welfare should something happen to Prince Peter. He saw the affection between the two of you and was concerned lest you should have a child. Theodora, you owe His Majesty, and me, an explanation.'

Theodora swallowed down the knot in her throat. 'Peter and I...we were afraid.' She sent an apologetic glance the Emperor's way. 'As you have realised, we married in the reign of your predecessor. Emperor Nikephoros was known to be...changeable—Imperial policy towards the vassal states was in a constant state of flux. Župan Peter wanted to confirm our alliance, and I—'

'You did not have to agree,' Nikolaos bit out. 'You are an Imperial princess. Whichever Emperor was on the throne, you should have waited until you received his final confirmation.'

Theodora lowered her eyes. 'I was wrong. I know I should have waited.'

'Yes, Princess, you should have,' the Emperor said. His voice was frighteningly quiet. 'An Imperial princess does not get married in the dark. Choosing the date of your marriage to Prince Peter was the responsibility of the Emperor—it was not Prince Peter's, it was not yours. In politics, timing can be all; you overstepped the mark and you know it.'

'Your Majesty—'

'Silence! I have not finished. You were betrothed to Prince Peter for years. You must have known the agreement would be ratified at the best moment for the Empire. For the Empire, my lady, not to fulfil your whim or that of Prince Peter's.'

'Your Majesty, I can only apologise. I should not have married Prince Peter so soon. I—'

'This is no trivial transgression, my lady. A matter of state such as this cannot pass unpunished.' Thoughtfully Emperor Alexios stroked his beard.

Theodora found the softness in the Emperor's tone more alarming than overt fury. She stared at his purple riding boots and wondered what her punishment would be. Imprisonment? Exile? Or worse...

'A moment, I beg you, Your Majesty,' Nikolaos said. 'Theodora, you were a child when you were sent off to Rascia, were you not?'

'Yes.'

'It must have become home to you. It is no surprise you grew fond of Prince Peter.'

Theodora found herself staring at her husband in astonishment. *He understands, Nikolaos understands why I married Peter!*

'What I cannot fathom—' the Emperor cut in '—is why you did not seek an audience with me the moment you returned to the City? And as for your child—when are you going to tell me if it is a girl or a boy?'

'She's a girl, Your Majesty, her name is Martina.'

'A girl—I see.' The Emperor gave her a look that made her want to curl up with shame. 'Your daughter is the legitimate Princess of Rascia. By concealing your marriage, by allowing the world to believe she is illegitimate, you deny Princess Martina her birthright. Why?'

Wildly, Theodora wondered whether this was the moment to prostrate herself before the Emperor. She was conscious of Nikolaos standing with his arms folded across his chest.

She twisted her fingers together. Neither the Emperor nor her husband would accept her reasons for continuing to conceal her marriage to Peter once Martina was born. They would dismiss them out of hand. They would condemn her, quite rightly, for putting personal desires before the interests of the State. *When I was shipped out to Rascia, I felt like a piece of merchandise. I don't want that for Martina. Far better for her to lose her birthright than be traded like so much silk. Martina is not a commodity, she is my daughter! I will not give her up, I will not allow her to be sacrificed to the interests of the State.*

'Your Majesty, when Prince Peter and Brother Leo were killed, I…I am afraid I panicked. The two people who knew of my marriage were gone.'

She looked earnestly at the Emperor, willing him to accept her explanation, praying that Nikolaos would find it in his heart to forgive her for deceiving him. 'I have explained why Peter and I kept our early marriage a secret. We knew we were courting Imperial displeasure, but we loved each other. And then, after Peter and Brother Leo were killed, Prince Djuradj's troops started massing on the borders. I believed that my unborn child would be safer if no one knew of the marriage.' She looked directly at Nikolaos. 'I am deeply sorry for misleading you.'

'You can no longer conceal your daughter's status,' the Emperor said. 'A public announcement will have to be made.'

Theodora's heart sank like a stone. *No!* 'But, Your Majesty—'

'This is politics, your daughter is the legitimate Princess of Rascia. A public announcement will give your daughter the protection of the Empire.'

'Your Majesty, I cannot agree. Župan Djuradj—'

'Your Majesty,' Nikolaos broke in, uncrossing his arms. 'With your permission, I should like time with my wife before we debate this further.'

The Emperor and his Commander-in-Chief exchanged glances, glances which revealed how close they were. If Theodora had not been so transfixed by her fears, she might have noticed this sooner. One of them might wear the Imperial crown, but they were warriors, comrades in arms. Alexios Komnenos and Nikolaos of Larissa would have had many a meeting over strategy and tactics; they would have discussed politics. And there was more to be read from that swift exchange of glances—these men liked and respected each other; they trusted each other. They were friends as well as allies.

'Niko, of course.' Emperor Alexios gripped Niko by the shoulder. 'I have to meet an envoy from Apulia, in any case. We shall speak later.'

'Your Majesty, before you go, I must make my position clear on one point. My wife has been living under a cloud for some time, it is my belief she has been punished enough.'

The Emperor's eyes narrowed. 'You are bold this morning, old friend. Your wife has put her interests first once—how do we know she will not do so again?'

'I will vouch for her, Your Majesty.' Nikolaos smiled crookedly at the Emperor and his gaze dropped pointedly to the neck of the Emperor's tunic where the top of his hair shirt was just visible. 'Alexios, few are perfect. Many of us have sins for which we need to seek forgiveness.'

A stunned silence followed his words. No one moved, no one breathed. For one sickening moment Theodora thought that Nikolaos had brought the Emperor's anger down on his head, too. There were those in the City who called Alexios Komnenos a usurper for seizing the throne, but it was surely sheer folly to remind him of that?

The Emperor broke the silence with a bark of laughter. 'That's good, Niko, very good.' He clapped Nikolaos on the shoulder and lowered his voice. 'Only you would dare, my friend. Only you.'

'Alexios, I dare because I know you,' Nikolaos said, simply. 'The Empire needed you and you answered the call. I merely point out that here on earth there is no such thing as perfection. You know you have my wholehearted support.'

The Emperor shook his head and, for the first time, he smiled at Theodora. 'Do you have friends like this, my lady?'

'Your Majesty?'

'Old friends who tell hard truths?'

'Yes, Your Majesty, I do.'

'Then you are as blessed as I.' Chuckling to himself, Alexios Komnenos made to leave.

Theodora sank into a deep curtsy. The doors clanged behind the Emperor; the golden eagle on the Imperial standard shifted in the sudden draught. Someone barked a command and the Varangians' footsteps retreated down the corridor.

'So. You were a widow when you married me,' Nikolaos said. He was rubbing his forehead. 'When were you going to tell me? Were you ever going to tell me? I did not marry an Imperial princess, I married the widow of the Prince of Rascia.'

'My lord—'

'His Majesty is, fortunately for you, not merely my Emperor, he is like a brother to me.' He fixed his gaze on the letter lying on the purple cushion. 'You must have had this planned for some time. I expect you thought you had me on a string. Well, Princess, let me tell you how wrong you are—you don't have me on a string.' He swung back, mouth a thin line. 'You didn't reckon on my cousin's letter, did you?'

'My lord, I was going to explain…this morning when you woke—'

He cut her off with an exasperated wave of his hand. 'No more lies, I have had my fill of them.' He took her shoulders, his grip was like iron. 'I was beginning to believe that you were different. I was beginning to hope that with you…' He stared in a puzzled way at her mouth. 'I was beginning to hope…'

Crushing her to him, he covered her mouth with his. For a moment the kiss was calculated. Angry. Theodora held her ground, neither accepting nor rejecting it. Oddly, her spirits lightened.

Nikolaos is angry. Which means he is hurt. Which means he has feelings for me, feelings he does not wish to acknowledge. There is hope, there has to be.

She slid her arms round his waist and waited.

He gave an inarticulate murmur and his mouth gentled. His tongue ran over her lips, moistening them, seeking a response. When she relaxed her jaw and opened her mouth, his tongue slid against hers. Her breasts tightened with longing, she ached to feel his hands on them, his mouth. She ached to have his love.

He is angry, but the passion between us has not died, there is hope.

He drew back, breathing hard. 'Holy hell, I should have known better than to touch you.' He shoved his hand through his hair, dark eyes watchful. 'You befuddle me, Theodora. From the moment we met I have had no peace.' He laughed—it was a bitter sound. 'I thought you nervous and shy. I thought you innocent. And after our marriage, when I learned that you were not innocent, Lord, you befuddled me even more. I accepted your lack of innocence—'

'You are a generous man, Nikolaos, a kind and generous man.'

'And then there was Martina. I accepted her, too.'

Theodora smiled, her heart must be in her eyes and she did not mind. She had married this man because she needed him, love had been quick to follow. 'As I said, you are beyond generous. I love you, Niko.'

He scowled.

'Truly. I do love you.'

'You love Peter. You are using me and you have been from the beginning.'

Swiftly, she shook her head. 'Nikolaos, that's not true.' She gripped his sleeve. 'When we met,

I admit I planned to use you. I was afraid what Djuradj might do if he realised Martina was Peter's child. I was afraid he might kill her. As it turns out, I was right to fear that.' She took a deep breath. 'And whilst your character was unknown to me, I thought if you learned I had a child, you would reject her. Is it so terrible a thing to want to keep one's child?'

His lips twisted. 'Not just any child—your daughter is Princess of Rascia, and you are an Imperial princess.'

Anger filled her. She snatched her hand from his sleeve. 'Is an Imperial princess not also a mother? Is a princess of Rascia not also a daughter? All my life I have put duty to the Empire before my own desires. And what was my reward? The Empire stripped me of everything I knew and loved.'

He drew his head back. 'Everything?'

'My home was here! I was uprooted and sent to Rascia. I never saw my parents again.'

'Privilege comes with a price, you know that. It was scarcely the fault of the Empire that your parents drowned.'

She clenched her fists. 'Is it not? They were coming to visit me. They would not have been on that ship if I had not been sent away. The Empire traded me in much the same way as they would trade a bolt of silk from the Imperial workshops. Peter understood how I felt. Peter was kind to me. Peter—'

'Yes, yes.' Nikolaos looked weary. 'The saintly Peter, how you loved him.'

'It's true I loved him. Peter made me welcome in Rascia, he loved me. And—' Theodora was appalled to hear a break in her voice '—he gave me Martina. I shan't give her up, Nikolaos, I shan't. You may say what you like to the Emperor, but I will not have Martina treated as I was. Martina is not a bolt of silk to be traded because the Empire needs a new alliance.'

He blinked. 'That's it? *That's it?* You were prepared to deceive the whole Court, to risk lying to your Emperor, to me, simply because you didn't want Martina sent away.'

She gritted her teeth. 'How many apologies do you need? My lord, I am deeply sorry.'

'So you should be.' Nikolaos was looking at her as though utterly bemused. 'You, an Imperial princess, put your desires as a mother over those of a princess. You put love before duty.'

'Martina is the world to me.'

'And you would do anything to keep her, including making a fool of me before my Emperor. I would have preferred hearing I had married a widow from you, rather than His Majesty. You might have warned me.'

'Please believe me, I was going to tell you. If you had woken a little earlier, I would have done.'

'That's easy to say.' Nikolaos stood in front of the gilded throne, dark eyes boring into her. 'Theodora, I have given you the benefit of the doubt a number of times, but I am afraid it stops here. To gain your ends, you were prepared to lie.'

'I did not actually lie.'

'Don't be disingenuous. You let me believe you were unmarried; you let me believe you were childless. Lies of omission, Princess, lies of omission. And there seems to be no end to them. Lord, you were even prepared to mislead the Emperor. I cannot trust you.' His chest heaved. 'I think it best you retire to Larissa.'

She blinked. 'Larissa?'

'Lady Verina will accompany you. You should enjoy each other's company.' His lip curled. 'It would seem that deceit comes as naturally to you as it does to my mother.'

Theodora gasped.

Nikolaos frowned down at her, mouth a thin line. 'My insolence offends you, my lady?'

'You forget my status.'

'Your status…and what exactly is that? Oh, forgive me, you are an Imperial princess, one who has so forgotten herself that she is prepared to ignore protocol and marry on a whim—'

'I did not marry on a whim!'

'You married in the dark, in haste. Were you already bearing his child?'

'No!'

'You were prepared to deny your daughter's birthright, not for great reasons of State, but because you want to keep her. Theodora, I think you had better tell me what you are, because I have no idea. Are you a princess or a peasant?'

Chapter Fifteen

'Are you a princess or a peasant?'

For a moment Theodora was struck dumb, there were so many words piled up inside her, so many emotions fighting for expression. 'That's a loathsome question,' she managed, swallowing down a mouthful of bile. *Calm, I can be calm. I can control what I am feeling, I have had years of practice. I am a princess, and I will not be sent to Larissa.* Nikolaos shrugged and turned away, but not before she had seen a muscle working in his jaw. Like her, he was clenching his fists so tightly, she could see white. He was rigid with anger. An anger that surely must match hers?

He is goading me. Why?

He wants to send me away. Why?

While she struggled for calm, she watched him. Those warrior's shoulders were filled with tension. She heard him swallow. Walking round him, Theodora put her hand on his chest, she might as well have touched a rock. He did not look at her, he did not move.

'Nikolaos?'

He grunted. Theodora took it as a sign he was at least listening to her.

'Nikolaos, I have no wish to go to Larissa unless you are with me, I would like us to have a real marriage. I am sorry I had to deceive you— you already know the reasons for that. I will do my best to make amends.' She lightened her tone. 'And as for your question, I am neither a princess nor a peasant. I am a mother. Motherhood transcends all else. Except…' reaching up, she cupped his cheek in her palm '…what I feel for you. I do love you, don't shut me out of your life.'

Theodora had misled him before, but the need for evasions was gone. It was uncomfortable admitting her vulnerability to him; love made her vulnerable, but it was a relief to be able to give him the truth. The urge to touch his heart overrode fear. *My love for Nikolaos equals my love for Martina.* Naturally, it was not the same kind of love, but it was equally powerful, equally irresistible.

It struck her that convincing Nikolaos she loved him might be as hard a battle as the one she was fighting to keep Martina. She would need to take this step by step, but she *would* win him, just as she *would* win the battle to keep Martina.

He looked down at her, eyes wary. Unconvinced. 'I can't trust you.'

'Do not send me away.' It went against the grain to beg—Theodora had never begged for anything in her life. However, she could not think how else to convince him that what she felt for him was true. 'Give me a chance to prove you can trust me.'

The muscle twitched in his cheek and he said nothing. Theodora waited. Light was pouring through the arched windows, bright splashes fell on the mosaic walls and floor. Red tiles glittered, golds, greens... Theodora could not understand it, but in that moment the tessellated scenes on the floor and walls no longer sparkled with the rich, intricate beauty she had always admired. Today they looked vulgar and gaudy, they were crude simplifications of the subtleties of creation.

I love him.

'Trust has to be earned,' he said.

She drew a deep breath. 'I accept I have to earn your trust. I shall go to Larissa with your mother. At the least I would have your promise that you will not surrender Martina to the State, or to Rascia. Let her come to Larissa with me, as my daughter.'

Dark eyes watched her, unblinking. 'Very well, you may take our daughter with you to Larissa.'

Relief rushed through her like a tidal wave, it was so powerful she almost staggered. He would allow her to keep Martina! And by saying '*our* daughter', he was reiterating what he had said the day before, that he accepted Martina as his. Martina was not to be bartered like so much silk.

Theodora felt like hugging him, but his expression—aloof, unapproachable—held her at bay. She was not wrong about Nikolaos, she knew it. Under that bluff, soldier's demeanour, there was a kind and generous man. And he did love her, she was sure of it. Only there was some impediment in his mind, some reason he could not admit to love.

He is shielding himself from hurt. Someone he loves has hurt him and he thinks to protect himself from further hurt by denying he loves me.

His mother! The key to Niko's reluctance to love her lay in his relationship with his mother… If matters could be resolved between Nikolaos and Lady Verina, there would be hope for Theodora's future as his wife. First, however, her daughter's place in the world must be assured.

'Nikolaos, will you swear the Empire shall not have Martina? She will not be given back to Rascia?'

'I swear it. By Saint Giorgos and all the angels, she is our daughter.'

'Thank you! Thank you!' Impulsively, she caught his hand. 'I could not bear it if she was sent back. There are many warring factions in Rascia—they would tear her apart.'

'Her identity cannot remain hidden, however. Envoys will have to be sent to Rascia to negotiate with the Council. We will find a way to satisfy them.'

'Don't forget Djuradj. What if the Emperor needs Martina to forge an alliance?'

'His Majesty must use someone else. I have promised that you may keep Martina. I shall not change my mind.' His fingers curled round hers, he was looking at their joined hands, face unreadable.

'What is it? Niko?'

His gaze slowly lifted, skimming up her body. He took his time, appearing to study her—waist, breasts, shoulders, neck. He touched her hair, winding a stray tendril round his finger. He smoothed an eyebrow and looked at her mouth.

Theodora's skin burned. They were standing so close, she was sure he must feel her blood heating. That familiar masculine scent filled her nostrils, blended with a faint hint of rosemary— and for a moment she was back in the bathhouse, aching with need. Peter had never wrung such intense reactions from her. 'Niko?'

His appraisal finished, Nikolaos cleared his throat. His eyes were dark with desire. 'I want you.' He shook his head as though to clear it and gave her a twisted smile. 'It should not be, I do not trust you, but I want you. When you are in a room, you are all I see. Even when I am not with you, you fill my mind.'

Sensing her moment had come, that it was now or never, Theodora took a deep breath. 'Niko, I want you to tell me everything that was said between you and your mother.'

Abruptly, he stepped back. 'No.' He released her hand.

'That was very…definite.'

'Yes.'

'Please tell me.'

He tipped his head to one side. 'I don't see why I should.'

'You know very well. You feel more for me than lust. There should be no secrets between us.'

His eyes narrowed. 'You have the gall to say that?'

'I was wrong to deceive you, I freely admit it. You must understand that when I came back to Constantinople, I was accustomed to being self-reliant. For years I had been in the habit of relying on no one but myself.'

'Not even Peter?'

Theodora shook her head. 'Not even Peter. I thought perhaps I might come to put my complete trust in him, but—'

'You loved him.'

'I married Peter because I was fond of him. At the time I mistook that for love. It was affection, though, not love.' Theodora swept on. 'Nikolaos, my dearest wish is to find my way into your heart as well as your mind. I am praying that you love me. I should like you to tell my why you refuse to see your mother.' Theodora put her hands together and sank on to her knees before him. 'Please.'

'For God's sake, Theodora, there's no need to debase yourself.' Taking her elbow, he tried to raise her.

Shaking him off, she remained on her knees. 'There is every need—I *must* know! Why won't you speak to her?'

'Get up, Theodora.'

'I will when you tell me.'

'My mother has nothing to do with us, I refuse to discuss her.'

'Very well, you give me no choice.' And then Theodora did what she never thought to do in her life—she prostrated herself before her husband. The tiles were cold against her nose and palms. Hard.

'Lord.' His voice came from somewhere above her. 'Theodora, there's no need for that.'

Large hands attempted to lift her, she shrugged them off and raised her nose off a cluster of blue mosaics. 'There is every need. It's the only way I can think of to show you how important this is. You have to tell me why you will not speak to your mother.'

When Nikolaos gripped her waist, she batted ineffectually at him. 'Don't touch me!' If he touched her, he would bend her to his will and she was not going to be bent. Not until she had mended matters between them.

He sighed. She heard rustling and felt him settle cross-legged on the floor beside her.

'Theodora, do get up. Someone might come in—what will they think?'

'They are bound to think,' she said acidly, 'they are looking at a peasant.'

He shifted close, his knee nudged her ribs. 'I should not have said that, I apologise. Theo, please get up, or we shall have to stay here for ever.'

His voice was warm, he had called her Theo. She looked up and caught the tail end of a smile, quickly repressed. Her heart lifted. 'Only if you te—'

Without warning, he lunged. She squealed and he took no notice, manhandling her until she was firmly on his lap.

It was, Theodora thought, a very nice lap, warmer and softer than the mosaic floor. But since it wouldn't do for him to know it, she huffed out a breath and folded her arms, just in case they were tempted to wind round his neck. She might love this man, but she knew instinctively that the barrier to do with his loving her was somehow tied up in his relationship with his mother. Until she had his agreement to listen to what Lady Verina had to say, she wasn't going to give him an inch.

He didn't seem to notice she wasn't holding him. Leaning towards her, he kissed her neck.

'You are a stubborn, wilful woman,' he said softly and kissed her again.

Before she knew it, Theodora was angling her head to allow him better access. Since she wasn't kissing him back, that was surely allowable. She closed her eyes, smiling and surrendering to the sensations. Those ripples of feeling, that delicious melting inside…

'Stubborn.' He eased aside her pearls. A soft kiss landed on her collarbone and her nipples tightened. 'Wilful.' Warm fingers slid inside the neck of her gown and he pressed his mouth to the top of her breast. Her hidden, secret muscles clenched. 'But most of all rebellious.'

Her eyes snapped open. 'Rebellious?'

Niko covered her cheek with his hand, steady brown eyes smiled into hers. He kissed her nose. 'Your hasty marriage to Peter of Rascia was your way of rebelling.' When Theodora made an impatient movement, a strong hand slid round her neck and held her in place. 'It is all of a piece with your hatred of being manipulated and your resentment at being shipped hither and yon like so much merchandise. I'd wager a galley full of bezants that it was *your* idea to marry early. You were asserting yourself. Well?'

Theodora stared in amazement. He was right, of course—Peter had brought their marriage forward at her insistence. She had been concerned that the Emperor's predecessor might change his mind about the alliance with Rascia and she had been determined to gain some control of her life. How had Nikolaos known? 'Am I so transparent?'

With a smile, he smoothed his thumb over her cheek and jaw. 'I am coming to know you, my love. You do not like being manipulated.'

'I do not.' Absently, she rubbed her cheek against his hand. His use of the endearment had not passed unnoticed. She caught herself raising her mouth for a kiss and pulled back. 'Not in any way.'

'Kiss me, Theo.'

'I thought you wanted to send me to Larissa.'

'Lord, no.' He groaned. A warm hand was stroking her back, the other had loosened a long lock of hair and wound it about his wrist—he was using it as a rope, to keep her close. 'You know what I want.' Gently, he tugged at her hair. His eyes were dark, full of warmth and want.

Theodora felt her limbs weakening. 'In a moment. Your mother...'

His nostrils flared, his expression hardened. 'I have explained that my mother broke her marriage vows. She insulted the man who I believed was my father—I have no wish to reconcile with her.'

Theodora nodded, though she had yet to understand his total rejection of Lady Verina. 'Niko, I can see it must be hard to learn that the man you thought of as your father was no such thing. However, illegitimacy will not strip you of land or power. It is clear that Emperor Alexios holds you in the highest esteem.'

'That is beside the point. Lord Gregorios was my idol. He taught me to ride, he gave me my first sword, he—' Niko's skin darkened '—saw that my first taste of a woman was good, he—'

'You loved him.'

'Yes.'

She put her hand on his shoulder. 'Lord Gregorios was your father in every way that mattered. Nikolaos, you must forgive Lady Verina—Lord Gregorios clearly did.'

'Did he? I wonder if he even knew.' He turned his head, face shadowed. 'I believed them happy and contented together and all the while he was not my father.'

Thoughtfully, sensing that they were coming to the heart of the problem, she looked at his profile, a profile that might have been taken from the side of a Corinthian vase. *This is about deceit. Nikolaos thinks Lady Verina deceived his father and he cannot stomach it.* 'There was never any sign of constraint between them?'

'Never.' His eyebrows formed a dark line. 'I should have known. For a woman to deceive her husband in such a way—it is unforgivable. A child has a right to know the identity of his real father. All she would tell me was that he was born outside the Empire.'

'Niko, do you think it possible that Lord Gregorios knew you were not his son?'

He made a dismissive sound. 'Don't be ridiculous.'

'I don't believe I am. Niko, there may be good
reasons for a man to condone his wife's affair.'

'Good reasons?' He looked at her, eyes wide.
'Are you mad?'

She gripped his shoulders, thinking aloud.
'I wonder…do you think your mother wanted a
child and Lord Gregorios could not give her one?
What if they *both* wanted a child?'

'You are mad.'

'I don't think so. Niko, do you have brothers
and sisters?'

'I am the only one.' Niko was shaking his
head, she could almost see his mind wrestling
with her suggestion. 'My father *was* married before,' he said slowly.

'Did he have children with his first wife?'

'No.'

'There you are, then!' She looked expectantly
at him. 'Is it so far-fetched that your mother might
long for a child and that Governor Gregorios
might turn a blind eye whilst she found someone to give her one?'

'My father—that is to say, Lord Gregorios—
always seemed besotted with her, it was common
knowledge he would have given her the world if
he could. However, it's something of a reach to
suggest that he would accept another man's by-
blow as his own…'

'I see it would rankle if you thought she had deceived him.'

Nikolaos stared at the floor, his focus was miles away. 'I have to confess, the possibility of my father condoning my mother's affair never occurred to me. When my mother told me my father was foreign, a barbarian, I was blind to everything except the idea that I had been a mistake. An unwanted child. It so shocked me, it overrode all else. But you are suggesting that my mother might have wanted a child…that she…that she and Lord Gregorios might have agreed…' brown eyes lifted '…do you really think it might have happened that way?'

'The only way to know is to allow your mother to speak to you. She is eager to see you. Niko, you must hear her out.'

'If my father knew all along, why not tell me years ago?' Reaching up, he absently stroked her neck, sliding his fingers into her hair.

'They may have decided that the fewer people knew about it, the better. Perhaps it simply was not important—they both wanted a child.' Theodora pressed a kiss to his cheek. 'That is my belief, at any rate.'

Nikolaos fell silent again and Theodora leaned against him, giving him time to think, time to work out for himself that for Governor Gregorios to have invested so much love in him, he must have wanted him, too.

'I believe both Lady Verina and Governor Gregorios wanted you,' she murmured. 'From the little you have told me, I am sure your father was proud of you. As is your mother. Speak to her, Niko, let her tell her story—you are breaking her heart.'

'Yes, I do believe I will.'

A sigh left her. It was going to be all right, they were going to be all right.

'Theo?'

'Mmm?'

'I love you.'

A flash of joy ran through her. Curling her fingers into his hair, she covered his face with kisses. 'And I love you, Niko. So much.'

Still on her husband's lap, Theodora's breasts were pressed against his chest. Her skirts had ridden up about her knees and, at some point during their conversation, Nikolaos had found the skin beneath. Long fingers were caressing her calf, though from the distant expression in his eyes, Theodora doubted he was conscious of what he was doing. His mind was running over their conversation; he was thinking about Lady Verina and Governor Gregorios.

'Niko?' She kissed his neck.

'Mmm?'

'You are not going to send me to Larissa, are you?'

His eyes focused on her mouth, his lips curved, 'Not this week. Not unless that rebellious streak shows signs of re-emerging.'

'Then with your permission, my lord…' She fitted her lips to his.

He twisted his head and gave a throaty groan and his lips moved against hers. 'I love you, Theo.'

Theodora wriggled shamelessly against him and opened her mouth and a warm hand cupped her breast. When he drew back in order to run a fingertip with delicate precision over the point where her nipple lay beneath the green fabric of her gown, she moaned.

'We are a little hampered in here, my love,' he murmured. 'I do believe a visit to the bathhouse is in order.'

Theodora glanced about them, at the glittering mosaics, at the throne with its purple canopy, at the gold-fringed Imperial standard…her eyes fastened on the throne. It was very large, and most inviting with all those cushions…

'Oh, I don't know.' Suddenly out of breath, she dragged his tunic clear of his belt, desperate to explore the warm male skin beneath it. 'I think we are in the perfect place.'

His fingers went on teasing her nipple through the silk of her gown. She shifted and her skirts crept up over her thighs. His other hand was sliding over her leg, higher, higher…

She could feel how much he desired her. He was pressed hard against her belly. She was reaching for him when his hand abruptly covered hers.

'No.'

'No?'

He flinched and shifted beneath her. 'Theo, love, have mercy. These mosaics...it's like lying on a bed of nails.'

Theodora caught his chin and turned his head in the direction of the throne.

'I wasn't thinking of the floor,' she said, lifting an eyebrow.

A reluctant grin appeared. 'Theodora, that's the suggestion of a peasant, not a princess.'

'You like the idea. Admit it.'

His grin widened. 'What do you expect? Barbarian blood runs in my veins.'

Shifting her to the side, he rose lithely to his feet. And then she was in his arms, and he was striding to the throne and setting her down among the purple cushions. 'It would seem we are well-matched then, the peasant and the barbarian. With your permission, Princess, I shall put a guard on the door. We don't want interruptions.'

* * * * *

So you think you can write?

**Mills & Boon® and Harlequin®
have joined forces in a
global search for new authors.**

It's our biggest contest yet—with the prize
of being published by the world's
leader in romance fiction.

Look for more information on our website:
www.soyouthinkyoucanwrite.com

So you think you can write?
Show us!

MILLS & BOON® Book Club

2 Free Books!

Get your free books now at

www.millsandboon.co.uk/freebookoffer

Or fill in the form below and post it back to us

THE MILLS & BOON® BOOK CLUB™—HERE'S HOW IT WORKS: Accepting your free books places you under no obligation to buy anything. You may keep the books and return the despatch note marked 'Cancel'. If we do not hear from you, about a month later we'll send you 4 brand-new stories from the Historical series priced at £4.50* each. There is no extra charge for post and packaging. You may cancel at any time, otherwise we will send you 4 stories a month which you may purchase or return to us—the choice is yours. *Terms and prices subject to change without notice. Offer valid in UK only. Applicants must be 18 or over. Offer expires 31st January 2013. **For full terms and conditions, please go to www.millsandboon.co.uk/freebookoffer**

Mrs/Miss/Ms/Mr (please circle)

First Name

Surname

Address

Postcode

E-mail

Send this completed page to: Mills & Boon Book Club, Free Book Offer, FREEPOST NAT 10298, Richmond, Surrey, TW9 1BR

Find out more at
www.millsandboon.co.uk/freebookoffer

Visit us Online

0712/H2YEA

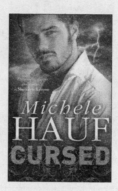